Snow-Flakes

Out of the bosom of the Air,
Out of the cloud-folds of her garments shaken,
Over the woodlands brown and bare,
Over the harvest-fields forsaken,
Silent, and soft, and slow
Descends the snow.

Even as our cloudy fancies take
Suddenly shape in some divine expression,
Even as the troubled heart doth make
In the white countenance confession,
The troubled sky reveals
The grief it feels…

—*Henry Wadsworth Longfellow*

DEAD OF WYNTER

SPENCER SEIDEL

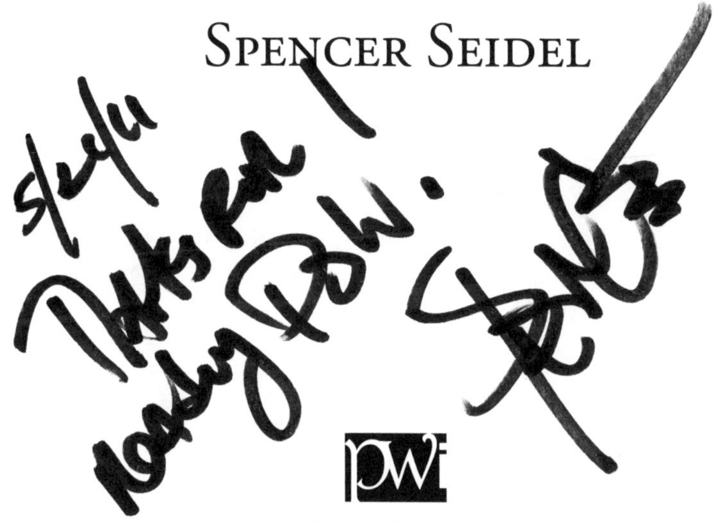

PublishingWorks, Inc.
Exeter, NH
2011

Copyright © 2011 by J. Spencer Seidel.

All rights reserved. No part of this book may be reproduced or transmitted in any form or by any means, electronic or mechanical, including photocopying, recording, or by an information storage and retrieval system—except by a reviewer who may quote brief passages in a review to be printed in a magazine or newspaper—without permission in writing from the publisher.

PublishingWorks, Inc.,
151 Epping Road
Exeter, NH 03833
603-778-9883

For Sales and Orders:
603-772-7200

PublishingWorks titles are distributed to the trade by Publishers Group West, a division of Perseus Book Group

Designed by: Anna Pearlman

LCCN: 2010937285
ISBN-13: 978-1-935557-69-2

For my mother, Annie Seidel, my constant reader

PROLOGUE

The ghost, the dead man, was still following. Chris Wynter swore and stumbled on, concentrating on putting one foot in front of the other and trying to ignore the pain in his bloody knee. It felt like it was filled with broken glass. He'd slammed it on the asphalt trying to get out of the damn car, to get away.

He was out in the Maine countryside. Camp country. Country he had no business being in this time of year. This was no place to fool around in the winter. Having grown up here, playing in and among these trees his entire life, he knew that. But here he was. His breath came rapidly in big white clouds that seemed to hang in the frigid January air forever.

"Damnit!" Chris shouted to no one when the pain in his knee flared.

He was too drunk to focus or care about all that. He had to get away from Ray and car. That was all that mattered now.

The heavy gun in his jacket pocket banged on his leg as he lurched forward, arms swinging from side to side for balance against the awful limp his hurt knee had given him.

An inner voice of clarity, not yet numbed into silence by his liter-a-day vodka habit, told him that none of this was right—screamed it actually—and that he should keep right on stumbling on, one foot in front of the other.

Impossible, Chris thought. *It can't be. This is fucking impossible. Ray died a long time ago.*

Chris focused on the ground and watched his feet as he swayed violently to the left and right, trying to stay upright.

He tripped on a root and went down on his bad knee. His right leg exploded in pain. He felt the fabric of his jeans crack where the blood pouring from his knee had frozen into a bloody patch like a malignant version of the ones his mother used to iron on the knees of his pants when he was kid, when things were better. A million bright lights flooded Chris's eyes, and he screamed in agony. Grayness crept into his peripheral vision. He was losing consciousness.

Desperately, frantically, he checked on the bottle of vodka he held in his right hand by holding it up in front of the silver eye of a near-full moon. The plastic bottle hadn't split open. It was the biggie. The three-liter version. The weight of it felt good in his hand. Reassuring. The grayness receded.

He glanced behind him again.

The Ray-ghost was closer now.

"Shit. Shit," Chris said into the night and struggled to his feet once again.

He thought he might take a pull from his bottle to strengthen his resolve but decided against it. The bottle had to last. Two, three days at least. After that? Well, Chris didn't want to think about that.

He'd gotten bad again, probably worse than he'd ever been in his life. He'd already detoxed once at the Salvation Army Men's Rehab in Portland and wasn't anxious to do it again. That was court-ordered and kept him out of jail after a fight at Flynn's. He hated the city. It was dirty and filled with immigrants. Bums were everywhere, hanging around looking for handouts and leaching off the government. He and Papa did just fine with very little, thank you very much. Didn't need any handouts.

He spent the better part of two weeks in that rat hole of a place, sitting on a dirty sofa, watching TV, smoking cigarettes, scratching his itchy legs like crazy, and twitching like an epileptic. In group, he listened to the other sad sacks talk about how their fathers beat them or raped them or whatever the hell. He didn't care. He had his own problems, but that was his damn business.

The day he got out, he walked a mile and half or so to the Hannaford's on Forest Avenue, feeling a little like he was blowing a pretty good chance to shake this thing off him, but he went anyway. Didn't think about it. Booze was like that. Sometimes your body just did the buying no matter how hard your brain told you not to. The rehab center had given him ten bucks for transportation, and that was good enough for his liter.

Chris gripped the bottle of booze now with both hands, determined to keep it safe, as if warding off the memory of those terrible days.

And then a thought popped into his head: *What if the ghost is death? What if this is how it happens? The end?*

Chris shook his head and rambled onward, towards what he wasn't sure. He'd know when he knew. He wasn't stupid. He'd grown up here. Sooner or later he'd see some familiar trees or recognize the landscape.

Death still followed. That's what it was, he was sure now.

Chris Wynter began to cry then. Big, spitty gasps. He was having one of his moments, those all-to-brief moments of real clarity and panic when he realized just how bad things were. How bad he was. He was a boozer. An alcoholic. Down and outer. No better than the stew bums he'd met passed out in the gutter on Preble Street.

He realized how far he'd fallen to be out here in the middle of fucking winter clutching a plastic three-liter bottle of vodka to his chest like it was going to save his life. He was running from someone who'd died twenty-five years ago and refused to think about what had gone down out there on the road. It would get him far worse than the goddamn Preble Street rehab.

His cloudy thoughts returned to the gun in his pocket. He reached to take it out but thought better of it. He thought if he saw the missing bullet or smelled the powder from the recent firing, he might lose it altogether and decide to blow his brains out all over the frozen Maine ground.

But you have to get rid of that gun, the voice of clarity said. *It's evidence. Just do it. Take it out of your pocket and throw it. Don't look at it. Just get rid of it. Out of sight, out of mind. Like you do with your bottles.*

And then he did. Stumbling, lurching forward, crying like a baby, Chris Wynter reached into his pocket and took out the gun. He didn't pause for a second and heaved it as far away from himself as he could, screaming.

There. Gone. Done. He felt better.

His tears dried up and he blinked his vision clear. His head felt lighter but now his chest hurt. His heart was racing. He wouldn't last much longer. He looked behind and saw the Ray-ghost a quarter mile back.

Chris tripped after turning his head. The dizziness was overwhelming. He went down hard on his bloody knee, falling forward. The bottle of booze bounced on the frozen ground, skidded beyond his reach and fell down a ravine. Chris toppled in after wondering how in the hell he was going to find the damn booze. He didn't care about himself, just the fucking bottle. Then his head hit something. Hard.

Before he blacked out, Chris thought, *I'm dead already. No two ways about it. Dead already.*

ONE

Alice Dunn watched as the fully loaded, Behemoth of a dump truck in front of her began to back up.

Beep-beep-beep-beep.

The backup warning blared in her ears. It sounded louder than it should. She took her hands off the wheel of her Mercedes (E Class) and held them up against her ears. The beeping wouldn't stop. The dump truck rolled backward. Dumb. Blind. Huge. Like a circus elephant sitting down.

A wave of panic rushed through Alice, and she punched the steering wheel with both hands to honk the horn.

What does this dumb-ass think he's doing? She thought. *He's going to roll right over me.*

But her horn wouldn't sound. The dump truck continued to roll backwards. A fine curtain of dirt and rocks poured from the back of the truck and lined the road. Several pebbles bounced up and landed on the Merc's shiny black hood. The driver hadn't properly secured the back of the truck.

The reality of it struck her. She thought, *He's really going to hit me! He really is going to back up and hit my Merc, the Merc I worked so hard for, the Merc I spent long hours at the office for, kissed ass for. My fucking Merc!*

"You going to do something about that?" a tinny voice said from the dashboard radio.

She paid no attention to the voice and instead struggled with the door. It wouldn't open. Her hands moved with agonizing slowness. Like they were—

"Hon, are you going to do something about that?" the voice said again, louder.

—numb. Tingly even.

The dump truck rolled backward. It was a foot away. She wasn't going to get out in time. She'd be crushed.

Beep-beep-beep-beep.

Why couldn't she move? She felt as though she was under water.

"Honey, please. Seriously. Can you do something about that?"

And then she was awake. She wasn't in her Merc. She was lying in her bed in Chatham, New Jersey, way up on Washington Avenue, with Gerald, her husband. In the pitch black of night. And he was saying something.

The phone's shrill electric ring cut through the night. It was offensive. Jarring. She lashed out, wanting to silence the noise that cut straight through to her panic button, but all she managed to do was to knock it off the nightstand. It crashed on the floor, the sound amplified in the dead quiet of the house. She'd slept on her arm and it was numb. As dead as bricks.

"Fuck," she said under her breath.

"What?" Gerald said sleepily.

"Just go back to bed. I'll get it," Alice said, angry.

I'll get it. Alice's famous words. She got everything these days. *Don't worry, Gerald, I'll get it. I'll handle it. We wouldn't want you to miss work. Or the squash game at the club. My job? Not as important. Don't worry, Gerald. I'll get it.*

Gerald had been missing-in-action in their marriage for months now. Alice suspected he was having an affair with his work-wife but didn't really know. She'd learned about her this past Christmas, when they'd met at Gerald's company's holiday party in New York City. He was a Wall Street lawyer. A good one.

"This is my friend, Tiffany. She's an administrative assistant. For Colson. I'm sure you've met him," he'd said.

Tiffany? Alice had thought. *Tiffany? Seriously? Her career singing at Malls not working out? Is that it? She decide to become a secretary? Or administrative assistant, as they call themselves now?*

Tiffany was in her late 20s, had big, perky boobs, white smile, long legs, the works. A complete package. Alice was in her mid 40s now and just couldn't compete. Any man would have found it hard to resist Tiffany, and Gerald was any man.

He was supposed to be Alice's Gerald forever. That was the agreement. They'd met at Boston University one night in the food court when they got to the last table in the crowded seating area at the same time. They decided to share the table. Theirs was a fate thing. A relationship born out of thin air that was supposed to last. But lately, that was changing, and Tiffany with the perky boobs and long legs wasn't helping.

Oh, yes, she'd learned all about Tiffany that night at the Christmas party, mostly from Gerald's coworkers, who stared at Alice with strange looks on their faces. Home wives and work wives are never supposed to meet. It made everyone uncomfortable but Gerald. Clueless, MIA Gerald. He hung on Tiffany's every word. They shared their inside jokes, which Alice chuckled at just to make it seem like she wasn't a total gimp. Alice felt as if Gerald was showing Tiffany off in some weird way, as if trying to tell her that she should be more like her. It was an incredible spectacle.

The fact that he was smitten with a pretty young thing at the office wasn't what upset her most. It was the fact that he didn't even acknowledge Alice's feelings, that she might be hurt, jealous. He just didn't seem to care. He couldn't empathize and that drove her crazy. In a weird way, it was almost as though Gerald resented Alice for growing old and not being Tiffany, double-D, blowjobs-every-other-day sex goddess, who would bear him 2.5 beautiful children, instead of frumpy Alice, who could not, or would not, sacrifice her successful career as a marketing executive in New York for a couple of kids, no matter what the current fashion. And, frankly, she could take or leave sex with Gerald.

These thoughts passed through her mind in an instant in the dark, as they did more and more often nowadays, while she tried to locate the cordless phone she'd knocked off the nightstand with her useless arm, which was now tingling like crazy.

Finally, she gave up and flung the covers off, shivering at the rush of cold that assaulted her sleepy body. She picked up the cordless phone with her other hand, which wasn't numb. She was sure this was going to be another hang up.

They'd been getting a lot of those. The paranoid part of her brain thought it might be Tiffany, but she hadn't quite worked up the courage to ask Gerald if he could please tell his girlfriend to stop calling them at home.

She clicked the Talk button and said, "Hello?" She walked out of their bedroom and into the hallway, shaking her right hand, desperately trying to make the tingles go away. She needed a blanket. Fast. It was freezing in the house on this early-January night.

"Dolly? It's your mother." The voice was deep and thick, like she'd been crying. The pack-a-day cigarette habit didn't help her either.

Mutha. Her mother's thick Maine accent struck some deep, hidden panic in Alice. Alice had come a long way since Redding, Maine, and didn't speak with her family much. On purpose. The last time had been ten minutes on Christmas day.

Something was wrong. *It must be Chris,* Alice thought.

"Ma?" Alice said.

"Dolly, it's your mother."

Dolly. Jackie Ruth Wynter had called Alice that for years. Alice hated it. Her mother loved to tell the story that when Alice was born, her father, Papa, had been singing that tune, "Hello, Dolly," by Louis Armstrong, the one that was popular when her mother was just a kid. And it stuck. Sometimes, when Jackie Ruth got into her jug wine, she said the name with a little smirk that curled up her lips on the edges, knowing that it pushed Alice's buttons.

"I know, Ma. What happened? What's wrong?"

"I need you home here. I need you here. It's your father."

"Ma, tell me. What happened?"

"Your father's dead."

The words took a moment to sink in. Papa was dead. Hard-drinking, selfish old bastard, rough-dried, old crank. Any of these things would describe Papa. He was a rotten old man. Local legend. End of story.

"W-what happened?" Alice said.

"There was an accident of some kind. They're still up there on Route 6. An officer came to the door to tell me . . ." her voice deteriorated into gentle sobs. A moment later, she said, "Dolly, I need to you here. I don't have anybody now."

"Where's Chris?"

"I need you here, Dolly. Please, Alice."

Alice's reaction was to put the phone on her shoulder and stare out the picture window in their living room, where she'd gone to find a blanket. The moon was bright and lit up their manicured lawn. She thought of every reason she couldn't go. They'd miss her at work. Gerald would forget to leave a check for the landscapers. He'd bring Tiffany home, screw her in their bed, and play house while making fun of Alice's dismal collection of lingerie. Alice's workout schedule would get screwed up. They don't eat right up in Redding. She'd gain weight. Any of these could work.

But in the end, no reason was good enough. Her father was dead, and that was really all that mattered, tough old bastard or not. Plus, she was worried about her twin brother, Chris. It could be a chance to put some things, old things, to bed forever. Make peace, as they say. She hated to admit it, but this could only help Chris, who had lived under Papa's thumb for years.

"Okay, Ma, okay. But where's Chris? Can he stay with you until I get there?"

Jackie Ruth sighed into the phone. Alice heard her light a cigarette, inhale deeply and exhale into the phone. "Chris is nowhere. He's gotten worse."

"Can you tell me what happened?"

"You know your father. How he gets."

Her mother was infuriating, and Alice guessed she'd been drinking her beloved jug wine. It tasted like watered-down white-grape piss-juice to Alice, who rarely drank.

"Fine. You can tell me tomorrow. I'll leave first thing in the morning."

"I love you, Dolly."

Alice hung up the phone. Her mother's words, *how he gets*, hung in her mind. She lay down on the sofa and stared out at the moon, remembering her last nightmare trip north several years ago.

She arrived in Portland, Maine late in the afternoon. The rain that had been pounding her car all way from New Jersey had eased and given way to a colorful sunset. She poked her way along Forest Avenue in the rush-hour traffic, headed into town, trying to remember where her mother had said the rehab was. Was it Preble Street?

Yes, that was it.

She was staying at the Holiday Inn by the Bay on Spring Street and would be able to walk to the rehab from there, so she left her car in the garage. She allowed herself a few minutes of relaxation in one of the hotel chairs before heading out, staring out at the fiery oranges, pinks, and reds that the sun had begun to paint on Casco Bay. She watched the fishing boats coming in for the day, chugging along in the black water, and lost herself in the scene for too long. Now she was late.

Alice left the hotel in a rush, walking northward up Oak Street towards Cumberland Avenue. It had been quite a while since she'd been to Portland, but she remembered her way around well enough. Before long, she saw the long brick building running a few hundred yards down Preble Street: The Salvation Army Men's Rehabilitation Center.

Her twin brother Chris had gotten into another fight at that damn bar he and Papa were always in and was arrested. He had nearly killed a man. The judge ordered Chris into rehab. Into detox.

The word scared Alice. Detox. It made her think of shaking sweaty men strapped onto gurneys and down-and-outers sticking themselves with needles in run-down apartment-building doorways. It was hard to imagine exactly what it was really, but she was sure that if anyone needed it, it was Chris. His blood was a toxic soup and God knew if he was taking drugs or pills or what now.

Chris occasionally wrote to Alice in long letters, carefully penned in his shaky handwriting. He never called, never emailed. Alice supposed he found some comfort in writing them. In the last, he'd asked her to come here for family night. He'd made promises about cleaning up his act before. He'd always made promises and lied and drank and lied. She'd tried to help for some time by writing back but had mostly given up. Now, she just read the letters and hoped her mother, Jackie Ruth, was doing him some good.

Alice figured it was a lost cause, but who knows? Maybe being there would teach him a thing or two. Maybe at least get him pointing in the right direction. The only reason Alice had agreed to be here this time was because she thought it might force Papa to take a look at himself. He was as bad as Chris, if not worse. It was a long shot, but what the hell.

Alice opened the rehab's side-entrance door, feeling stared-at and self-conscious as her heels clicked on the floor while she walked towards the reception area. The building had seen better days, and Alice imagined they didn't receive much funding. Sad-looking men sat on metal chairs in the hallway and watched her go by. One smiled and said, "You married?"

A short, fat woman sitting at the reception desk pointed Alice in the right direction with barely disguised disgust, furrowing her brow and frowning at Alice's clothing and tardiness. Or so Alice imagined.

She entered the meeting room slowly, embarrassed at being late. It was filled with smoke that hung in the air like smog on a hot morning. Several rather beat up men sat in worn-out chairs. Some lounged on the floor. Nearly all smoked cigarettes. A relatively healthy counselor-looking man wearing a backwards cap stopped talking when Alice stepped into the room and looked at her impatiently. He was sitting backwards on a folding chair, giving an introductory speech he'd likely given a hundred times or more before.

Jackie Ruth and Papa sat on the opposite side of the room. Jackie Ruth waved her over. Alice groaned quietly as she walked towards her parents, having to pass by so many sets of judging eyes.

She threaded her way through the tangle of destroyed people.

Jackie Ruth, under her breath, said, "You're late."

Alice shrugged. "Traffic."

"Hi, Alice. Thanks for coming," Chris said, looking up at her from where he was seated on the floor. He didn't smile. He didn't seem capable of smiling.

Alice gently touched his shoulder. His round face was redder than the last time she'd seen him. He looked almost as though he was sunburned, and she noticed a slight tremor in his hand, the one holding a nearly burned-out smoke in yellowed, swollen, dirty fingers. His disease, or whatever they called it nowadays, had him. It was obvious. From the look on his face to the complexion of his skin, he looked beaten. Her twin brother, younger by just a minute or so, was fading. He was transforming into something else that she and probably no one else but the other sad men in this dingy room could ever understand.

Her father, whom everyone called Papa, merely looked in Alice's direction and grunted. She smiled and whispered sarcastically, "Father, so nice to see you again. You look wonderful."

He'd never approved of her. Thought she was too smart for her own good. But she knew the truth. He couldn't control her and run her life the way he did Chris's and Jackie Ruth's. Alice thought she'd stopped caring about this years ago but felt a small twinge of hurt now just the same. She hated him for what he was helping Chris to become.

Alice sat down.

Her eyes stung from the smoke. She wondered if

this was doing any damn good at all, whether she'd ever get this smell out of her coat, if they offered coffee, or if it was too late to help Chris. She listened to the men in the room talk about their feelings; how their families made them feel; how alcohol or drugs helped them to not feel that way. She was uncomfortable and soon regretted coming.

She heard Chris give some rather pat answers to questions that should have been harder to answer and knew this was not it for him. He was making promises and lying. He was saying things they wanted to hear. He wasn't going to stop drinking. He was here because he had to be. She'd come for nothing and would leave first thing tomorrow morning after indulging in a quick trip to LL Bean. She should have known better.

Alice turned to look at her mother. Jackie Ruth looked both sorrowful and hopeful, like a woman who knows she can't make a difference but goes to bed every night praying that this time her son would get better anyway. Alice wanted to scream at her that it wasn't Chris. It was Papa. He was as addictive a thing for Chris as the booze was. Couldn't her mother see that? They kept each other down. All these years. It made no sense to Alice. It never had. After all, she'd escaped. Why hadn't Chris?

Alice's only consolation was that this meeting must have been torture for her father

At last, just as the morning sun was beginning to break, Supervising Detective Lt. Don Lambert drove down his long dirt driveway in what he called the "company car": a black 2007 Ford Crown Victoria, complete with all the trappings of law enforcement. He was tired. Bone, dog tired.

The car's tires skidded a little on the dirt outside the garage when he stopped. After turning the car off, he sat, staring out ahead, trying to process, trying to turn it off before he went inside his house. He didn't like bringing his work home, but sometimes it got the better of him.

After a few minutes, Don got out of the car, squeezing his huge belly out from under the steering wheel, and walked slowly to the back door of his ranch in Redding, a few towns away from Madison, Maine, where he worked. Redding was a sleepy little rural town and suited Don and Gaye just fine. Don was a detective for the Somerset County Sheriff's Office and was damn lucky to have the job. He was supervising detective and also their lone homicide detective. Unit 3. The truth was, what kind of detective you were in Somerset County didn't matter much, since all four of them worked together at various times. Crimes tended to overlap. Plus, there was the simple fact that there weren't many murders in Somerset County. Usually less than 10 a year. Far less in some areas.

He was "from away," as the Mainers say. You weren't from Maine in their eyes unless your parents were from Maine. Or, more accurately, unless your parents' parents were from Maine. Don had crossed the border from New Hampshire, where he was born and raised. After a stint in the military, he came over with his wife, Gaye, to look for a job in law enforcement when budget cuts had dried up such jobs in his home state. He found one as a patrolman in the Somerset County Sheriff's office. But that was a long time ago.

He paused at the back door and took a deep breath. He walked into the mud room and instinctively stamped his boots, though there was no snow on the ground yet, a pleasant but foreboding miracle in this neck of the woods. Mother Nature would pay back dearly, Don was sure of that. It was just a matter of time now.

Though it was just now a little after 6:00 A.M., Don found Gaye in the kitchen in her robe. She'd made coffee and was frying up some Canadian bacon, Don's favorite. He smelled the good decaf coffee they picked up a couple of times a year and used only special occasions—Don's doctors made him swear off the high-octane stuff on account of his blood pressure. Normally they just drank the store brand. Gaye was making it special because he'd been out all night. He smiled at the warmth of his kitchen and remembered the days gone past when his two daughters, Kim and Erica, both now out of college, had filled the air in the house with noisy kid stuff. He was fifty-five now. Gaye just a couple of years behind. Nowadays it was just Gaye and him.

"Made you some bacon," Gaye said.

Don hugged her from behind and gave her a little goose, surprised to feel a little stirring in his loins, something that happened less and less these days. "Thanks."

She batted his hand away, giggling a little, likely knowing *exactly* what it meant after all these years, and said, "Oh, you do sound tired."

Don poured himself a cup of coffee and said, "I am."

"You want to talk about it?"

Don sat down at the table and pulled a Merit Ultralight cigarette out of a pack he kept in his shirt pocket. He lit it and inhaled deeply. It was his first smoke in hours. (He had a little more trouble swearing off the smokes, doctors or not.)

He said, "Papa Wynter shot himself out on 6 sometime last night. CSI from Augusta is still going over the scene. Seems like a pretty clear-cut deal to me, though."

"*The* Papa Wynter?" Gaye said, walking towards Don, holding a sizzling pan.

"One in the same."

Gaye scooped out a couple slices of bacon and set them gently on Don's plate. "You know I don't like you smoking in the house. Or at all, for that matter."

"Yes, dear," Don said sarcastically and stubbed out his smoke. She *was* right, after all, and he knew it. He looked down at his plate. "Just two?"

"You remember what the doctor said. Got your blood pressure to worry about, and that cholesterol. Gotta drop that weight."

As far as Don was concerned, that doctor could jump off a bridge. He felt fine. He'd always felt fine. Fifty was the new forty. Isn't that what they said? Or was it sixty? Besides, everyone in his family was a little overweight. Okay, so maybe he was a little more overweight than everyone else, but what's twenty or thirty pounds?

Gaye dropped a single slice of unbuttered white-bread toast on Don's plate and said, "Eat up now. Before it gets cold. I want you in bed. You're too old to be gallivanting around all hours of the night. Catch your death of cold. And that reminds me. Did you give any thought to what we talked about a couple of days ago?"

Retirement. That's what they'd talked about. He *hadn*'t given it any thought at all. In fact, Don figured she'd forgotten all about it. He figured he'd just about go damn crazy if he had nowhere to go in the morning and nothing to do all day. Don held up the toast and said, "Butter?"

Gaye gave him a smirk.

God love her, Don thought. *She's a royal pain in the ass sometimes, but I love her to death. No doubt about that. I should tell her that more often.*

Instead, Don said, "Gotta be in Skowhegan for court at 3:00. Figured I'd head down to the Chief Medical Examiner's office in Augusta after to get an early read on Papa. Carol said she'd do me the favor."

Carol was the new, young doctor over there. Sharp as a tack.

Gaye rested her head on her hands and watched Don eat. She said, "Was it bad?"

Gaye was always doing this. She wanted to know the gory details but just didn't have the stomach for it. Don gave her the watered-down version: "Shot himself in the head, fell out onto the road. Froze himself solid."

The truth was that old Papa Wynter's head was half blown apart and what was left of it was frozen fast to the goddamned asphalt. They'd had to use warm water to get him up and into the coroner's van. Even then, his arms and legs wouldn't budge. But Don didn't mention any of this to Gaye.

"Oh, dear."

"Uh, yuh," Don grunted. It was a little Maine-ism he'd picked up over the years.

"Doesn't surprise me a bit," Gaye said. "Those Wynters. Always been trouble. Especially that awful Papa."

Don nodded. The Wynters had a long history in Redding, where Don lived. They were *that* family, the family who never had any money, the family whom everyone knew was abused by the alcoholic father, the family you felt sorry for and hated all at once.

"Going to have to interview the lot of 'em," he said. "Jackie Ruth and the son—"

"Chris."

"Uh yuh."

"What's going to happen next?" Gaye asked.

"Well, not much. Routine stuff. We'll wait for the ME's ruling, which will take a day or two, and then release the body to the family."

"I don't know whatever happened to that boy of theirs," Gaye said, thinking. "And I haven't seen Jackie Ruth in quite some time. You think maybe I should take a collection at church? You know, to pay the expenses?"

Don nodded grimly. "Might be a downright nice—"

"Now just a minute…"

Don arched his eyebrows, waiting.

"They had a daughter, didn't they? That's right! Chris was a twin. Now what was her name? Alice. Alice Wynter. I haven't thought about her in years. Used to break my heart, looking at her."

Don looked at her quizzically.

"Don't tell me you don't remember her? She was just a slip of thing. And pale as a ghost. Used to wear those big, black glasses and hand-me-down dresses. I'll never forget her. Oh, my. That was back when I was volunteering at the library down at school. When Kim and Erica were in the system."

"What happened to her?"

"Smart as a whip that one. Smarter than Jackie Ruth and

the rest of them put together. Used to read like crazy. Always had a book in her hands. I never saw a kid read that much to this day. Last I remember, she high-tailed it out of here. And you know what? I don't blame her a bit. I wouldn't be the slightest bit surprised if she ended up doing good for herself, I'll tell ya."

"Well, I suppose you may get a chance to find out. We told Jackie Ruth last night what was going on, so I suspect she spoke with Alice. Assuming they're still speaking, of course."

Gaye was shaking her head slowly back and forth. She said, "What a shame, these things. Well, Wynter family or not, I'm going to take up a collection at church on Sunday. They had their fair share of problems, I'll give you that, but everyone deserves a proper burial. We're equal in the eyes of the Lord."

Don soaked up the last bit of juice on his plate with his toast and then drained his coffee cup. Truth be told, he'd never had much of a head for religion, but he figured if there was a God, he'd be looking out for Gaye. "That's why I love you," he said, and he meant it.

Gaye smiled and said, "Come on, now. Into bed you go."

Don pushed his chair back and stood up. He felt his tiredness now, especially after getting something warm in his stomach. He said, "What are you staring at?"

"You," Gaye said and smiled. "I'll tuck you in. Maybe get under the covers with you. Leave the dishes for later."

Don watched her walk past and just managed to catch the belt that held her robe together in the front.

"Now stop it! You need your rest. You're terrible!" she said, laughing. But she didn't close her robe and she climbed in after him into their warm bed.

Friday, September 28, 1984

Chris Wynter, his cousin Ray Wynter, and Victor Acree spent most Friday nights over at Plaza Lanes, bowling, drinking, and playing video games. Sometimes girls would show up to look at. Usually not. There wasn't much else to do in Redding, Maine, on Friday nights.

Ray was nineteen and could pass for a guy in his twenties, so he always bought the booze. He'd go in and start bullshitting with the guy behind the counter like they were old buddies. Next thing you know, the guy at the counter would forget all about asking for Ray's ID and they'd all have their booze for the night.

But Ray was too big and awkward to be popular with kids his own age, especially girls, who mostly seemed terrified of the big kid. Ray got his dark skin, height and dark black hair from his mother, who was part Penobscot Indian, and even a member of the tribe. Ray's father was Chris's Uncle Bruce. Ray played up his imposing looks for all it was worth. Most people were scared of him, and he knew it, but inside, he was just as insecure as the rest of them.

They were all like that in their own way. Chris was pudgy, had messy dirty blond hair and freckly cheeks. He looked years younger than other kids in his senior class, who looked like grown men to him. They got all the chicks.

Vic was nearly as tall as Ray, and they could have passed as brothers. But where Ray was filled out, Vic was gangly and had sunken features. He had dark skin, black hair, and looked vaguely Italian or Greek, but he didn't know what he was and didn't care.

Chris was playing Pengo, his favorite game, even though he wasn't very good at it, when Ray and Vic appeared on either side of him, smoking cigarettes.

Ray poked Chris's arm and made him lose a guy.

"Hey!" Chris said. "Fuck off!"

"What's on the agenda, boys? We gonna spend the whole night here with our thumbs up our asses or what?" Ray said.

Vic said, "What do you want to do, Ray?" Vic spent most of his time in school doodling sex pictures on his notebooks. And they were good. Masterpieces of depravity. Once, in freshman year on a field trip, he'd snuck onto the bus after everyone had gotten off and filled the fog covered windows of their bus with all manner of sexual imagery, like the Kama Sutra from hell.

Ray took a deep drag off his smoke. He tapped his fingers on the side of the machine and bobbed his head. He was forever moving and tapping and bobbing his legs up and down, as if dancing to some hardcore metal soundtrack in his head. He said, "Fuck if I know. You want to go cruise? This blows."

Chris lost his final guy and said, "Yeah, let's get outta here. Go toke. You got the papers?"

Ray gave him a of-course-I-have-rolling-papers look and patted his leather jacket pocket. Ray always had the best weed. He knew a big-time dealer Down East who supplied most of Maine. He said, "Let's go boys."

Chris and Vic followed Ray towards the bowling alley entrance. Coming in were a couple of jocks and a pretty cheerleader named Nora Strawser. The jocks looked disdainfully at Ray's long hair and motorcycle boots.

"Hey Nora," Ray said. "Why you hanging around with

these losers?"

Nora said, "Shut up, germ."

Chris and Vic groaned.

Vic said, "C'mon, Ray, don't start."

"I heard something about you, Nora. Something maybe you might want to know about," Ray said.

Nora looked up at him suspiciously. "What?"

"Come out to the car. I'll tell you out there. In private."

Nora said, "Fuck you, Ray."

Ray moved aside to let them pass. "Okay, you want me to say it right here?" He raised his voice. "I heard you gang-banged Nathan Gabbard and Fred Hamlett in the back of Fred's pickup truck after the game last weekend. At least, that's what Fred told me. How was it? Did your boyfriend mind or did he just watch and jerk off?"

Several older men at the alley's food counter turned around and stared at Nora.

Nora's boyfriend, Sean Wayman, muscled his way in front of Ray and said, "You better watch your mouth, scumbag."

The other jock, Billy Cate, walked up behind Sean and looked scornfully at the three misfits. Ray's smile faltered and twitched. He hadn't expected to be challenged.

Ray said, "Fuck you, huh?" He turned, trying to pretend it was all no big deal.

The minute he did, Sean was on him, knocking him to the floor, face down, holding one of Ray's arms behind his back. Chris saw Ray's mouth stretched into a grimace of pain.

"What'd you say, Ray? Huh? What was that?" Sean said, laughing and turning to look at Billy, who was also laughing.

"I said your mother's a whore."

"What was that?" Sean said.

"Fuck you!" Ray said.

"Lick the floor, asshole," Sean said, digging his knee into Ray's back.

"Get off me you dumb jock asshole!" Ray said. He squirmed and tried to shake Sean off, but Sean was too strong.

Nora Strawser laughed and said, "Ray, I heard it was you in the back of the truck with your friends. I always knew you were a homo."

Ray said, "You watch your mouth you fucking bitch!"

"Don't talk to her like that, scumbag!" Sean said, pushing Ray's face down on the floor. "Lick it! Lick the fucking floor."

Ray struggled harder and grunted loudly in frustration. The men eating at the counter laughed. One of them said, "Best do what he says, long hair."

Finally, Ray touched his tongue to the dirty floor.

Sean let him up. The men at the counter started clapping and whistling.

Ray spat and said, "C'mon." He walked up the stairs and pushed open the door hard enough that it banged the wall. Chris and Vic followed him out to his Chevy Nova.

Chris climbed into the back seat. Vic always got shotgun. He was older than Chris. When they got into the car, Vic said, "Ray, was that true about Nora?"

"Fuck off! What do you think? Where were you guys back there? Huh? I'm gonna kill that fucker, Wayman, I swear to God."

Ray took off into the night, tires screeching. The boys

cruised Redding for what seemed like forever. Ray wasn't talking. He was fuming. Pissed off at being humiliated. Chris was bored. Vic said it first. "This fucking sucks."

A few minutes later, Ray parked the Chevy behind the high school and rolled a joint. They passed it around, silent.

Finally, Ray said, "I'm gonna fucking kill them, I swear. Did you hear those tired old shitbags laughing at us? We should form a gang. Make people know their place."

"What do you mean?" Vic asked.

Chris leaned in closer between the driver and passenger seats.

"I heard about these guys down in Boston. Started a fucking syndicate, man. Like five guys."

"What's a syndicate?" Chris asked.

Ray said, "It's like a gang. Like the masons or the fucking skull-and-bones society."

"That's cool." Vic nodded.

Chris said, "You should make a logo, Vic."

"I could do that. What's our name?"

Ray shrugged and got out of the car. Chris and Vic followed, watching.

"This town sucks," Ray said. "All we do is go to school. That's it. They force us to stare at chicks like Nora Strawser all day. I mean, how are we supposed to take that? And the fucking jocks! What the fuck? They get everything. We get shit. We get the shit jobs after high school while they get to go screw sorority chicks at fancy colleges."

Vic and Chris remained silent. Sometimes it was better to let Ray rant. He was scary when he got like this.

Ray bent down. He picked up a rock. "It's not fucking fair! You know what I mean? I'm fucking tired of this shit. And the fucking teachers! Jesus Christ! Jocks get away with fucking everything."

Ray's voice lowered. He said, "I'm not gonna take it. From now on we stand for a society of fear. No laws. Anarchy. Chaos. Where guys like Sean Wayman are afraid of us."

Vic said, quietly, "The Masters of Chaos."

Ray smiled and snapped his fingers. "Masters of fucking Chaos, baby. That's us." He reached into his jacket pocket, took out a bottle, and took a long pull. He passed it to Chris, who did the same, and finally to Vic, who finished the bottle.

Chris felt good. It felt good to feel stronger and tougher. It was like all the failed quizzes about shit he didn't care about anyway, the dirty looks from teachers, the perfect Sean Waymans who got to touch Nora Strawser's tits when Chris had never even so much as kissed a girl didn't matter any more. Because he was bigger than that. They had themselves, and they could do whatever they wanted to do. At least that's what Chris felt like at that very moment. Like no one could touch them.

Ray smiled and said, "And, as your leader, I shall now commence our official inauguration ceremony." He lifted the rock and threw it as hard as he could through a cafeteria window. Chris and Vic followed suit, laughing. Within minutes, nearly every window was broken and alarms were screaming. The boys heard sirens in the night.

Ray smiled and said, "Time to go."

TWO

"Who the hell was that last night?" Gerald said.

He padded past Alice, who lay on the sofa, awake, staring out the picture window, wondering what other people's lives were like in their neighborhood. Did Lizzy Nyman, who lived across the street, have an alcoholic brother she'd abandoned years ago because it was just too painful to watch him become his father? Did Lizzy's husband, Tom, have a work wife and all but ignore her at home? Would she stand for it if he did? Lizzy Nyman probably visited her family a couple of times a year—certainly more than Alice, who'd returned home only a handful of times since leaving twenty-four years ago.

Gerald poked his head back into the room and said, "Hey! I asked you a question. You okay?" Then, he went back into the kitchen, where Alice heard him opening the fridge.

Would you really care if I wasn't? Alice wondered. Instead of saying that, she said, "No. Not really. My father died last night."

Gerald came in and stood next to her. He said, "What happened?"

Alice shrugged. "Don't know. My mother wouldn't really tell me."

"What do you mean? She must have told you something."

"Well she didn't. Just that it was an accident."

Gerald sniffed and said, "That could mean anything." He turned and went back into the kitchen. A minute later he said, "We're getting low on coffee."

Alice turned her attention back outside. Lizzy Nyman's husband probably wouldn't complain about having no coffee when *her* father died.

Stop feeling sorry for yourself, she thought.

Alice sighed, depressed, resolved. She stood up and walked into the kitchen. Gerald was sitting at the breakfast bar, the TV turned low to CNBC, the financial channel, the paper opened up before him, just another day dealing in imaginary money.

Alice picked up the remote and turned off the TV.

"Hey! What gives?" Gerald complained.

"Gerald. I want you to listen carefully to me."

He made his fine-get-on-with-it face. Alice felt like punching him. He was impossibly self-centered.

"My father died last night. I'm upset. I was hoping you might provide me some comfort."

"Well, if you're expecting me to go to the funeral, forget it. I never liked your Dad. Plus, work's really bad right now. I mean, you know that."

Alice smiled a little in the face of this proof that her husband wasn't really that. They were strangers. But they'd loved each other once. A great deal. There had been a time when they couldn't keep their hands off each other, and Alice would have done anything for Gerald.

Alice gritted her teeth, trying not to turn this into a blowout fight. She said, "Gerald. Listen to me. He was my father and—"

"—What do you want me to say, Alice? You don't like your family, remember? Now all of a sudden we're supposed to give a rat's ass?"

"He was my father. For better or worse, he was my family."

"I don't see why you're getting all upset. I mean—"

"That's not the point, Gerald!"

This isn't working, Alice thought. She didn't expect comfort. Not from Gerald. She didn't know what she wanted from him. Maybe nothing. Maybe just to prove that the marriage was failing. Why was everything so complicated?

"I'm leaving for Maine today," she said.

"You know I can't go, right?"

"I don't want you to go. I'm leaving for Maine this morning. As soon as I pack."

"How long you gonna be gone?" Gerald asked.

"I don't know. A couple of weeks. We need time apart. I need time to think about things."

"What things?" Gerald said, his brow wrinkling, as though he really didn't have the slightest clue.

"Us. And this . . ." Alice waved her hand to indicate the house, everything. "I'm not happy anymore, Gerald. We're different. We've grown apart, and we need to think about that."

"Is this about Tiffany? 'Cause that's nothing. I've told you that a million times. She's just someone at work. A friend. Nothing."

"No, this isn't about *Tiffany*." Alice said her name with as much disgust as she could muster. "This is about me."

"You really want to do this, huh?"

Alice nodded. "I do."

"What about your job?"

"I'll tell them the truth."

"You told them you grew up in Connecticut!"

She had, it was true. She hadn't thought of that. She'd habitually lied about where she grew up, where she came from, for years, fearing that if people found out she grew up in some backwater dump like Redding, Maine, they'd think less of her. She didn't even have a trace of a Maine accent now. That part of Alice was gone. Forever. Maybe Gerald was right. Maybe she should stay in Chatham. Chris would come home eventually. And her mother had uncle Bruce. Was it really so bad here with Gerald?

Of course it wasn't. She had a big house, nice car, great job, a few good friends. They'd been closer once. They could find it again. Right? They had a lot, but lately Alice had felt that something was missing. Like she had reached some great destination, some great place, but had forgotten how she'd gotten there. It was the journey, the connection to the past that was gone. And she'd carefully constructed her life that way. And now that curtain was being pulled back, just a little, to remind her that the lies she'd told herself and others over the years where just that: lies. She wasn't a real person. She was a facade. Even to Gerald. Gerald didn't know her completely. No one did. She'd done a damn good job of hiding things from others but mostly herself. And that would make a person hard to love. But Gerald had, in his own way. Had to give him credit for that.

Alice looked hard at her husband, who had returned to his financial ticker, paper, and cereal. The more Alice thought about traveling up north, the more she resolved to herself that she would use this opportunity to put some things to rest, make some things right in her life. Maybe really help Chris, get him into treatment again, be there for him. Confront her past and be honest about it. After all, she'd proven herself better than how started out in life, hadn't she?

"I'm going to Maine. I'll call you when I get there."

Gerald looked up from his cereal and studied her face a little. He nodded and said, "Be careful, okay?"

The genuine sincerity in his voice and on his face touched her. Somewhere, the old Gerald was still in there.

"I will," she said.

And then she was in her Merc, her Kindle on the front seat set to read a hefty Ken Follet novel to her during the six-hour trip. Gerald was behind the front storm door, waving goodbye. She wondered if their marriage was really over and if he'd call Tiffany when her car was out of sight.

"Thanks, Don. Sorry you had to drag ass all the way here for that," a tall man in a neat grey suit said, extending his hand.

Detective Don Lambert took it and shook it firmly. He said, "Not a problem. Just glad it ended soon. I'm headed down to Augusta on business anyway. Congrats on your conviction."

Peter Eldridge shrugged and said sarcastically, "Yeah, this one was a beaut."

Don had known Peter for years and frequently testified as a witness for him. Today had been a more-or-less routine burglary case, which Don had happened to investigate, but he'd been called here on murder cases, molestation, assault. The works. You see a lot in law enforcement. And usually not the best sides of humanity, although that comes through sometimes as well.

"Okay, Peter. I'm sure I'll be talking to you soon. I gotta get rolling if I'm gonna catch Doc Carol." He felt a bit of trepidation at the thought of meeting the Chief Medical Examiner in Augusta. Her cool handling of death was unsettling.

"Tell her I said hello."

Don nodded.

Peter winked at him and snapped his fingers in a mock gun shape. "See you soon." He turned and disappeared. On to another case.

Don left the building, fishing a cigarette out of his shirt pocket, feeling guilty. Someday he'd quit. He then headed south, towards Augusta, hoping he was too early for any traffic, listening to talk radio. He didn't care much for the music they played on the popular stations nowadays, more evidence that he was getting older.

Maybe Gaye was right. Maybe he should retire. Although he wasn't too keen on the idea, he had been thinking about retirement for a few years now. He'd been in the county sheriff's department for nearly 30 years, about half as a supervising detective. He'd had opportunity for advancement, but who wanted it? He loved dealing with people, loved solving crimes. They were like puzzles sometimes.

And even though it was probably just in his mind, the Maine winters seemed to be getting longer, snowier, and colder. He spent more time shoveling than he liked and had lately begun to wonder if maybe he and Gaye would be better off wintering in Florida or maybe out west in Nevada or New Mexico. The west had always appealed to him, although he was sure Gaye would vote for Florida. As distasteful an idea as it seemed at times, he couldn't quite shake the thought of it. It wouldn't be, after all, as though they'd abandon Maine altogether. Certainly not. They'd just hide out until the snow cleared.

Besides, there were plenty of younger guys waiting to take their turn. Detective Sgt. Matt Ivey, for example. Don worked with Matt frequently. He was his unofficial partner. The kid was young, smart, and eager. A go-getter as they say. He'd probably make supervisor if Don left.

A little while later, Don pulled onto the unassuming little street that housed the CME's office, just behind the State Police Crime Laboratory. Visiting the CME's office was never a pleasant job. The doctors who worked in there had a special brand of tolerance for the human condition that Don could never quite work up to. He'd seen his share of horrendous accidents, but nothing quite prepares you for the clinical coldness of how these doctors regard the victims.

He entered the little brick building and made his way down the main hallway towards the back to Carol's office. He knocked gently on the door. Dr. Carol Farington was a good looking woman with a smart, stern look about her. Neat. Controlled. She wore her dark brown hair short. She smiled a little upon seeing Don filling up her doorway.

"Be right with you, Don, just trying to finish up here. You almost missed me."

"Yeah, sorry about that. Had to testify up in Skowhegan. Hope I didn't waste a trip."

Carol laughed in a way that made Don nervous. She said, "Oh, no. You didn't waste a trip. That much I assure you."

Don watched her scribble for a minute or two. Then, she signed her name with a flourish and made a point of dotting the 'i' in Farington.

"Done," she said, putting the small pile of papers in a metal tray on her desk. She stood up and put on her lab coat. "Follow me, please."

Don did as he was told and followed Carol down a flight of stairs and through a large set of wooden swinging doors labeled *Authorized Personnel Only*. She headed towards a wall of stainless steel doors on the left, simultaneously clicking on a set of intensely bright overhead lights.

"Your friend here surprised us, Don. Now, you understand that we haven't done the full work up. I'm just giving you my impressions. Off the record, of course. As a favor."

Don tried to say, "Of course," but what came out was more of a dry-throated grunt. He would rather Carol not refer to a dead body as his "friend."

She reached out and pulled open one of the coffin-sized drawers to reveal a black body bag within. With swift, practiced motions, she pulled on a pair of clear gloves from her lab-coat pocket and wiggled her fingers to get the fit right.

Don's stomach dropped a little as he prepared for Carol to casually unzip the plastic bag that covered Ed "Papa" Wynter's corpse.

Dr. Farington drew down the zipper gently, perhaps sensing that Don wasn't as comfortable in these situations as she, and pulled the edges back to reveal the startlingly grey flesh within.

Don breathed outward in disgust. Much of Papa Wynter's head was missing.

Carol, now oblivious to Don's unease, pulled out a telescoping wand from her coat pocket and extended it six-or-so inches. She pointed it at the obvious entry wound and started to explain.

1984

"Vic, don't be such a wuss," Ray Wynter said, looking across at Victor Acree from the front seat, where he sat driving the Chevy Nova.

Chris sat in the back seat and watched the overhead street lights streak by. He fished out a cigarette and lit it. Truth was, he didn't think what they were planning on doing was such a good idea either, but something felt good about it. Like they could do anything they wanted to so long as they stuck together.

"I'm not being a wuss, okay? I just don't know if this is such a good idea."

Ray shook his head and turned his attention back to the road. "You're being a wuss," he said again softly.

"Chris, right?" Vic said.

Chris shrugged.

Ray said, "Oh, for fuck's sake. Don't tell me your pussying out too."

"I didn't say anything," Chris said.

"Dudes, we didn't get caught last week! We're the fucking Masters of Chaos! Vic, tell me it didn't feel good to stick it up the school's ass. Those fuckers didn't even know what hit 'em. We blew out almost every goddamn window in that place. Stupid assholes."

Chris laughed. Ray was right. It had been *good.*

Ray took a swig from a bottle he was holding between his legs and passed it to Chris, who swigged it and then passed it back to Vic, who took a deep gulp.

Ray said, "So, we gonna fucking do this thing or what?"

Vic lit up a joint and passed it around. He said, "Masters of Chaos, motherfuckers!"

"Masters of Chaos!" Ray and Chris yelled back.

The Chevy Nova raced on as the boys got higher and rowdier. Before long, Ray pulled the Nova into the Plaza Lanes parking lot and around the back. The place was crowded as usual this Friday night.

"Ray, how are we going to do this without getting caught?"

"Just trust me, okay? I saw this in a movie once. It's fucking brilliant." Ray stopped the car and turned it off. "Ready, boys?"

Chris and Vic got out while Ray popped the trunk. Normally, only employees used the back lot. It was dark and just a few cars were parked in the spots closest to the Plaza Lanes building where the dumpster was. Their target.

Chris looked down into the trunk and saw three gasoline filled bottles, the kind with the resealable tops for people who make their own beer and soda. Ray pushed past him and picked up a rag, tearing it into three strips. He handed one each to Vic and Chris and kept one for himself. He did the same with the bottles.

Ray said, "Anyone catches us before we get in the dumpster, ditch the bottles and say we're just headed in to bowl."

Vic and Chris nodded.

Chris's stomach curled up into a tight ball, and he felt lightheaded. Before, it was all talk. Now they were doing it. Really doing it. They were going to give the Nora Strawsers of the world something to think about. Same with her boyfriends or whatever they were, Billy Cate and Sean Wayman, the asshole jocks who'd made Ray lick the bowling alley floor last Friday in front of Nora, who'd stood there in that stupid cheerleading outfit laughing and smacking her gum.

They got everything they wanted. Chris felt like he never did.

Not even from his own family. Except maybe Alice, but she was smart in a way that he wasn't. And then there was Papa. Papa was a loud, mean drunk who seemed on most days to hate Chris. Even Chris's Uncle Bruce, Ray's father, seemed to think Chris was a loser. They sure loved Ray, however. But they didn't know about Ray like Chris did. They didn't know that he smoked pot and drank and talked about stuff like being in the Masters of Chaos. They didn't know about the time last year when Ray almost killed a guy after stringing up a wire across the road between two signs to see what would happen. (He didn't expect the guy on a moped to come along, a guy who was damn lucky to still have a head.) They didn't know that Ray liked to watch videos in his basement of girls getting tied up or that he had a whole grocery bag filled with such porno videos and magazines. No, they didn't know Ray like Chris did. Ray was a bad kid, and that's why Chris liked hanging around him and Vic. They just knew stuff and made Chris feel like he wasn't such a loser. They were like family.

And now, they were going to get even with Nora Strawser, Billy Cate, and Sean Wayman. Chris was tired of all the shit they got and he didn't.

Chris looked over and saw Vic, whose eyes were wide with fear and excitement. Vic was getting off on it too.

"C'mon, douche bags, let's go, let's go, let's go!" Ray motioned towards Chris and Vic with a wave of his arm. He was already twenty-five feet ahead and walking towards the dumpster just next to the back door of the place. When he got there, he tried to climb up into the dumpster himself up but couldn't manage it. "Boost me up," he whispered.

Chris locked his hands together and held them down for Ray to step on. Soon, Ray was in the dumpster. He said, "See, the thing is, I'm gonna clear out a spot and set the bottles down. Then, I'm gonna light a fuse I made out of matches that'll burn down slow enough that we can get outta here."

Vic said, "Hurry up! What if someone comes?"

"Stuff the rags in the bottles and hand 'em over," Ray said. "Make sure the cloth hits the gas."

Chris and Vic each unstopped their bottles and poked their cloth strips down into the hole. Chris watched the gasoline climb up the cloth. He handed his over the lip of the dumpster to Ray. Vic followed.

"Holy shit!" Vic said. "Someone's coming. I can see him coming down the hallway. Some fat guy. He's the cook!"

"Fuck!" Ray said from inside the dumpster. "Block the door with your foot!"

Vic slammed his foot next to the door and tried to keep away from the little window. He said, "Jesus, Ray, hurry!"

Ray climbed over the edge of the dumpster and fell

down to ground in a heap. He groaned and picked himself up.

Chris was already halfway back to the car and panicky. If they got caught, there'd be hell to pay. They'd get juvenile hall for sure. Chris shot a look backwards. Ray was running towards him. Chris saw the cook. He was a lumbering fat guy with a greasy apron hanging in front of him dragging a overstuffed garbage bag. He was about halfway down the hall.

Ray yelled out, "Vic! He's got a way to go, let's get outta here! He can't see outside! There are no lights out here."

Ray was always thinking stuff like that. Smart.

Vic didn't need any more encouragement. He took off for the Nova. Chris was in the back seat. His heart was racing. He felt excited and powerful. Good.

Chris said, "Start the engine, Ray!"

Ray shook his head. He said, "Too late. The cook'll see us."

Vic hit the front seat the moment the back door slammed open and hit the outside wall.

The fat cook's chin jiggled as he tried to haul the garbage bag up and into the dumpster. He stopped suddenly and looked around, out at the parking lot, like he was smelling something.

"Down!" Ray said. "Fuck. He smells the fire or the gas or something."

Chris poked his head up just above the window line. "He's throwing the bag in."

The next seconds were a blur. There was a sudden rush of air and low *whoomp* as the gasoline caught. That was followed by a loud pop. The cook screamed.

They boys looked up and saw flames shooting up out of the dumpster, licking the roof's overhang, searing the edges.

Chris's stomach sank and he thought, *We just lit the whole fucking building on fire.*

Ray was laughing.

The cook stumbled backwards, shielding his face from the intense heat of the blaze and fell backwards into the building. He was screaming bloody murder but was so far unable to get off his fat ass and onto his feet to warn everyone inside.

Vic said, "Jesus, Ray, let's get outta here!"

Ray just laughed. "Not yet."

Chris said, "C'mon man, let's go."

"Not until we hear the first siren."

"Ray! C'mon!" Vic said.

Chris heard a second pop from the dumpster and watched the flames intensify. The back side of the building was on fire now and had spread to the roof. He wasn't scared anymore. Hell, he *wanted* the building to burn down. They did this. Just the three of them.

Chris began to laugh with Ray and thought about Nora Strawser panicking inside. That stuck-up bitch deserved it. They all did. Chris felt a powerful erection pressing against his jeans.

Vic turned his head towards Chris and Ray and said, "Fucking Masters of Chaos."

They were one in destruction.

A siren cut through the night. Ray fired up the engine and took off.

Chris watched Plaza Lanes burn out the back window and felt like a fucking million dollars.

THREE

Alice Dunn crossed into Maine on the Piscataqua River Bridge with mixed emotions. A part of her *was* really glad to see her home state again. It was, in many ways, an indescribably beautiful place filled with friendly, wonderful people. In another place and time, she imagined Gerald and her driving to some little camp on a lake with two kids fast asleep in the back seat.

But this was not that time. She was going to a place she'd spent the better part of her life trying to forget. This was the *other* Maine, the part they don't advertise in the brochures in the Freeport Hampton Inn lobby. She was headed to Redding, where she'd grown up under the oppressive, drunken rule of her father, a man she was now to bury.

The Maine Turnpike stretched out in front of her like a long fuse, and Alice raced towards Augusta, where she would turn off and travel northwest towards Redding. She was hoping to make Redding by nightfall, which was now rapidly approaching. She'd been driving for over five hours and was tired and had to pee badly, but she wouldn't stop. She was afraid if she did, she'd lose her nerve and turn around.

At last, well after the sun had lost its battle with night, Alice Wynter reached Redding and wound her way through the little streets lined with new quaint Cape Cod- and ranch-style houses. It was a typical Maine small town, and one that had come a long way since her childhood. But there were holdouts. Set back from the road, she saw a few run-down trailer-style homes among the newer houses and thought of her family's house, which wasn't new. Or quaint. There were a few more obligatory strip malls and chain stores, which she normally didn't like, but here they somehow provided her a sense of familiarity that reminded her of her other home. And then she passed a Starbucks and let out a long breath, unashamedly relieved to have a source of decent coffee while she was here. But it was the foreignness of it all that struck Alice most. A mask of newness covered the town, but this was a literal ghost town for Alice. Around every corner, her mind's eye filled with memories. Some sweet and innocent but most not so. She'd come a long way from this place.

And then she was on Gardiner Avenue with just a few hundred feet left. She turned slowly onto a well worn dirt driveway with a Mohawk of brown, winter grass down the middle. Her tires crunched on the frozen ground and the overgrown bare shrubs seemed to close in on her as she made her way towards her old house.

She put the black Mercedes into park and stared at the dashboard, trying to gather her thoughts and relish this last moment of sanity before turning back the pages in the book of her life. Before her mind could argue, her body moved and stepped outside into the chill, clean Maine air. She locked her car and walked towards the house, wondering if she'd made the right decision.

Jackie Ruth Wynter stood on the porch, her face concealed in the darkness. Alice saw a thin line of cigarette smoke curling upward.

When Alice was close enough, Jackie Ruth said, "Dolly. Look at you with your fancy car. You look like a movie star."

Alice said, "Hi, Ma."

"You gotta hug for your mother?"

"Of course," Alice said and embraced her rail-thin mother. Alice stared down at the worn paint on the porch and thought about her cousin Ray and a brief moment long ago.

When she was twelve, she and her mother had spent hours together creating a Halloween princess costume for Alice, complete with sparkly wand, tutu, and tiara. They'd planned it for weeks before buying the fabric and glitter from Pete's Hardware in town, which also sold craft supplies. It was the only time Alice could remember she and her mother getting along well, talking about boys and life. Chris and Papa had mercifully left them alone.

And when the costume was finished, she waited patiently for Halloween, counting the days. Finally, the day came, and she put on her costume and stood in the mirror admiring herself, knowing she'd find a life for herself, dreaming that she'd be able to wear a real princess gown someday, perhaps at her wedding.

She stood out on the porch holding her goody bag, waiting for Chris to get ready, when her cousin Ray stepped out. He was fourteen, and much bigger than she was. They were alone on the porch. Ray told her she looked pretty in a way that made Alice's insides squishy. He moved closer and pushed her against the house, forcing his body close to hers. He touched her breasts, or what there was of them then, placing a hand outside her costume. He touched himself beneath his hobo costume and whispered dirty things in her ear, most of which she didn't understand, things about her. She tried to tell him to stop, tried to push him away, but he was too strong, so she gave up and did nothing. She stood stone-still like a statue, confused and scared and wanting him to stop. She told him he was gross, but he just told her to be quiet for a minute. So she was. Then, all at once, Ray breathed heavily into her ear and seemed to twitch. He pulled his hand away from her chest and went into the house.

She hadn't thought much of it then. She'd just blocked it out, forgotten about it. He was a boy. Boys did gross things. She forgot all about it until high school, when the memory should have served as a warning but didn't. Now, Alice could never forget it.

"Let's get you inside," Jackie Ruth said, interrupting Alice's thoughts. "Get you warmed up."

When they entered the house, Alice saw Uncle Bruce, who stood up and smiled. He was thinner and older. He looked worn out. Run down.

He said, "Well, I'll be. Alice Wynter."

"Dunn."

Bruce raised an eyebrow.

Alice smiled. "I'm Alice Dunn now." She held up her left hand and twiddled her ring finger.

Bruce shook his head and walked towards her with his arms out. "Well, around here you're still Alice Wynter. Can't change that, I'm afraid."

No I can't, Alice thought, gloomily.

Jackie Ruth said, "Have a seat, Dolly. Can I fix you some coffee?"

"Actually, I need to go to the little girls' room. I'll just have a glass of water, okay?"

Jackie Ruth nodded and fetched a tall glass.

When Alice returned from the bathroom, she interrupted the conversation. Both Jackie Ruth and Bruce sat at the kitchen table and looked at her and smiled guiltily.

"What's going on?" Alice demanded.

Bruce shook his head as if to say: *nothing*. Instead he bit his lip.

Jackie Ruth said, "Alice, you know how your brother is. Well, he—"

"—He's gotten worse since the last time you saw him," Bruce finished.

Alice said, "But I thought he was doing better. In his letters, he said—"

"It's just not that simple, Dolly dear," Jackie Ruth said, lighting up a Carlton and taking a deep drag. "He and your father had been hitting it pretty hard lately. More than . . . well, normal."

Alice was confused. She assumed he was getting better. He said he was getting better in his letters. Even talked about rehab again. It was Papa. It was always Papa keeping him down.

"There's, uh, more," Bruce said. He exchanged a worried glance with Jackie Ruth.

Alice waited expectantly.

Jackie Ruth said, "Alice, dear, your brother's gone missing. Since your father . . . passed. We're worried sick. He must've been drunk as a skunk. The police are looking for him but . . ." She shrugged. Her face was creased with worry.

No more need be said. Alice grew up in Maine. She understood more than most that the middle of January at night is no time to wander off into the woods, especially after you've been drinking.

She thought about Ray again. What had happened to Ray his senior year of high school.

And then her emotions came forward in a rush and tears streamed from her eyes. She apologized, but it was no use. Her twin brother was in trouble. Or worse.

1984

Chris's feet slipped on the wet interior of another dumpster. Fire licked up and curled around his forearms, singing his hair. Immediately, the air was filled with the sickening smell of burning flesh. He screamed and began to panic slightly as the gasoline soaked rags burned black and threatened to ignite the bottles. If that happened, he'd have no chance.

He jumped and slipped again, his flat sneaker treads unable to gain traction on the sloped side of the dumpster.

"Hurry up, man!" Vic said from outside the dumpster.

Ray was laughing.

Chris, completely panicked now, jumped and caught the lip of the dumpster with his hand. He clung for dear life and pulled himself upward. Then, he felt a sharp pain in his hand that raced down his arm, and Chris let go, sliding back down into the burning dumpster. Ray had hit his hand! He heard Ray laughing. He fell again and tipped one of the bottles, which spilled out and caught fire immediately, joining the other blaze.

Vic said, "Ray, man! What the fuck are you doing? Why did you do that?"

"Relax, I'm just fucking around!"

Through sheer adrenaline, Chris jumped high enough to hook his elbows on the lip of the dumpster. Vic helped pull him over. Chris fell and landed painfully on the asphalt just as the first of the bottles exploded with whoosh.

Earlier that evening, Chris had snuck out of his bedroom window to meet Vic and Ray late to get fucked up and do another fire. He guessed it was now two or three o'clock. The air was cool and clear. It was a good night to be out screwing around and getting into trouble.

Sirens.

"We better get moving," Ray said calmly and turned toward the running car.

Vic said, "Ray, man, that was not cool. He could have died."

"Gimme a break man. Don't be so dramatic. Does he look dead to you?"

Chris was paying no attention to the argument. He was too busy taking inventory of his body, trying to figure out how badly he was injured. His ribs hurt like anything and his forearm was covered with little black balls of singed hair. Other than that, he seemed fine. Behind him, a second bottle burst and sent forth a wave of heat. Chris couldn't help but giggle a little.

Ray turned back and stared up into the flames and said, "Holy shit, that was good one!"

"Yeah," Vic agreed.

"We fucking did that, man," Ray said.

Even Chris had to smile. This dumpster was the third of the week. They were starting to make the papers. The Kennebec Journal had a story on the arsons just this morning. They were big time now. Vic was even working on a logo so they could leave it behind. As a warning.

The boys piled into the Nova and sped off.

Ray said, "Let's park across the street and watch them."

"What are you, fucking crazy?" Vic said. "Ray, man, seriously, we're gonna get caught. What if someone saw us?"

Ray laughed. "No one saw us. We're not gonna get caught."

He pulled into a parking lot about a block away from the Redding Library, where they'd lit up the dumpster. Ray parked under a Ronnie's Auto and Truck Repair sign and turned the car off. The three boys hunched down in their seats and waited. The sirens were getting closer.

Their first fire at Plaza Lanes had spread all across the roof and burned a good portion of the back wall. All the Sean Wayman and Nora Strawser assholes had run out screaming like chickenshits. That part always made Chris smile. Thinking about Nora Strawser scared made him hard. Hell, thinking about Nora Strawser in any way made him hard. He thought about her a lot. He also thought a lot about setting fires. Sometimes he jerked off thinking about the fires. Setting fires made him feel good. Made them all feel good. They shared something together. Like brothers. It was them against this piss-ant town.

A police car raced by and turned into the library parking lot. Chris's heart raced. They'd get juvi-hall for sure if they got caught. Probably for a long time. He looked back and saw Vic's wide eyes and bright smile. He felt it too. Only Ray seemed bored.

A second later, a big fire truck raced by and followed the police car. This was soon followed by another. Then another.

Chris began to worry. "We better get out of here."

Ray said, "No way, man. It's too late."

Vic said, "Chris is right. They'll see us."

"Of course they'll see us," Ray said. "You think they'll catch us in the Nova? No way. I could fucking take them."

Chris knew better than to challenge Ray. He was talking shit, but he'd do it just to prove a point. He was getting worse like that lately. Since the fires started.

A few minutes later and the bright orange glow at the back of the library was gone. The fire was out. An hour later and they boys were passing around a celebratory joint.

"Fucking unbelievable," Vic said.

Chris nodded.

"Dumpster fires are nothing," Ray said, out of the blue. "Kid stuff."

Vic said, "What do you mean?"

"We gotta do something big. Make news. Big news."

Chris said, "Like what?"

"I don't know, something bigger."

Chris was afraid to ask what. He was happy with the dumpsters. But still, he'd never felt this way before. When he was out with Ray and Vic and being Masters of Chaos, he didn't give a shit about school or his stupid father or the fact that he couldn't get a girl to look at him, much less touch him. All that mattered was the fire, sticking it to them. The bastards.

Vic said, "What, like a house?" His voice was calm.

Ray nodded. "Yeah, maybe a house. Or something. I don't know. Yeah, maybe a fucking house."

Alice spent most of the next day in a haze, trying to make sense of things. Her brother was missing, but she felt in her heart that he wasn't dead, that he *couldn't* be dead, because she'd know. They might be estranged, and he might be a down-and-out alcoholic, but they were twins. So, he wasn't dead. That was that.

So where was he?

Alice kept herself busy with mindless chores around the house for her mother, who padded around until mid-day in her bathrobe and slippers. The house was dirty, and Alice felt vaguely guilty, as she always did, that she wasn't closer by to look after things. Chris wouldn't be any help even without his problems.

No. Alice stopped herself. She refused to feel guilty about wanting better things for herself than Redding. It wasn't her fault that her mother had married a drunken tyrant. It wasn't her fault that her twin brother had a serious alcohol problem, which he was likely to die of.

You could have at least checked up on him, Alice thought. *Maybe encouraged him a little, especially after senior year, after what happened.*

Alice shook her head to clear her mind. Her thinking was wrong. She was blaming herself for the world's problems when the truth was she'd had her own set of terrible problems then. But she wouldn't even entertain a walk down that particular memory lane. Not today.

Jackie Ruth watched her from the kitchen table. Her lunch plate and empty glass sat in front of her. A stubbed out cigarette butt protruded from the remains of her tuna-fish sandwich. She said, “You got something on your mind, Dolly? Come. Sit.” She patted the chair next to her.

Alice sat and said nothing. Her mother looked worn out and tired. Sad. But she wouldn’t shed too many tears over losing Papa. She’d had a hard life living with him and his excesses and abuses.

Alice said, “You doing okay, Ma?”

Her mother stood and grabbed her plate to take it to the sink. “What does okay mean, anyway? My okay might not be someone else’s.”

“You’re sad about Papa.”

“ ‘Course I’m sad. But I’m not gonna lie to you. Not a day went by I didn’t think about leaving him.”

“Why didn’t you?”

Jackie Ruth lit up a cigarette and sat down again at the table. She took a long drag and said, “Lots of things. You kids. The house. I don’t know.”

Alice pursed her lips and nodded, agreeing.

“It wasn’t easy. After you left, you know, things . . .” Her voice trailed off and she looked out the window thinking. “Things just changed for your brother and father both.”

“They drank more?”

“Yeah, that. Always that. But something else as well.” She shrugged. “Water under the bridge, I guess. Right?”

“Something like that,” Alice said.

“He loved you, you know.”

“I know.”

"No, I don't think you do," Jackie Ruth said. "He was always proud of you."

Alice smiled. "He hated me."

Jackie Ruth smiled right back. "You're wrong. Your father was a monster in a lot of ways, but he did love you. You had a connection."

"What about Chris?"

"Oh, Chris too, I suppose. But things were different with him. Your father didn't respect Chris like he respected you."

Alice laughed bitterly. "Papa Wynter didn't respect anybody."

Jackie Ruth shrugged. "Maybe you're—"

A knock at the kitchen door.

Alice looked up and saw a huge man in a dark suit standing on the porch. He looked like a cop. Her stomach dropped to the floor.

Chris. It's going to be about Chris. He's dead. Please don't let that be true, Alice thought. She glanced at her mother, whose brow had furrowed deeply.

"I better get that," Alice said. She stood up and opened the door.

The officer took off his hat and said, "Ma'am? I'm Detective Don Lambert from the Somerset County Sheriff's Office. Is, uh, Jackie Ruth in?"

Alice stood aside and said, "Please," inviting the man in with her hand.

The big man stepped into the house and looked around. He said, "Nice cozy little place you got here."

Alice said, "I'm Alice Dunn. Or Wynter. I'm Alice Wynter. Was Alice Wynter. Oh, hell. I'm sorry. I'm Jackie Ruth's daughter." She was suddenly nervous and scared like a little kid.

Jackie Ruth didn't stand up. Instead, she lit another cigarette and said, "What can we do you for, Detective? Lambert was it? Care for some coffee or tea?"

"No. No, thank you. I can only stay for a moment or two. Ma'am, I'm afraid I've got some bad news."

Alice's stomach churned.

Jackie Ruth said, "Oh, dear Jesus. What now?"

The detective said, "Do either of you know the whereabouts of Chris? Is he here?"

Alice shook her head. She didn't understand. If he was dead, the detective wouldn't be asking about him. "You mean he's not dead?"

"Frankly—Alice was it?"

Alice nodded.

"Alice, we just don't know what's going on."

Jackie Ruth said, "What's the bottom line? What does Chris have to do with anything? He's got some problems. Booze."

"Ma'am, your husband didn't commit suicide. He was shot. At close range. Based on a cursory analysis at the scene, we assumed it was suicide. We were wrong."

Jackie Ruth held her hand over her mouth in shock.

Alice was thinking the same thing: Chris did it.

"So," the detective continued, "Do either of you know where Chris is?"

Alice shook her head. She tried to say, *no*, but all that came out was a squeak. She cleared her throat and said, "No. We have no idea."

The detective looked hard at Jackie Ruth and said, "You're sure on this?"

Jackie Ruth nodded.

"Okay. That's fine for now." The heavy detective fished a business card from his pocket and handed one each to Alice and Jackie Ruth. "But if Chris makes contact, we need you to call us right away."

Alice and Jackie Ruth nodded in stunned silence.

"And we'll need to talk to the both of you at some point. Down at the station. Now, I know what you're thinking but stop yourselves. It's just routine. Homicide cases are a little different. We're just trying to touch all our bases here."

Homicide.

The ugly word repeated over and over in Alice's mind.

FOUR

Flynn's Bar and Grill was a favorite haunt of Papa and Chris Wynter. It was a dive favored by the local working class and did a good business most nights. Hell, Don had tossed back a few there himself. But it was a rough place, a real townie bar. As a patrolman, Don Lambert had broken up his share of fights outside as well as arrested countless drunk drivers coming out of the little parking lot in the back. It was a rite of passage. He'd once even busted a guy who'd fallen asleep shortly after getting behind the wheel and let his car roll across the street and through a chain link fence.

After his meeting with the Wynters, Don decided to check the place out, maybe grab a cool one after talking with Andy Flynn.

The humid, beer-soaked air engulfed Don when he opened the back door to the bar. He stepped up two crooked steps and nodded at a scraggly, serious-looking man in a dirty green baseball hat playing pinball in the back hallway near the door.

The patrons quieted considerably when they saw the detective. He was a formidable presence and took advantage of it. Lately, Flynn's seemed to attract a younger crowd, perhaps drawn to the sheer desperateness of it. It was so unhip it was cool.

"Well! I'll be. Don Lambert!" A grotesquely fat man yelled over the deafening strains of some heavy metal tune or another.

Don held a hand up to his ear. The bartender reached under the counter. The music quieted.

"Don, you don't get in here enough," the man said.

Don grinned. "Andy, you old dog. How you been?" He stepped forward and shook Andy Flynn's hand. He was an old, old friend whom Don had known since arriving in Maine years ago. "You got a couple minutes?"

"For you, sure. You want a beer?"

Don tapped his watch. "Maybe when we're done here. I'm still technically on the clock."

Andy waved him over, indicating that they could talk in Andy's kitchen, upstairs. Andy had a back problem so severe he couldn't walk upright. It gave him the unmistakable gait of a silver-back gorilla. Don would have found it comical if he didn't know how much pain Andy was in most days. In many ways, working behind a bar was perfect for him. He was bent over most of the time anyway and could hold up his beefy upper body on the bar.

Don's eye gazed over Andy's wife, Rose. The woman hardly ever moved from her stool at the end of the bar. She nodded at him suspiciously, her eyes half shut, a long cigarette burning in her drink hand. She didn't like cops. She didn't like Don. He'd been against Andy's marrying her, way back when. They'd just never hit it off. He guessed he was still in the right there. But, the two of them made a pair and stuck with one another all these years. That says something.

Don said, "Hiya, Rose."

She sniffed, tapped her cigarette, and said, "What the hell would you know about it?"

Don smiled at her and said, "Lovely day, you know?" He followed Andy up a narrow staircase, slowly, cringing a little watching his friend struggle.

When Andy reached the top, he pulled out a cheap metal chair for Don and then sat in his own abruptly, breathing heavily. He took a handkerchief out of his pocket, wiped his forehead, and then coughed thickly into it. He stuffed it back into his pocket after examining the contents.

Don said, "How's business?"

" 'Bout the same, I'd say. Usually picks up after the holidays. Don't know why."

"Yeah-uh. The wife?"

Andy nodded. "Been better. You?"

"Gaye is doing pretty good," Don said, rubbing his belly. "Been on my case about retiring."

"You? Retire?"

"Hey, I didn't say I was gonna!"

Andy nodded. "Bad Nor'easter coming, from what I hear," he said. "Coupla days off now."

Don nodded. Bad winter storms in Maine were nothing new to him. He said, "Listen, Andy, I'm here about Papa."

Andy shook his head and pulled the handkerchief out of his pocket again. "Damn shame," he said, blowing his nose. The handkerchief disappeared into his pocket again. "For what it's worth, he was a good customer. He and that boy of his."

"Was Papa here the night he killed himself?"

"He's here every night."

"What about his kid, Chris?"

"Him too."

"But did you see them here that night?" Don said.

"Yeah-uh. Came in about 7:30. Sat in their usual spots."

Don said, "You see anyone unusual that night? Maybe a hopped up kid or someone like that?"

Andy nodded. "We do get a few of those in nowadays. Mostly late night. They always pay and don't get into fights, so I don't have no trouble with them. What they do is their business. What do you care anyway? I heard the old guy shot himself."

News sure gets around in a small town. "Not exactly. Don't spread this around. I have your word?"

Andy said, "C'mon. It's me."

"Yeah, well, someone shot him."

Andy's face registered surprise. "You don't say."

"Yeah-uh."

"Who?"

"That's why I'm here. I figure Papa spent most of his time either here or asleep."

"Don, you're gonna kill me, but I wasn't here. I mean, I was here, okay, but I was up here in bed. My back was killing me. Took a Percocet and my lights were out. Been that way a couple times a week lately."

"What about Rose?"

"She was tending bar that night."

Don said, "Guess I'll have to go talk to her."

"I'm real sorry Don."

"Nah. It's nothing. Why don't you stay here? I'll go down and talk to Rose. Listen, you call me if you hear anything."

" 'Course."

"Take care of yourself, Andy. Oh, yeah, think you can come up with a list of people who were here that night? From Rose, I mean? I'd ask her myself, but—"

Andy held up a hand to stop Don. He nodded slowly as Don get up. He said, "No sweat. Take 'er easy."

Don gave him a little backwards wave and headed back down the steps, holding onto the railing for dear life, listening to the steps creak and groan under his weight. When he reached the bottom, he sat down next to Rose's seat. She was behind the bar now, closing the register. She put a beer down in front of Don and started fixing herself a drink.

Don picked up his beer and took a long sip. He told himself it was okay, that he was off the clock. It tasted good.

He said, "Rose—"

She held up a hand to stop him. "Before you say it, I know why you're here." She shook her head slowly and deliberately. "I tended bar, but I didn't see or hear anything from those two all night."

"Chris and Papa you mean."

"Who do you think I mean? Yeah, Chris and Papa."

"Can you tell me when they got here?"

She shrugged. "7, 7:30. Chris came first. Papa came in later. Usually does."

"So you did see them?"

"Well of course I *saw* them. I mean I didn't *see* them, if you know what I mean."

"Were they arguing?"

Rose laughed. She sounded like a kitchen garbage disposal filled with rocks. "Don, honey, they're always arguing." She sipped from her drink to test it and then waddled around the bar to sit down. She climbed up on the stool and carefully arranged herself. Then she lit another cigarette from a pack on the bar.

"You know what they were arguing about?"

"They argue about everything. How the hell would I know?"

Rose and Don sat in silence a few minutes. Don sipped his beer, thinking about Papa and Chris sitting at the bar, trying to imagine the night and put himself there, like a fly on the wall. It's all about possibilities, things that could've been.

Minutes passed and Don surveyed the bar patrons, most of whom were keeping themselves to themselves, trying to forget about their lives for a couple hours.

Then, across the bar, an old man Don knew to be Jimmy Bible barked, "They were arguing about Bruce's kid, Ray. Heard it clear as day."

Don got up and took his beer over to Jimmy. Don said, "You say they were arguing about Ray? Ray Wynter?"

Don hadn't thought about Ray Wynter in years. The kid was no good. But he'd died years ago. Why would Chris and Papa be arguing about Ray Wynter? Why would they even be talking about him all these years later?

"Yeah-uh. Heard 'em." Jimmy Bible wouldn't look Don in the eye. He didn't look anyone in the eye. A half-consumed beer sat in front of him. His hard-worked, leathery hands were folded next to it and a pack of Marlboro Reds with a lighter neatly arranged on top. He wore an expression, as did most of the people in Flynn's, that said he didn't trust Don much.

"What were they saying?"

"Couldn't tell you that. Nothing specific. But I heard 'em talking about him. Papa's boy got real mad and stormed out. And Papa weren't far behind him."

"You know what time?"

"It was late." Jimmy shrugged. "Don't know for sure."

"Thanks, Jimmy," Don said. "You think of anything else you call, okay? And take care of yourself."

"Yeah-uh. You got it, boss."

Don said loudly. "Anyone else hear anything like that?"

Many blank stares.

Don set down his beer and turned to walk out. When he got to the hallway that led to the back door, Don decided to relieve himself in the bathroom next to the pinball machine.

When he got out, he noticed the scraggly looking man he'd seen on his way in was gone. He found him the moment he stepped outside.

The man blew out a lungful of smoke and said, "There was someone else with them."

"With who?" Don said.

"The two you was asking about. I didn't know 'em."

Don thought, *he's from away. His accent.*

The man nodded vigorously. "When they left, I was out here smoking. I don't like smoking in all that hot air in there. Better out here."

Don nodded. He was a smoker. He knew. He pulled one out of his pocket and joined the man.

"They came out," the man said. "Met someone out here. Had a little argument or something like that."

"What did the other guy look like?"

The man shrugged. "Couldn't tell ya. Too dark. Just a guy I guess. Skinny fella. Tall. Long hair."

"Did they leave together?"

The man smiled. He said, "Don't know. I finished my smoke and went back in. Didn't think one way or the other about it."

Don nodded and said, "Appreciate your help." He took out a small notebook, writing down the details. He looked up. "Can I get your name?"

"Not unless you're gonna run me in for not telling you."

"Fair enough," Don said and flipped his notebook shut. "Don't drink too much tonight. You hear?"

The man grinned. He was missing a canine tooth on the right side of his face. "Naw. I'm good."

Don got in his car, glad to be back out in the cold, away from the moist, hot air in Flynn's. He thought about what Jimmy Bible had said. And Ray Wynter. He was a bad kid. Then he remembered the crime spree. The fires. And the teacher. But that was a long time ago, and he couldn't remember the details. Gaye would remember. She remembered things like that.

He started the Crown Vic and pulled out of Flynn's, heading home. Gaye would be getting worried, and he needed to kick back in his La-Z-Boy, watch the tube and relax.

1984

His old man was staring at him that way again. Chris knew that look better than anyone, except for maybe Alice, who was sitting across from him at the dinner table staring down at her food, her long, black hair covering all but a small window of her face.

Finally, Chris couldn't take it any more. "What?" He said to Papa.

Papa took a long pull on his beer and belched. It was Thursday evening, and Thursday evenings were drinking nights, although Papa usually got started a fuck of a lot earlier in the day. He smirked at Chris and nodded.

"What?" Chris said again.

"You're a little shit, you know that?"

Jackie Ruth said, "That'll be enough."

Under his breath, Chris said, "Fuck off."

"What was that? I didn't catch that, little shit."

"I said, 'Fuck off,'" Chris said.

Alice tittered.

Papa glanced at Alice, and then in a flash, he was on his feet. He took a swing at Chris and caught him full in the eye. Chris felt the dull explosion of pain his head. He was going to have a black eye for sure. He folded in on himself, hoping his father had gotten it out of his system, but he was inwardly angry. Very angry. One day he would get even. His father couldn't keep him down forever.

"Edward Wynter!" Jackie Ruth said, staring at her husband defiantly. "Enough!"

Papa poked his finger in her direction and said, "I'll deal with you later. You and me are gonna have a long talk after the kids go to bed. Been a while since you and me had a long talk."

Jackie Ruth reached back and grabbed the phone.

"Don't you fucking dare," Papa said. "You say one word to my brother, and I swear to God, woman, I will kill you in your sleep."

Jackie Ruth put the phone down quietly and returned to her dinner.

Papa smirked in disgust.

Chris just willed him to go away. He would eventually. He always did when he got like this.

Papa said, "Fucking unbelievable. Fucking unbelievable. I'm going out." And then he was out the door.

I hope he dies in a car wreck on the way there, Chris thought, watching his father leave the house. The moment he was gone, Chris got up and bolted from the table, grabbing his favorite Army jacket. He was meeting Vic and Ray to do another dumpster. Tonight, he felt more than ever like watching the world burn.

"What the fuck happened to you?" Ray said, laughing when Chris pushed his way into the backseat of the Nova.

"Just drive," Chris said.

"Lemme see," Vic said.

Chris didn't budge. He just sat and fumed.

Vic turned around, flicking the overhead light on. He said, "Holy shit, what happened?"

"Can we just fucking drop it? Christ. Where we going anyway?"

"Orange Products," Ray said.

"Well all right!" Chris said.

By the time Ray pulled the Nova into the back of the large, flat warehouse, the boys were pretty well lit up and feeling good.

Chris said, "This is gonna be good tonight."

"Fucking-A," Vic said, smiling and passing Chris the rest of a fast dwindling joint.

"You got the cocktails?" Chris said to Ray, who had opened the trunk of the Nova and was rummaging around.

"Nope," Ray said. "I got a better idea." He pulled a crowbar and a metal gasoline container from the trunk. He said, "We're going to do the whole building."

Vic said, "What?"

Despite his mood, Chris was nervous. He said, "Ray, I don't know. We could get in a shitload of trouble."

"Like we aren't already?" Ray said. "Dumpsters are kids' stuff. I want to see the fucking place burn." His eyes shone in the dark like little black suns.

Chris felt his nervousness change to excitement. He thought about Nora Strawser, as he always did, topless and running out of the building scared. His erection grew until it raged under his jeans. He began to nod. "Yeah," he said.

Ray said, "Well all right! Let's do it!"

Vic held back, unsure. "Guys, I mean—"

"You coming or what, Vic?" Ray said. "We can't wait all night."

"It's just that I mean, shit, man. This is fucking arson. In a big way, I mean—"

"Never mind," Ray said to Chris. "It's just you and me."

Ray believed in Chris. Chris thought of his father sitting at the bar, hating the world. His father didn't know excitement like this. He thought the world had beaten it right out of him and maybe it did. But Ray believed in him and that was all that mattered.

Chris and Ray left Vic in the car and walked to the back of the Orange Products building. They stuck a crowbar underneath a chain-link screen in front of a window and pulled as hard as they could. It popped off easily. A moment later they were inside lurking around in what looked like a small office. Chris saw papers left on desks from the day's work. They poked around a little but found nothing interesting. But the excitement Chris felt was mounting.

The boys crept down a long hallway and stopped before a set of swinging doors that led into the main warehouse. Rows and rows of boxes lined the wide, open space. Chris imagined it all burning and felt good.

A snap. Bump.

Ray whispered, "What the fuck was that?"

Chris shrugged, scared.

Bump. A footstep.

Chris said, "You think there's a guard?"

Ray shook his head. He said, "Let's get in the warehouse."

Chris nodded. They pushed in the doors as quietly as possible and held one slightly ajar so they could see out. A dark figure appeared in the hallway.

Chris said, "Someone's coming." His excitement had turned to fear. Near panic. They were about to get busted for breaking and entering with a can of gasoline.

Ray held his fingers up to his lips to quiet Chris.

The figure approached and stopped. "Guys?"

It was Vic. He'd followed them in.

Ray said, "Jesus Christ, Vic, what are you trying to do? Give us a fucking heart attack?"

"Sorry. I changed my mind," Vic said.

Chris said, "Let's do it."

The boys ran up and down the aisles filled with boxes, dousing the place with gasoline. It only took a few minutes. They stopped by the doors.

Ray said, "You ready to do this? We gotta run like hell when this baby lights up."

Chris and Vic nodded, laughing nervously. Chris

thought his hard-on was going to break off in his pants. He'd never been this hard in his life.

Ray lit the match.

Chris studied his cousin's face in the orange glow. He looked crazy.

Then the match hit the floor and the purple orange fire spread like napalm across the cement and curled up around the first of the boxes. The fire began to spread. Chris felt the heat of it on his face even now. It was unbelievably hot. The flames licked up the stacks of boxes and took hold. The fire spread and built.

They stood mesmerized by the sight, consumed by the magnitude of what they'd started. Chris thought about Nora again, this time on top of him, fucking him in the middle of the flames, her big tits in his face, and he came in his pants, just like that. He'd never felt anything as powerful, and his knees nearly buckled with the pleasure.

There was no going back now. They'd crossed a line. That's how it felt. Chris looked at his companions, and they too seemed to be fascinated with the destruction. Their jaws were slack, eyes wide with surprise and delight.

Vic broke their temporary hypnosis and said, "We gotta fucking get outta here. Run!"

And so they did, back the way they came, out through the window and to the Nova. Ray peeled out and shot across the street to a self-storage facility, where he parked, out of the way. The boys got out and lay out of sight but within view of their latest crime in among some trees. Chris saw the orange light flickering in the front windows. Then an alarm went off.

Ray said, "The sprinkler system. Lotta fucking good

that's going to do."

The boys stayed put for hours watching the flames, the fire engines, the police cars.

They'd done all this, Chris thought.

His father was probably sitting in his own piss at Flynn's. Chris bet his old man had never seen anything like this or came in his pants thinking about a girl just watching a fire.

Chris wasn't a loser. He was a king.

On her second full day in Redding, Alice wanted to get out of the house, so she decided to spend the morning running errands in town for her mother. It felt good to slip behind the wheel of her black Mercedes and made her think to call Gerald. He hadn't been home when she'd called from the house upon arriving, so she'd left a message. He hadn't called back.

She tried to push the image of Gerald waking up in Tiffany's bed out of her mind, of them canoodling naked together, Tiffany providing soothing I-know-Baby-it-must-be-hard-for-you comfort to Gerald, who would be explaining to her that Alice just didn't get him. Alice pursed her lips glumly at the thought. It was a hard thing to shake off, and by the time she arrived at a little strip mall in town, she was downright angry at her husband, although she had no reason to be. She'd just made it all up. Or had she?

She leaned over and opened the glove compartment, fishing for her phone. Alice prided herself on being seemingly one of the last people on earth to embrace the culture of the cell phone. She despised the idea of always being connected, and texting was out of the question. Why not just call the person you're trying to text? She supposed it was generational. She owned one (at Gerald's insistence) but mostly kept it in the glove compartment for emergencies. She always made sure it was charged, but she just didn't use it often. Having it handy up here might be a good idea, as it would allow her to check in with work.

She sat in her car, pleased at the warmth of the morning sun streaming in through the windshield. But she shivered just the same. The thermometer in her car told her it was twenty-five degrees. She thought she'd treat herself to a decadent Starbucks concoction of some kind after speaking with Gerald—*if* she spoke to Gerald.

She flipped open her phone and dialed his cell phone (he refused to answer the house phone and couldn't understand why they even needed it). She put the phone to her ear and waited for it to ring.

Nothing.

Is the phone dead? She wondered. No, it wasn't. The little screen was on. The buttons were lit up. Then she realized. No bars. No signal. Her cell phone was useless out here in the boonies. T-Mobile. So much for modern technology. Great. She shoved the phone back into the glove compartment. As she did, she spotted across the street what struck her as a quaint anachronism: a pay phone. The kind you could close.

She bundled herself up against the cold air and walked across the street to the phone, sealing herself in. She called Gerald collect. He picked up a few rings later and agreed to let the call through.

"Hey," Alice said. "It's me."

"Oh, hey. What, uh . . ."

Pause. Muffled scratching. A muffled voice.

" . . . are you doing?"

His voice was tired and thick. A few notes deeper than normal.

Alice said, "I guess I should ask you that question. Were you just talking to someone?"

"No, I was just trying to clear my throat."

"Why aren't you at work?"

"Taking the day off, okay? What's up with the twenty questions?"

Alice resisted the urge to tell Gerald that he was getting the twenty questions routine because she suspected that he was using all this as an excuse to stay out late drinking and doing God knows what else. She could just imagine Tiffany walking her skinny butt into the bathroom while Gerald made his oh-baby face.

"I don't want to fight, okay? Just thought I'd check in," Alice said. She would play nice. After all, she told herself, she didn't really know if Tiffany was there. Or what Gerald had been up to the night before.

"How are things going up there?"

"Not good. They think someone killed my father."

"What? Are you serious? Who?"

"Don't know. Chris maybe. But he's gone."

Gerald said, "Jesus, Alice. Are you okay?"

"Not really. Oh, I guess so. It's just hard, you know?"

"So they think it's Chris?"

"We just don't know. We're all going in for questioning. Everything's just so crazy right now."

"So when do you think you'll be home?"

Alice paused, thinking. She hadn't thought about it. It

could be several weeks. Her heart sank thinking about her house in Chatham, about her snooty neighbors. She said, "I don't know. I guess a couple of weeks."

"Oh, man. Is there anything I can do?"

"No, I don't think so. They're looking for Chris now. There's not much to do except wait for them to release Papa for a funeral. I guess we'll just go from there. It's such a mess."

An awkward silence passed. Things went this way lately in their marriage.

Alice said, "Okay, I guess I'd better get going. Who knows how much this phone call is gonna be."

"Yeah, okay. I gotta get going anyway."

"Where you going?"

"Nowhere, I just gotta get going. You know, get up."

"I'm sorry if I'm acting funny, Gerald, I just—"

She hated herself for apologizing for it, for the weirdness they seemed stuck in. She wanted something from Gerald that he was simply unable to give her. At least for now.

"It's okay. We'll talk tomorrow. Well, I better get going."

"Yeah, okay," Alice said. "I'll be in touch. I love—"

But she was too late. He was already gone. She hoped it wasn't back to Tiffany.

She hung up the phone and cried quietly in the phone booth, knowing that she had a mountain to cross and no idea where to start. Their marriage was not getting any better and they both knew it. It might be just a matter of time.

She looked out at Redding and felt an odd detachment, like she wasn't really there. She couldn't believe she was here to bury her estranged murdered father, that her twin brother was gone, and that she'd spent half her life trying to convince herself and the world that she wasn't from this place.

She took a deep breath and wiped her eyes. Crying about it wouldn't help. She decided to call work to tell them that her mother was sick, that she'd be out for a few weeks. She could spare the time. She hardly ever took vacations.

She dialed the operator and spoke for moment, figuring out how to pay for the calls without a mountain of change, and then waited to be put through to the office.

She nearly fainted when she saw him.

It was Ray.

That's impossible, Alice thought. *It can't be. Ray died years ago.*

But the man was across the street, leaning against a telephone pole, smoking a cigarette. She hung up the phone and struggled trying to open the door on the phone booth. Finally, she burst through the door and out into the parking lot.

But he was gone.

1984

"Mr. Wynter!"

Ray looked up. Mr. Gartlin, his history teacher, was staring at him angrily. Gartlin was a little man with long out-of-style hair. He called everyone Mr. This and Ms. That.

"Ms. Rochon? Is that a note? Pass it up."

Ray groaned and said, "Fucking-A."

"What was that, Mr. Wynter?"

"Nothing."

Gartlin took the note and read it. He laughed. He said,

"Mr. Wynter, may I make a suggestion?"

Ray didn't say anything. His face was red with anger.

"Mr. Wynter, might I suggest that you'd have a better chance with women like Ms. Rochon if you actually paid attention in class and exercised whatever's left of your brain matter?"

"Fuck off," Ray said.

Gartlin charged him. "You say that again, Mr. Wynter and you're outta here."

Ray looked at the man defiantly.

Quietly, under his breath, and right at Ray, Gartlin said, "Be careful, Mr. Wynter, or you'll find yourself a lifer here in Redding. You're a smart kid, and you can make it out of here. Make something of yourself."

1984

It was different after the Orange Products burn. Chris felt the relationship and what they were doing was darker somehow. They couldn't explain or understand why they were doing what they were doing, and maybe a part of them didn't want to. It didn't matter. What did matter was how they felt when they were out there, cruising around in Ray's Nova saying fuck you to the world.

But Chris was scared because he couldn't stop thinking, how will it end? He'd told no one about what they were doing, but tonight, before he left, he paced in front of Alice's room. She was in there with the door shut. Chris heard that Flock of Seagulls tune playing behind the door. She was probably doing her homework.

He knocked gently, half hoping she wouldn't answer.

The door opened. Alice said, "Oh, hey, Chris."

Chris looked at the floor and said, "Can I talk to you? I just have a few minutes before I gotta meet the guys."

Alice shrugged and opened the door a little wider. Chris squeezed by. He sat on the bed.

Alice turned down the music and slumped into an old beanbag chair. Her homework papers and books were scattered around her. She picked up a can of coke and sipped at it. After a couple of minutes of silence, she said, "Well?"

Chris said, "I've been feeling bad."

"About Papa?"

Chris shook his head. "Nah. He's just a dick like always."

"So what, then?"

"Me and the guys, we been…" *How could he tell her?* Chris thought. *I can't.* "Doing stuff."

"Whaddya mean? You mean like drinking beer? I know that."

Chris shook his head. "No, different stuff. Bad stuff."

"Chris, what? What is it?"

He stood up and said, "Never mind. It's too complicated."

"Chris, what? Are you in trouble?"

Chris shook his head and left. He felt guilty and stupid. He and Alice had always been close. They were twins after all. If he couldn't tell her, he wouldn't be able to tell anybody.

He banged out of the house, ignoring his father's half-ass where-the-fuck-are-you-going and ran down his dirt driveway to wait for Ray. The weather was getting colder and Chris bundled up his old army jacket. He lit up a cigarette.

Soon the Nova roared up and over the hill and stopped in front of the driveway. Mountain's "Mississippi Queen" blared out from the windows. Vic got out of the front and waited for Chris to tumble into the back before climbing back in.

After he was in and Ray had peeled out, Vic opened the glove compartment and fished out a joint. It was the evening ritual.

Ray was quiet.

Chris said, "Ray, man, what's up?"

Ray looked over at Chris. His face was deadly serious.

"What is it?" Chris said.

"He's been that way all night," Vic said.

Chris shrugged. He said, "What's it gonna be tonight, boys?" But it was half hearted. Nothing could top Orange Products and they knew it. Was it the end of the Masters of Chaos?

Then, as if reading Chris's mind, Vic said, "Guys? Maybe tonight we just, I don't know, go bowling or something."

Ray jammed on the brakes and the Nova bucked and shuddered to an abrupt stop.

Chris flew forward and hit the front seats. Vic dropped the lit joint when he crashed up against the dashboard.

Chris said, "Jesus fucking Christ, Ray! What the fuck?"

"We are NOT just going to go fucking bowling!" Ray said. "What the fuck is wrong with you guys?"

"I-I was just saying, Ray," Vic said. "I mean shit, we've been out every night. My parents are really starting to give me shit about it. And what if we get caught?"

Ray shook his head, incredulous. "We're the fucking Masters of Chaos, and you're worried about your parents? Don't be such a goddamned pussy wimp, Vic."

Chris said, "What the fuck is your problem, Ray? You been acting like a douche bag all night."

"I'll tell you what my fucking problem is," Ray said. "I'm sick to hell of this shitful town. I'm sick of everyone in that goddamned school of ours."

Chris nodded.

Ray said, "Especially fucking Gartlin."

"The history teacher?" Vic said. "I kind of like him."

"He's a fucking jerk off," Ray said.

Chris hadn't ever had him, but he heard that Gartlin was a hard teacher. He was famous for wearing a stupid denim tie that looked like a pair of Levi's jeans, complete with a back pocket stitched onto the front. Gartlin wasn't nice to people like Chris and Ray. But a smart guy like Vic? Gartlin probably loved Vic.

Chris said, "Something happen?"

"He fucking said I wasn't going to amount to anything, that I'd never get out of this town. I was passing a fucking note to Cheri Rochon, man. I wasn't even doing anything. I hate that short little fuck. Who does he think he is?"

Chris said, "Hey, man, relax. He's just an—"

"No! Fuck that. I hate that hippy freak. We're gonna egg the fucker. At his house. Tonight."

Vic nodded and giggled.

Chris smiled and said, "He's gonna know who did it, man! Right?"

"He won't know shit," Ray said.

Chris shook his head.

"Do you even know where he lives?" Vic said.

"Of course I fucking know where he lives. Jesus!" Ray said. "But we gotta get some eggs first."

And off the boys went to a 7-Eleven just outside of Redding, where they bought their supplies. Ray put everything in the trunk.

Then, a few minutes later, they were a couple of houses down from Gartlin's. Ray turned off the headlights and coasted up alongside some tall shrubbery that ran the length of one end of Gartlin's lawn. Ray said, "Here's the plan: you guys are going to go up and knock on the door and run to the side of the house. I'll be back here with the mask on holding the eggs, ready to chuck them."

Something wasn't right. Ray was too serious, too dark. The vibe in the car was poison, and the air felt hot and foul like something bad was oozing out of Ray's skin. Chris said, "Maybe this isn't such a good idea, Ray."

"Oh, no. It's a wonder-fucking-ful idea. Besides it's too late. We're already here."

"Yeah, but—" Vic started.

"Get going," Ray said. "And give me a minute once your up there. I gotta get the eggs out of the trunk."

Chris glanced at Vic, who shrugged.

Chris and Vic got out of the car and approached the darkened house. The grey flickering light of a TV strobed in the picture window that jutted out from the front of the little yellow house.

Now on the front porch, Chris was shaking like a leaf. Vic's face was white as snow. Chris tried to ignore the bad feeling he had. He thought about Orange Products and about Nora Strawser, and it didn't make him feel good. Not any more. It made him feel guilty as hell. He wanted nothing more than to be anyplace else but here now with Ray and Vic. After all, Orange Products was just a building. Gartlin was a person. This was different.

He looked behind him, towards Ray, who had his hands down behind the car. He brought one up and gave the okay sign.

Chris looked at Vic before pressing the bell. Vic's face was a picture of concentration and fear. He nodded slightly, urging Chris to do it, to ring the bell.

Chris did. Loud electronic chimes came from within in the house.

From inside: "I got it!"

Vic mouthed, "It's Gartlin."

The boys ran off the porch and off into the side yard. When they were clear, they turned to watch Ray egg Gartlin. Only Ray wasn't holding eggs. He was holding a compound bow and arrow. And then the front door opened.

What happened next changed everything. For everyone.

FIVE

Alice's blood ran cold as she stood next to the phone booth looking for Ray. Goosebumps raised on her skin, and she shivered.

Ray.

Her mind swirled with memories from that terrible time, and Alice tried pushing them away. She was seeing things. She must be. Ray was dead. Long dead. Missing after a snowmobile trip, something she'd actually been glad of at the time—for Chris, for both of them. When Ray died, most of those terrible things went with him.

Could it be? Alice thought. *Stop it! No time for this. What's done is done. It was just a man who looked a little like Ray. You're seeing things because you're here in Redding and because you're under a lot of stress. That's all there is to it.*

She willed her jumpy mind quiet, refusing to allow herself to wade into the murky waters of her memories, or all of them, anyway. Some things are better left alone. She was here to bury her father and make sure her brother and mother were okay. That was all.

She wiped her face on her sleeve and rubbed her temples, wishing that, Gerald notwithstanding, she could be at home in Chatham, New Jersey, brewing some freshly ground coffee in her kitchen instead of out here in the cold standing in a dirt parking lot, trying hard not to think about things that she had no business thinking about, not after all these years.

As her mind began to clear, she wondered how long she had been standing here. Best to get a move on.

She hurried across the street, noting how the Maine drivers stopped dead in their tracks to let her walk across, something she'd forgotten about after living in the New York area where pedestrians were sometimes open game, or at the very least inconsequential.

Alice had a few things to buy in the CVS: soft toilet paper for one—the stuff her mother used may as well have been strips of sandpaper—and other odds and ends she'd forgotten to pack in her haste to leave. She also figured on picking up a good paperback. Maybe a juicy romance novel. She was in no mood for a murder mystery.

Soon, Alice's basket was full, and she was waiting in line. She picked up the romance novel she'd chosen: Victoria's Regret. On the cover was a bare-chested man looking longingly up towards a woman (presumably Victoria) who happened to be riding her horse wearing just a sheet by the looks of it. It was silly and stupid. Perfect.

"Alice? Alice Wynter?"

Alice heard her name and guiltily tossed her trashy novel back into her basket, turning her head. Behind her, a couple of customers back, stood a man about her age and height. Alice recognized him immediately. Michael LaPage had aged well. Very well. He wore faded blue jeans and a worn L. L. Bean field jacket. His ruggedly handsome face was beaming at the sight of her. Suddenly, Alice wished she'd spent half a minute fixing herself up this morning.

Alice said, “Michael. I can't believe it! It's been so long.”

“Since high school.”

They'd dated years ago, before she'd gone to Boston University. That had been a terrible time in Alice's life for a lot of reasons and Michael had been the perfect distraction. They'd grown steadily closer the more they'd talked in the hallways between classes and slid into an easy relationship. But it had ended badly. She'd left him with no explanation. How could she have explained?

Alice was flustered. She said, “Let me just . . .” She held up her basket.

Michael nodded and waved a little, indicating that he'd wait.

Alice paid for her things and stood by the door, waiting for Michael, who was paying for a prescription. He glanced in her direction at the counter, still smiling, face still filled with all those gleaming white teeth.

Alice felt dizzy. God, he was handsome. Age had hardened his features in just the right way and had given him a look of worldliness that she found unbelievably sexy.

Soon they were outside.

Michael said, “So, I just can't believe running into you here. Look, I heard about your father. I'm sorry.”

Alice nodded. There wasn't much to say. She changed the subject. “So, you're still living up here in the boonies?”

“Oh, yeah. Couldn't leave it if I wanted to. I'm making a pretty good living building custom cabinetry and whatnot for the snowbirds and camp owners.”

“Not too much business in the winter, though, huh?”

"Ah," Michael dismissed the comment. "I do okay. I build furniture in the winter mostly. It's what I love to do."

They stood in the cold for a minute longer and then Michael said, "Hey, look. It's freezing out here. You want to get a Starbucks?"

Alice smiled.

"Great! You remember where that old pharmacy used to be? Down on Old Granger Road? It's right there."

She said, "Yeah, I saw it on the way in. See you in a few minutes."

The Starbucks was warm and humid. It felt wonderful. Michael had managed to claim a couple of oversized chairs. Alice put her things down, and they walked up to the counter to place their orders. They didn't talk.

Michael ordered a latte and Alice a large coffee with a shot of espresso.

Michael said, "So, I can see by the Mercedes that you've been keeping busy."

"You might say that. I work in New York City at an advertising firm. Living in a suburb in New Jersey."

"Whoa! Really? Let me guess. Is there a white picket fence in your front yard? How can you stand it?"

Alice giggled. "What do you mean?"

"All those yuppies and taxis and busses. Went there once a couple of years ago to show a piece at a furniture show."

"It's not that bad."

Michael nodded, sipped his coffee and stared forward. They didn't talk for a few minutes.

Finally, Alice said, "You married? Any kids?"

"Was. No kids."

"Oh, I'm sorry."

"No, it's okay. Cancer."

"Michael, that's terrible. Did I know her?"

"Might of. Kerri Oram? She was a few years younger than we were. We started dating after you . . . well, after you left."

Alice knew of her. When Alice had been a senior, Kerri was a little freshman girl. Cute. "I think so. Michael, I'm sorry. So young."

"Yeah. It was a little over a year ago now. I mean, I still miss her. Every day. But I guess it's just one of those things, right?" He grew silent and thoughtful for a moment, then said, "Enough about that. What about you? You married? Kids?"

Alice hesitated for a moment, thinking about Gerald and Tiffany. She said, "18 years. No kids," and looked at the floor. When she finally picked her head up and looked over at Michael, he was staring at her curiously. "What?" she said.

He shook his head. "Nothing. I just can't believe I'm sitting her talking to you. What a world, right? One minute I'm buying Lipitor in a run-down CVS and the next talking to an old high school flame. You look great."

She smiled, happy to have the conversation moving on. "You too. I'm glad we're here."

"Me too."

A comfortable silence passed, and Alice sat in her comfy oversized chair sipping her turbo-charged coffee, glad for the company.

Michael said, "So, like I said, I was sorry to hear about your father, Alice. I wondered if you were going to come up. When I read the name in the paper, I couldn't believe it. Well, I guess that's not exactly true. I remember all those things you told me about him. Just a matter of time, I guess. Still, it's a shame." He fumbled a few words, nervous. Finally, he said, "Look, don't worry, I'm not a stalker or anything. I just think about our time together way back when sometimes, and when I read the name . . ."

Truthfully, Alice hadn't thought about Michael at all since those days and had in fact nearly forgotten about him altogether, but that wasn't surprising. She'd had a lot going on in her life then. A lot she wanted to forget. So, she remained silent for a moment.

Then before she could catch herself, she said, "It's a long story."

Michael shook his head a little. "What is?"

"Oh, never mind," Alice said. She was tempted to unburden herself to this man but quickly realized how silly that would be, talking to a near complete stranger, old flame or not, about who might have killed her father. *If*, that is, the police were right.

But Alice thought she knew who did it. Deep down. Chris. Who else? Really, who else could it have been? Papa had made a royal mess of Chris's life since high school. They were hard drinkers, fighters. No, not hard drinkers. Alcoholics. Her family didn't use that word enough, but there it was. Chris was a hard-core alcoholic who probably murdered his father in a drunken rage. And he was missing. But not dead. Alice would know if he were.

Michael, apparently noticing Alice's mood shifting, said, "Hey. I've got an idea."

Alice looked over at his handsome, innocent face and felt a wave of guilt. He was going to ask her out, and she was going to say yes. But she knew she shouldn't because she was married and because she would just be using him to escape from her mother. She would tell him that. Just as soon as she could. She would be honest.

"Maybe you could come over for dinner tonight. You know, to get away from your old house. Talk about things." He held up his hands and said, "No funny business. Promise. I have my own problems, believe me. Plus, I'm one of the good ones. Small-town guy. That kind of thing. I'm safe. Whaddya say? I cook a hell of a seafood stew."

He'd read her mind, and despite her better judgment, she felt a strong attraction for this uncomplicated man with his uncomplicated life.

It had taken a little doing, but Detective Don Lambert had finally prized a list of customers from Rose Flynn, who'd been tending bar at Flynn's Tavern the night Papa was shot. She'd remembered quite a few. Andy Flynn, Don's old friend and owner of the tavern had said he was happy to do it, but Don knew better. Andy's severe back condition wasn't the only kind of pain he lived with.

Don's junior detective and unofficial partner, Matt Ivey, a good kid (if you can call a 32-year-old professional detective a kid, and at Don's age, he supposed he could), held the list, written in a shaky cursive that resembled a child's chicken scratch, studying it. He squinted at the paper several times, trying to read Rose's terrible hand writing.

The duo were driving in Don's Crown Vic, headed back from court where Matt had testified in a traffic violation case. The weather had taken a turn for the worse, it seemed. The temperature had ticked up a degree or two and the air felt moist. Dark grey clouds blanketed the sky. It looked like snow was coming. Bad snow.

Don said, “You recognize any of the names?”

Matt shrugged. “A few. Nothing jumps out at me. You think we should hit all of these?”

Don nodded. “I do. There aren’t that many, and we don’t need to go crazy. We’ll split up the work.”

“You got it boss. I’ll set something up when we get back.”

They drove in silence for a few minutes.

Finally, Don said, “What do you think about me settling down?”

“Retiring?”

“Uh yuh. Maybe getting a place in Florida or out west.”

“I think it would make me supervising detective.”

“C’mon now, I’m serious,” Don said, chuckling. The kid was right.

“I don’t think you’d ever go through with it. You love it too much. You’re one of those types who’ll just drop dead one day on the job.”

Don nodded and said, “Maybe. Just maybe.”

Matt opened the top of a Dunkin Donuts coffee and pulled it from a cup holder where he’d planted it. He took a long sip.

“Gonna kill you, all that caffeine,” Don said.

Matt ignored him. He said, “What do you make of what old Bible said?”

“You mean about Chris and Papa arguing about Ray?”

“Uh yuh.”

“I wish we knew what the hell they were arguing about.”

Matt laughed bitterly. “No kidding. Jimmy Bible’s probably 90 percent deaf, and that’s when he has his hearing-aid turned on.”

"And that's why we have to make it through that list. Someone else is bound to have heard them. More details."

"But what do you make of it? Ray, I mean. I mean, let's just say for argument's sake that they *were* arguing about *that* Ray. *The* Ray. What of it?"

"You remember him at all?"

Matt shook his head. "He was a lot older than me."

Don had spent last evening talking with Gaye, his wife, about good ol' Ray Wynter and his gang of merry men, remembering. And there was a lot to remember. He said, "Ray Wynter was a bad kid, Matt. You know I don't say that too often. Kids aren't born bad, they're made bad. At least, that's what I believe. But Ray wasn't like that. Oh sure, he started off okay, I'm sure. But something happened to that boy. Snapped like. When he was in high school."

Matt sipped his coffee and stared out the windshield at the ominous clouds, lost in thought.

Don continued. "Ray was best buddies with his cousin. Any guess as to who that was?"

"Chris Wynter."

"Bingo. There was another kid in their little gang, but neither Gaye nor I could come up with his name. Doesn't matter, though, I guess. Not really. I was just a patrolman then. Young and dumb, as they say."

Matt laughed and said, "Hey! Watch your mouth. I'm still young."

"Anyway, it was like one day Redding went to hell. Fires, vandalism, you name it. The worst one I recall was the Orange Products warehouse on Congress Street. Burned to the ground. And it all happened one fall. I'm not exaggerating when I tell you that the town was at war that fall. I mean, *at war*. Only we didn't know who with."

Matt said, "You ever pin anything on them?"

"Wait. I'm not finished. That wasn't the worst of it. Not by a long shot. No sir. And *no*, we never did. Not officially. But we knew what was what. Teachers saw things. Talked. Students talked. We heard a lot of it. But before we could make a move Ray was gone. Just gone. Snowmobile accident. At least we think so. Like the hand of God came down to make things right. Things settled down after that."

Matt shot Don with a concerned look.

"Now, I know this was before your time, but I'm thinking even you might remember the worst of it. Before Ray died, that is."

Matt thought for a minute and then shook his head. "I'm gonna need more help to remember. I was just a k—"

The police radio sparked with static. An electronic voice said: *"Unit 3, we have a 901s involving a juvenile. The patrolmen on scene say they need you, Don. Three-five-nine Hollister Rd. Repeat: Unit 3, we have a 901s involving a juvenile. Assistance requested. Three-five-nine Hollister Rd."*

Don picked up the mic and said, "Dispatch, unit 3 responding. I'm with Ivey."

"Roger that, unit 3."

"10-4, dispatch. Thanks."

He replaced the mic in its cradle, lit up the Crown Vic, and turned on the siren. He said, "Speaking of. Story time is over, I guess."

Matt said, "Must be a doozey if they have an ambulance en route. Jesus, I hate when a kid gets shot. But why do they need you?"

Don shrugged and gunned the car.

1984

What happened next was a blur of seemingly disconnected snapshots for Chris, who couldn't quite process what was happening, really fucking happening, right before his eyes. In the weeks and months after Gartlin's house, he would play them out late at night and wonder if he was going to hell: *the look on Gartlin's face when the arrow from Ray's compound bow pierced his neck; how Gartlin's blood pumped from his neck between his fingers; the panicked, confused look on Gartlin's face as he tried to speak, to say, "Why?"; Gartlin shaking like a leaf, knowing he was dying out there on his front porch; Ray laughing like a lunatic. Vic's stunned,* holy fuckin' crap, *look. Gartlin's wife saying from inside the house, "Honey? Who's that at the door? Is everything okay?"*

No. Everything was most certainly not fucking okay. Nothing would ever be okay for Chris Wynter again, and he knew that then. At that moment. What he wasn't sure of was how it would end. How something as big as what Ray had just gone and fucking done like a psycho could possibly resolve itself without everyone knowing what they'd done. Chris would wear this memory on his face forever like a bad scar. He already felt the impossible weight of guilt crushing him like a giant foot on a bug.

And then, reality came washing over Chris like a rogue wave rolling over a helpless boat lost at sea. He heard Ray shouting, "Let's get the fuck out of here!"

Vic was tugging on Chris's arm, jumping up and down, saying, "C'mon. Jesus Christ! We gotta go! We gotta go!"

And they went. Chris had to jump into the already moving car onto Vic's lap and scramble to the backseat. Behind them, Chris heard Gartlin's wife scream when she found her dying husband on the front porch. Chris wondered if they got to say goodbye to each other. Then the kids. Her scream must have awakened them because he heard them screaming as well. Chris wondered if she'd seen the car.

"What the goddamned fuck, Ray? I mean, Jesus! You fucking killed him, man! You fucking killed Gartlin," Chris shouted as the car gained speed.

"Just shut up, man," Ray said. "I didn't mean to, okay? I was just trying to scare him a little. It was a fucking accident. A fucking accident!"

"It doesn't matter, douche bag. That doesn't matter because the cops aren't going to give a crap that you didn't mean to do it. You had the bow in the trunk. You were planning to do this. Jesus Christ, we're fucking screwed, man. We're fucking screwed." Chris was really losing it now, no doubt about that. He felt as though he were sliding off a cliff.

Vic said, rather more calmly, more out of shock than any actual calm, "You shouldn't've done that, Ray."

Ray said again, "I didn't mean to, okay? What's done is done."

"But, Ray—" Chris started.

"Would you just shut the fuck up, man?" Ray said. "I need to fucking think."

Chris thought about Gartlin's wife saying goodbye to her husband again and started to cry. *What the fuck were they thinking? What had they been doing? They'd burned down a factory, lit up the bowling alley, smashed windows, spray-painted buildings, and now this. And why? For what?*

Chris said, "Why'd you do it, man? What the fuck is your problem?"

Vic, in the front seat, was staring out the window. His face was pale but serene. He said, "Yeah, why?"

Ray shrugged. "I told you. I was just trying to scare him. Besides, it was fucking Gartlin, man. He was a dick. Who gives a shit about that asshole? You know what I mean? We're the fucking Masters of Chaos!"

Chris looked at Vic and wondered if he was thinking the same thing: *I sure as shit don't feel like a Master of Chaos. I feel like a scared kid who's been doing some pretty stupid things, and it's too late now to take them back.*

Chris caught Vic's eye and said, "We gotta go to the cops. We have to go right now and tell them it was an accident. We don't have to tell them about all the other stuff. Just this."

Vic was shaking his head no. He started to say, "No way, man. No fucking—"

Ray said, "Fuck!" and slammed his hand on the Chevy Nova steering wheel. He whipped the car into an parking lot behind an empty building, turned off the lights, and shut the car down.

"First of all, we're not going to the fucking cops. You hear me?" Ray said. His eyes were dark and angry. "Second of all, we're the Masters of Chaos. You know what that means?"

Tears had welled up in Chris's eyes. He saw Vic in the front seat, his eyes stone cold. He was staring at Chris. Chris shook his head back and forth—he didn't know what Ray meant.

"It means we stick together. One of us goes down, we all go down. We'll figure this out, just like all the other shit. We won't get caught if we stick together."

Chris said, "But Ray, man, it's fucking premeditated murder. People get the fucking chair for that."

"I told you, man, it was an *accident*. And they don't have the death penalty in Maine. Besides, you gotta get caught first. *And* they have to *prove* that it was premeditated. And it wasn't."

"Fine," Chris continued, "Life in prison. What's the difference? Jesus, Ray, what the fuck? Why did you do that?" He was crying again.

Ray said, "What about you, Vic? You with me?"

"Fucking right, man. Masters of Chaos strike again."

Chris felt at that moment that he no longer knew Vic, that the old Vic had died right there on Gartlin's porch. For that matter, Ray too. The air in the car was hot and sick. He wasn't friends with them and didn't want to have anything to do with them. Not any more. Not ever.

Ray clapped him on the back. "Good. See, Chris? Vic is cool with it. You in?"

Chris shook his head.

Vic said, "C'mon, man. You in?"

Chris turned to look outside but caught Ray glancing over at Vic in the reflection in the mirror. Chris had a bad feeling. A very, very bad feeling.

Ray said, "We need an answer man. Are you in or what?"

Chris said, "I'm in."

What else could he say? Vic and Ray didn't look right to him any more. How could they be so sure of themselves, of what they'd just done?

"Atta boy. Now, we got some stuff to do," Ray said.

An hour later, the Masters of Chaos were behind a garage barn in Ray's backyard. They'd hidden the bow and the rest of the arrows. They'd also washed out Ray's trunk for good measure, hoping to eliminate any traces of the Molotov Cocktails they'd used over the last few weeks.

Ray said, "I'm telling you, we're okay. No one saw the Nova, no one saw us, no—"

"What about Gartlin's wife?" Vic said clinically, detective-like.

"What about her?" Ray said. "She was still in the house when we peeled out of there. Gartlin's kids were asleep. She didn't see shit. They didn't see shit. By the time she found Gartlin, we were fucking outta there, man. I'm telling you, it was the perfect crime."

Chris wasn't convinced and wasn't digging the conversation at all. He said, "I don't know, man."

Ray started counting on his fingers. "One, Gartlin's wife didn't see the car. Two, no one heard anything because we were quiet. Three, there's nothing to link us to what happened. It's the same as Orange Products. It's totally fucking random. Chaos. You know what I—"

"Someone could have seen us drive up," Chris said. "You know, on the street."

Ray shook his head. "No way. You saw Gartlin's street. It was dark, man. Trust me, no one saw us. We're fucking gold. Plus, just in case, I'll leave the Nova out here for a while. In the garage back here. Shit, I've been wanting to do some work on it anyway."

Vic offered, "We should question each other. You know, like the cops would do. To test each other in case something happens."

"Nothing's gonna happen," Ray said. "Trust me."

Maybe Ray and Vic were right. Maybe it would be okay.

But how could Chris live with this? With what had happened tonight? A little voice inside him said, *yeah, but as long as you don't get caught, it's like nothing ever happened. No one has to know.* Despite this, he said, "I don't know, man. It just doesn't feel right. Like we should go to the—"

And then Ray was on him. Chris felt a white explosion in his head and a peculiar taste filled his mouth: blood. It was on his hand, which was now rubbing his jaw. Chris thought about the blood on Gartlin's front porch and winced. Ray had clocked him upside the head, hard. Vic watched coolly, nodding in approval. He was all in and not turning back, all aboard and on this fucking crazy train, Chris realized with growing unease. So that's what fucking Ozzy Osbourne was talking about. He thought again that these were no longer his friends.

Ray got right down low into Chris's face and said, quietly, "I swear to fucking God, Chris, if you fucking say anything, you little prick, I'll fucking kill you. I'm not fucking around. You hear me? This thing only works if we're together on this. And I mean all together. Not just me and Vic, but the Masters of Chaos, all three of us. I'm not going to jail because you feel fucking guilty."

Vic said, "Let him up, man. He's in. Right, Chris?"

Ray stood up and extended his right hand for Chris to help him up. Chris grabbed it. As he stood there in the dark behind Ray's barn garage, he racked his mind about what to do. He thought about Nora Strawser again then. About how the fires they'd set had made him feel. He wanted to feel right about this too, but it was too big. He hoped that he never saw Nora again, not ever.

SIX

Michael LaPage called Alice late in the afternoon to see if she was still interested in getting together to talk about old times over dinner. She'd immediately said yes, partly because of her attraction to him and partly just to get out of the house. Her mother had been acting funny all afternoon. Anxious. Scared even. Her mother's behavior at lunch had left Alice unnerved to the point that she was afraid to confront her about it. But before she had a chance to, Gerald had called. They'd had a good conversation that left Alice doubting her feelings towards him. Was he guilty? Maybe he wasn't seeing Tiffany after all—really seeing her. Maybe it was just a work thing. It happens all the time, she told herself.

Soon after, Michael had called. And now it was she who was feeling guilty. She resolved herself to enjoy his company and tell him in no uncertain terms that she was (for the moment at least) married. At the same time, she wanted to talk to him about what had been going on. See what he thought.

She left at 4:00 and arrived at his little colonial house at 4:30. The sun was disappearing rapidly. She parked in the driveway to the left of the house, got out, and admired the wrap-around deck and pleasant light blue color of the house. It looked immaculate. She imagined that Michael paid careful attention to that little house and took great pride in how it looked.

The front screen door swung open. Warm light flooded out from within. Michael took a step out and waved her in. He was smiling. He wore jeans and a blue flannel shirt with a white t-shirt underneath. He'd left his shoes inside and wore only socks.

Alice greeted him and stepped inside, feeling immediately cozy and at home in his warm living room. Of course, a fire burned in the fireplace. He'd already opened a bottle of white wine.

"You look nice," he said, taking her coat.

"Thank you. I hope you can forgive me. I didn't bring anything."

Michael waved dismissively. "Nah, forget it. Would you like some wine?"

"I'd love some."

"Have a seat," Michael said. "I'll get us a couple of glasses."

Alice made herself comfortable on the his soft leather sofa.

Michael returned with two wine glasses. He sat down, poured her a glass, smiled, and said, "So."

"So," Alice said.

A beat of silence passed. Then, they made small talk about Redding, their old high school, where they'd been since. The wine warmed Alice. She felt comfortable with Michael. Relaxed. He was definitely one of the good ones.

Before she could catch herself, Alice said, "Michael, there's something I have to tell you. About why I'm here."

"Is this the long story you mentioned in Starbucks?"

Alice nodded and looked at the floor.

"I'm all ears." He looked concerned, apprehensive.

"The truth is that it's not really a long story. My father passed a few days ago. I'm here to support my mother. You know this already. From the paper. I don't . . . Well, I don't get along with my family. And I hate Maine. I haven't been here in years. I don't mean to burden you with this, it's just that I feel like I'm all alone up here. And you seemed so—"

"Oh, Alice. Oh, man. Hey, no burden. I'm sorry. God, that's horrible. Are you okay? I mean, your family must be . . ." He stopped and seemed to gather his thoughts. "What I mean is, I'm here, okay?"

Alice felt like crying. She nodded and took a sip from her glass. "That's not all."

"Oh?"

"He probably didn't commit suicide."

Michael's face dropped in astonishment. He started to speak, but Alice held up a hand.

She said, "The police think he was murdered."

"How did it happen? I mean, if you don't mind me asking."

"He was shot. I'm pretty sure my brother did it. He and my father were . . . Well, you know. Everyone around here knows."

Michael nodded. "No, it's just a small town. People talk. I mean, you hear things from time to time but not this."

"Chris is gone. We don't know where he is. I feel like I'd know if he were dead. We're fraternal twins. I just feel like he might be. And I'm scared."

Michael looked at her with concern. Just listening.

"I just don't know what to feel. I hated my father. Oh, God! Listen to me. This is too much." She put down her wine and stood to leave. "I shouldn't have come here. You don't need to hear this."

Michael grabbed her arm gently. He said, "Alice. It's okay. It's nice to hear about someone else's problems for a change. Usually, it's just me. I get real tired of hearing myself think, you know? It's okay. Really. I want to help you."

Alice sat down again. She said, "I don't want you to get the wrong idea. I'm married. You just seemed like someone I could trust. Someone outside my family."

His brow furrowed in understanding. He said, "Of course. Please. Let's just sit and talk. Okay?"

And then it came out. Alice could hardly help herself. She told Michael about why she'd left him after high school (nearly all of it, anyway—some of those days even she didn't care to remember). Mostly, she talked about what had happened to Chris. His troubles after high school.

"It's sad," he said.

"It is. And I just feel so guilty for not being there."

"Alice, you had to save yourself. You know?"

"I know. But I could have come back."

"There was nothing you could do. By the sound of it, Chris and your father were trapped in some kind of spiral together."

Alice looked up at Michael. *Spiral. A death spiral.* That was it exactly. It was like they fed off each other's negativity. She said, "Yes. You don't understand what it was like. They were always together. Papa never let Chris alone. He was always criticizing, nagging. They fought constantly and yet they couldn't leave each other alone. I just couldn't bear it."

"So, you don't have to answer this, but do you think Chris . . . you know, did it?"

Alice nodded. "I think he snapped."

"Did you tell the police that?"

"They know he's missing, so I think they basically assume he's guilty. I guess we all do. We just don't know where he is. I've been wracking my brain to figure it out. I just need to talk to him before they question me." Alice thought of her mother this afternoon. There was something about her behavior that Alice didn't want to admit. But she had to.

She said, "But that's not the worst of it. I think my mother knows where he is."

Michael nodded. "This is . . . man, what a mess."

Alice nodded. "It is. That's what it's like. Being a Wynter. Everything is so complicated."

Michael poured the rest of the bottle of wine into Alice's glass. "Here," he said. "You need this more than I do. I'll get dinner."

He disappeared into the kitchen. She heard him bustling around, getting things ready. Alice sipped her wine and stared into the fire, feeling empty and yet slightly relieved that she had someone to confide in. It felt good to talk to someone, to share with someone. She thought about Gerald. It had been a long time since they'd talked openly.

"Soup's on!" Michael called from the dining room.

Alice brought her wine to the table, which Michael had set neatly. A bowl of seafood stew sat steaming in the middle of the table. A plate piled high with sliced crusty garlic bread sat next to it. Her stomach grumbled. All she'd eaten all day was a baloney sandwich on white bread at the house. Yick.

And he cooks? She wondered. *This is too much.*

Guessing what she was thinking, Michael said, "I confess. I didn't make it. There's a little deli down the road. Bella's. This little woman runs it. I don't know why she calls it a deli. I'm not even sure she sells sandwiches. Anyway, best seafood stew I've ever eaten. I picked it up a half hour before you got here. If this stew doesn't help your mood, nothing will."

Alice smiled and said, "I don't care who made it. I'm starving."

"Dig in," Michael said. He watched her eat. "Good, right?"

Alice nodded, thinking that she felt as though she could tell him anything and know that he wouldn't judge. She watched him dig into his bowl, satisfied that she was enjoying her dinner first. *No more wine*, she thought. *I wouldn't trust myself after this glass.*

Driving home in the cold dark, Alice found herself thinking about her conversations with Michael and surprised herself by admitting that she had feelings for him. At first, she'd dismissed it as nothing more than what happens when you reconnect with an old flame. But there was something more. She felt safe with Michael, comfortable. Things were easy.

Her relationship with Gerald wasn't like that and never had been. She'd always felt vaguely uncomfortable around him naked, for example, as if he disapproved of her body—or held it in contempt. It was nothing she could articulate, just a vague feeling. And their sex was sometimes mechanical, awkward and uncomfortable because it was all about Gerald. Not always, but more often than not. It had gotten better over the years as they discovered a routine, but not much. And this had always been a theme in their relationship, the sex, the control, Gerald's way. Love meant sex to him. But worst of all, however, was that Alice had never felt that she could tell Gerald everything about herself, the best and worst of it. She didn't think he'd care or accept it. The truth of all this was something she didn't like to think about, but driving home from Michael's after a nice evening just talking in their easy way, she had to admit: Gerald was likely part of the great cover-up in her life, that great big lie she told herself and the world; he couldn't and might never know her past completely. She lived with that uneasy balance in their relationship just as she lived with her past. So, she had to admit that the troubles in their marriage were perhaps her fault. At least in some ways.

After all, *she'd* created the facade and now lived every moment of it. She was Alice Dunn, a successful executive with a major advertising firm in New York City, who drove a black Mercedes that cost more than most people's yearly income and who lived in a big McMansion on the right side of Main Street in wealthy Chatham, New Jersey.

But here, in Redding, Maine, she was little Alice Wynter, and her alcoholic father was murdered, probably by her alcoholic brother, who had flown the coop and was God knows where doing God knows what, a victim of his own weaknesses and controlled almost completely his entire "adult" life by an overbearing father who took the reins of his son's life years ago. That was her life. Her real life.

Alice's thoughts quieted and she drove the rest of the way back to her mother's house thinking about nothing more than how dark it seemed to have gotten in the past couple of days now that the snow clouds had rolled in. Lucky her. Just in time for the first snow of the season, much later than normal. Alice turned her black Merc left into the Wynter driveway, vowing that she wasn't going to let her thoughts run away with her tonight and prevent her from getting a good night's sleep. She hoped her mother wasn't up. She couldn't deal with her right now.

She sat for a moment in the Merc after turning it off, enjoying, as usual, the peaceful quiet, *her* peaceful quiet, the smell of the interior, so much like home. She took a deep breath and got out of the car, bracing herself against the chilly, damp air that smelled unmistakably of snow.

He was back.

Alice let out a little scream and her breath caught in her throat. At the base of the driveway, a few hundred feet away was the unmistakable form of Ray leaning against the telephone poll next to their driveway. He was smoking a cigarette and smiling.

Marlboro Reds. He always smoked Marlboro Reds, Alice thought.

Alice instinctively fumbled for her keys, thinking to get her cell phone, but realized that it was useless out here and besides which, who was she going to call? She froze with panic. She was seeing things. She had to be seeing things. She blinked.

He was gone. There was no one there. Was she losing her mind?

She stood in the driveway for a few moments, gathering her thoughts. She was under a lot of stress. Being here was unhealthy, she realized. She'd put this part of her life away in a mental lockbox for a reason. But she couldn't leave. She had to bury her father. Help her mother. Help Chris.

Chris.

She had a feeling he was beyond help.

1984

After leaving Ray and Vic, Chris had walked home and gotten into bed. He didn't sleep longer than fifteen minutes at a stretch, and when he did, he dreamed of Gartlin's panicky face and his wife saying, *Honey, who's that at the door? Is everything okay?*

When the sun finally came up, Chris rubbed his eyes and got out of bed. His stomach hurt.

On his way to the bathroom, he passed Alice, who walked by rubbing her wet hair. She said, "What's wrong with you? You look terrible?"

Chris smiled weakly and shrugged as she walked by and into her room, slamming the door.

Then he was at the kitchen table, choking down a bowl of cereal. His mother was doing dishes. His father sat across from him, drinking coffee.

At least the old man is probably too hung over to bother with me, Chris thought gratefully.

The little black and white TV set on the kitchen counter blared: " . . . *in this small Maine community. According to a spokesman for the Somerset County Sheriff, the attack does not appear to be accidental, but they don't yet have a motive or a suspect. The Sheriff's office is encouraging anyone who might have more information about the murder to come forward. Randall Gartlin came to Redding nearly 15 years ago and quickly became on of the area's most popular teachers, incorporating theatrical techniques to inspire the . . ."*

Jackie Ruth said, "Can you believe it? I just can't believe it. Who could have killed that man?"

Papa Wynter growled under his breath and stood up. He said, "You got my lunch?"

Jackie Ruth handed it to him wordlessly.

He turned and left for work, currently at a construction company.

Jackie Ruth stood in front of Chris and said, "You okay?"

Chris nodded his head, staring into his cereal.

Jackie Ruth grabbed his chin and lifted it so she could examine his face. "You get into a fight? That's quite a shiner you got there."

Chris shrugged. He felt like crying but held back. His guilt felt like a thousand tons pushing down on his shoulders, and he felt as though he couldn't bear the weight of it a minute longer.

Alice bounced in, grabbed a banana, and said, "Hey! Did you hear about Mr. Gartlin?"

Chris couldn't take any more. He said, "I gotta get ready for school."

Jackie Ruth said, "The both of you get moving. I don't have time to drive you today if you miss the bus."

And then they were at school, where the entire student body it seemed was silent and morose. Chris's homeroom teacher sat at his chair and stared at his desk. He'd been friends with Gartlin, Chris knew. They were both history teachers. The students on either side of him, Ben Wolf and a cute redhead named Becky Daggett, whispered to each other before Chris sat down in between them.

"I heard he was cheating on his wife and his mistress got him," Becky said.

Ben thought a minute and said, "Could have been drugs or something like that."

Chris tuned them out and tried to think about something, *anything*, but Gartlin's wife saying, *Honey, who's that at the door? Is everything okay?* Those were the last words she'd said to him before he died out there on the front porch, the last words before her life was torn apart by Ray's arrow. A single arrow. A sob escaped Chris's lips before he could catch it.

What in the hell had they been thinking? He wondered. *How could we have let things go so far?*

Chris's homeroom teacher, Mr. Kump, stood up and said, "Please! Everyone! Please! Can we quiet down now?"

The students fell silent and stared up expectantly.

"Look, I . . ." Mr. Kump held a fist to his mouth and swallowed back his grief. ". . . I know this is hard. It's hard for me. Randall and I have been friends for almost ten years.

"All the homeroom teachers have been asked to spend an hour or so with you to talk about what happened and how it made you feel. After that, we'll have an assembly and then you'll be dismissed for the day.

"What happened to Randall was, well, one of those things that don't have an explanation or reason. You're all probably feeling bad. Scared maybe. Confused. Just know that you can talk to us. Any time. We'll listen and help if we can. If not, we can get you in contact with someone who can help."

The class spent the next hour remembering Randall Gartlin. Chris didn't participate and felt no bigger than a cockroach sitting in his chair, wishing he could slither away and die somewhere rather than endure the endless reminders that he'd helped to kill a man with a wife and children, a good man whose only crime was trying to be enthusiastic about his job. He was sure everyone could read it on his face. He felt as though he may as well be wearing a sign that said, "I DID IT." But the fact that no one could see that made him feel worse. What he and Ray and Vic had done was so terrible that it was far from what most people would be willing to believe about three high school boys. Chris was simply a bad kid. His father was right about that. And boy, what his father would have to say after this came out, if it came out.

Good ol' Dad will have a fucking cow, Chris thought.

An hour later, Mr. Kump dismissed them to the assembly, and Chris shuffled out of homeroom and into the hall. The other kids were starting to come alive more now that they'd talked about things. Chris looked for Ray and Vic because he wanted to avoid them. At all costs. But he had no such luck.

Chris felt a clap on his back and turned to see Ray smiling at him. He was a good foot taller than most of the other kids and seemed more threatening today. It was his eyes that made him seem so much more dangerous than usual. They'd changed. They were colder. Meaner. Something had awakened in Ray the night before, something that made a little voice in Chris's mind speak up and warn him about staying away from Ray.

Vic stood off to the right, his hands jammed hard into his pockets. He wouldn't look Chris in the eye. Or anyone for that matter. But he didn't look sad.

"Missed you this morning, Chrissy," Ray said, his hand still on Chris's shoulder.

Chrissy? Chris thought. *That's a new one.*

"Yeah, well, I decided to take the bus."

"Did you? Huh, that's weird. Isn't that weird, Vic?"

Vic shrugged and shifted his weight to his other leg.

Ray's grip got a little stronger. Quietly, he said, "I'm starting to worry about you, Chrissy. I think you know what I mean. I thought we had our little talk last night for a reason. We're the Masters of Chaos. Remember?"

Chris shook his head. He said, "I'm cool. Don't worry." But he wasn't cool. Something foul and evil was coming off Ray in waves. Something Chris had never felt before. Then it struck him: *Ray could kill me. He really could. Just like Gartlin. He could kill any of us. He doesn't even care about what he did.*

Ray said, "What's say we blow off the assembly and split early? Go cruising. I got my Mom's car."

"I don't know, Ray," Chris said. "I'm not sure it would look good."

Ray stared down at Chris, his eyes wild behind the thick lenses he wore. His greasy black hair fell down in front of his pocked face. He said, "I'm *really* starting to worry about this, Chrissy. I don't want to have to worry. You know what I mean?"

Chris nodded.

Vic said, "C'mon. Let's go, man. Quit fucking around."

They walked past Chris and stopped, waiting for him to join. Chris felt like he had no other choice. Plus, he couldn't imagine spending another hour talking about grief counselors and how he was feeling. No one could imagine how he was really feeling.

Chris caught up with his friends and walked out of the high school, wondering if maybe Ray and Vic had cooked up a little plan of their own about what to do with Chris. He felt sick to his stomach at the prospect of having to spend the rest of the day with the Masters of Chaos. What a fucking joke.

SEVEN

Eight-year-old Joshua McLain was lucky to be alive. He lay in a bed in the intensive car unit at Maine General, still unconscious. A bullet had punctured a lung and ultimately stopped just short of his heart. But it had rattled around a little. Lots of internal bleeding. He'd been EVAC'd there just an hour or two earlier. He was critical but stable after some emergency surgery to stop the bleeding.

That much Don Lambert had gotten from the patrolmen on scene. He and Mike Ivey sat uncomfortably in seven-year-old Ryan Crane's overheated living room, his nervous parents off to the side a little watching their scared little boy, who (Don had to give him credit) was putting on a brave, if a bit shy, face.

Out of earshot of the parents, a tall uniformed patrolman said to Don and Matt, "Could be nothing, but we figured you might want to handle it after the kid said he found it in a field. We couldn't get much out of him."

Don pointed at the gun the patrolman was holding and

said, "Be careful with that weapon. If it's the gun that killed Ed Wynter, I don't want any smudging."

Patrolman Parson nodded and put the gun little Joshua McLain had found in an evidence bag and sealed it.

It had taken Don nearly a half hour to calm the parents down. They were terrified that their son had killed his best friend, Josh. After reassuring them that he hadn't, they all agreed that the detectives could ask the boy a few questions. It was routine, and Don just wanted to make sure nothing funny was going on, but from the looks of things, this was all just a terrible accident. This particular accident would turn out better than most he'd investigated. Most involved one or more piss-drunk hunters whose total common sense couldn't have filled a thimble.

There was really just one question: "Can you tell the policeman where you found the gun, buddy? It's important." That came from the boy's nervous father, Jerry.

Little Ryan shook his head and stared at the floor.

"Ryan, dear, it's okay. You're not in trouble." That was Mom.

Don smiled. *Like hell this kid's not in trouble. The minute we walk outta here, he's going to get an earful and probably spend the better part of his childhood grounded in his bedroom.*

"I don't . . ." the kid mumbled something soft and incoherent and wiped his nose on his jacket sleeve.

"What's that, kid?" Mike said. Sometimes he was better with the kids, being a little closer to their age.

Soft as could be, Ryan Crane said, "But I don't want to go to jail."

"Jail?" Don said. "Aw, you're not going to jail. In fact, I was just thinking something."

The kid looked up hopefully, his eyes still red and swollen with tears. He looked embarrassed and a little more than ashamed at what had happened. Don felt for the kid.

Don said, “Mike, tell you what. Why don’t you give him that badge of yours. Just temporary.”

Mike smiled and winked at Don. He said, “Sure, Don.” He unhooked his badge from his belt buckle.

Don took it and said, “Now, just so you understand Ryan, this is just temporary. This is a pretty big responsibility for a kid your age. Why, I can’t remember the last time we gave one of these out to someone so young. Can you, Mike?”

Mike frowned and shook his head.

The kid suppressed a little smile. He nodded.

Don held out the badge but pulled it back at the last second, just as the kid was reaching for it. He said, “Now wait a minute. This is a big step. You have to come clean. You have to tell me all about what happened. We got a deal, deputy?”

The kid nodded earnestly. Don pinned the badge on the kid’s striped shirt. He said, “Well, it’s official now. You’re on the hook.”

The kid nodded again.

“You want to tell me where you got the gun? Was it here, at home?”

Ryan shook his head.

“Did Josh bring it over? Maybe his father had it, and you kids knew how to get into the gun safe? Was that what happened?”

Ryan shook his head again. He said, “Mr. McLain doesn’t shoot guns. He has a bow and arrow. Like this.” Ryan mimicked a hunter shooting a bow and arrow.

"Ryan," Don said, "You're an official deputy of the Somerset County Sheriff's Office, duly appointed by a Maine law-enforcement official. You're not lying to us now about that gun safe, are you?"

Ryan shook his head vigorously and said, "But we found the gun. Really."

Mike said, "Found it where?"

"Can you show us where?" Don said.

The boy nodded and stood up. He said, "We gotta go outside. It's outside. Can we go, Mom?"

Don stood up and said, "Put your jacket on Ryan, and me and you will go outside. You can show me where it was. That sound all right?"

Ryan nodded and ran to the hall closet to get the jacket. Don flicked his fingers to indicate that Mike should come. Don then said to Ryan's parents, "Probably better if you stay here. He's more likely to tell us the full story without you there. Mike, go outside and get the big candles from the back of the car. It's dark out there." Candles were the big flashlights, not the little Mag-Lites patrolmen sometimes wore on their belts.

Barbara Crane burst into tears and cried into her husband's shoulder. Jerry Crane nodded like he understood. His face was bone white.

Don and Mike followed Ryan out of the house into the freezing January air. It was dark. The sun had set behind the clouds hours ago.

Don said, "Why don't you tell us what happened while we walk?"

"Um, Josh came over after school."

"Did you go play outside?"

"Uh huh."

Despite the darkness, Ryan led them through a maze of vegetation, mostly just evergreen shrubs and bare trees, that only a kid could know so well. They walked down into a small ravine and crossed a frozen stream. The flashlight beams bounced ahead of the kid.

Ryan said, "You can pretend like your skating on this," and showed them by skating across to the other side.

"How far we going, partner?" Mike said.

Don was winded. The frigid air made him cough.

"You okay, Don?" Mike said.

"You just keep your eyes on your own paper. I'm fine."

"Not much further," Ryan said. When he reached the top of the hill on the other side of the frozen stream, he stopped. He said, "We're here," and pointed out into the moonless darkness.

Don and Mike walked up beside Ryan, shining the beams onto a field of dried ankle-high corn stalks. A white fence ran alongside the field, separating it from the road. Beyond it was forest, thick and dark. Route 6 was desolate in the best of times and downright creepy when it was this dark.

Ryan said, "I don't want to go over there."

"It'll be okay. Just show us where you found it."

Ryan let out a sob and said, "I didn't mean to. We were just playing like he was an outlaw, like we saw on TV."

Don patted Ryan reassuringly and said, "It's okay now. Just show us where the gun was."

As they walked closer to the spot, Ryan slowed and walked behind the two men. He said, "It was there. I'm scared of that place. I don't want to see it."

Don and Mike walked a few feet further ahead of Ryan, who stopped, pulled his gloves off, and popped his thumb into his mouth. He watched the men fearfully.

Don squinted at the ground. He didn't see any indentations. The ground was too cold. He said, "Here?"

Ryan nodded.

The policemen looked at one another and then to the road.

Don said, "You found it here? Right here?"

"No," Ryan said after thinking for a moment. "That's right! This was where I dropped it after it went off. When I ran back to get help. To my house. Josh was bleeding."

"Can you take us to exactly where you found it? Exactly?" Mike said.

Ryan walked carefully towards the road, considering every step. Finally he stopped. "It was like right here." He drew an imaginary circle above the ground. "Josh saw it first. Can we go home now? I'm cold."

Mike said, "Don, this has got to be—"

Don held up his hand to stop Mike and shook his head. *Not in front of the kid.* The gun was just a stone's throw from the road when the kid picked it up. Route 6. A mile or two from where Papa Wynter had been shot. They'd run a trace on the serial number, if one was left. And of course try to lift the prints, which might be mostly the kid's unless they got lucky and the kid was wearing his gloves the whole time. And lastly, they'd compare the bullets that shot Ryan's friend Josh and killed Papa Wynter. But Don had a gut feeling that all those pieces would fall right into place. This was the murder weapon, he was sure of it.

"Ryan," Don said. "I may just let you keep that badge after all. Now let's get you home. You've had a long day."

The morning after she'd eaten with Michael, Alice sat at the kitchen table, staring out into the cold, moist gloom that had settled over Redding and presumably over all of central Maine. Jackie Ruth was still in the shower. Bruce hadn't arrived. Alice was alone with her thoughts, and she wasn't sure she wanted to be.

Her emotions were jumbled. She'd safely buried the toxic sediment of her childhood under layer upon layer of her new life as Alice Dunn. The house, the car, Gerald, her job, Boston U., all of it. It wasn't until her evening with Michael that she realized just how close to the surface it all had been. Just being back in Redding had stirred up the waters and let some of those memories and feelings kick up from underneath.

She was scared that the truth about what Ray Wynter had done to their family, to her, would get out into the universe instead of staying safely locked away in her memories. Even Gerald didn't know about Ray.

But it was there, and it would come out in time. The part of her that was seeing Ray in the shadows and on the street would make damn sure of that. It scared her. What was happening to her?

Alice sipped her coffee and took a deep breath. She told herself that it didn't matter now, and maybe it didn't, but Chris was gone and her father was murdered. And that mattered. Things happen for a reason. Everyone knows that.

And what about Michael? What about her feelings for him? Maybe it was puppy love, a convenient crush during a stressful period in her life. But she'd shared a part of herself with Michael, and that meant something—to her, anyway. But she was sure it meant something to him as well, and she was equally sure that he was sitting at *his* kitchen table wondering why his feelings for her made him feel like he was betraying his dead wife, Kerri Oram, one-time junior cheerleader and all around Miss Perky. Alice just knew it. Intuition.

"Dolly, honey, did you find something to eat? Can't live on coffee, you know." Jackie Ruth shuffled into the kitchen wearing an ancient pair of dime-store slippers and a tattered robe.

"I had something earlier," Alice lied.

Jackie went to the stove and turned up a burner. "Make you some eggs," she said.

"Ma, I don't want any eggs. I'm fine."

"Umm hmm. Well, I'll just make myself some. Feel free to help yourself, you want any."

Alice rolled her eyes and returned her gaze outside, wishing she'd had just a few more moments of silence.

Jackie Ruth came to the table with four raw eggs, a bowl, and a fork. She set them down and returned to the coffee pot to pour herself a cup. When she sat down again, she pulled a long cigarette out of a crumpled pack on the table and lit up. She moved with that hypnotic slow deliberation reserved for the elderly.

Alice watched her mother crack the eggs one-by-one into the bowl and then whisk them, as she'd done a thousand, billion times before on countless mornings before school for the kids and for Papa.

The phone rang.

Jackie Ruth nonchalantly set her burning cigarette butt in the heavy black glass ashtray on the table and leaned back to grab the phone. She said, "Wynters."

"Yeah-uh," she said. "Speaking."

Pause.

"Oh, I don't think—"

Pause.

"But I-I-I'm not, it's not like that. This is family business. Family! Detective, no, I'm not—"

A long pause.

"I see."

Jackie Ruth hung up the phone. She took her cigarette out of the ashtray and sucked hard at the end. She flicked the ashes obsessively.

Alice said, "Ma, what is it?"

Jackie Ruth's face twisted up and a tear rolled down her right cheek, leaving a long, wet streak before it fell to the table.

Alice's stomach clenched in fear. Louder, she said, "Ma, what is it? Is it Chris? Was that about Chris?"

Jackie Ruth shook her head gently, crying, not looking Alice in the eyes. Alice let her cry for a few minutes, while her fear escalated to near panic.

Finally, Alice said, "What did the detective say, Ma?"

Jackie Ruth looked up at Alice. The tears stopped. Her mouth pooched out in a defiant pout. "The bastard wants to bring me in. Oh, he called it an interview, but we know what it really means. He's bringing me in like a common criminal—for questioning."

Alice shook her head. "Ma, it's just routine. Remember what he said?"

Jackie Ruth didn't say anything.

"Well?"

"You don't understand, Alice. He must think I had something to do with this. *Me!* This is family business!"

"It's not just family business. Papa was murdered. Don't you understand that?"

Jackie Ruth shook her head. "No. No. He wasn't murdered. He shot himself. Just like they said."

"But the—"

"Doesn't matter what any damn coroner says. They don't know everything."

"What did the detective tell you exactly? Did he mention a lawyer?"

"Of course he mentioned a lawyer! But I don't need a damn lawyer. This is just family business, and he'd do well to just butt the hell out of our problems."

Her mother was being irrational. Alice thought about calling Michael to ask about a good local lawyer.

Was this really happening? Could it be that she really should have one? Alice thought.

Alice said, "Ma, maybe that's not a bad idea."

Jackie Ruth stubbed out her cigarette angrily and stood up. She took the bowl of scrambled eggs with her. She said quietly, almost to herself, "Oh, what the hell would you know about it, anyway?"

Alice's mouth gaped in shock. "What's that supposed to mean?"

Jackie dropped the bowl in the sink loudly and turned. "You know damn well what that means." She took a juice glass from the cabinet and retrieved a container of store-brand orange juice from the fridge. She poured and drank it greedily, shaking a little.

Alice wasn't going to have this discussion here. Not now. She was above all this. She had a different life now. Besides, this wasn't about her. Alice said, "I'm not even going to justify that. You know why I left."

Jackie Ruth took another sip of juice and stared at the floor.

"What's going on here, Ma?"

"Don't know a damn thing," Jackie Ruth said quietly.

"When do you have to be there?"

"He said 10:30, but I'm not going."

Alice said, "Ma, we're going. I'll drive you. We'll go together. It's nothing."

Jackie Ruth looked up at Alice and started crying again. She said, "I'm sorry you left us. So was Papa. In his own way. I'm just sorry you never understood that." She turned to the sink and set her juice glass down carefully. She said, "I better get ready," and then shuffled off in her dime-store slip-ons to her bedroom.

Alice thought about what her mother said, about how much *stuff* was left unsaid that she could never tell her mother, even though it would make her understand, for God's sake, *finally* understand and forgive her. But it was too late for that.

Alice picked up the phone to call Michael about a lawyer and decided against it, choosing instead to call Uncle Bruce, who wasn't surprised. *Routine*, he told her. *Nothing to worry about. Just get her there on time.*

But, after she hung up the phone, Alice wasn't so sure. *Someone* had killed her father. *Someone* knew what happened.

The longer Alice stared out into the cold gloom, the more she thought her mother hadn't told her everything there was to know about that night Papa died out on Route 6.

Jackie Ruth sat quietly in the passenger seat of Alice's Mercedes, staring out at the passing sights as Alice drove to the Sheriff's office up in Madison, about a half hour drive from Redding. After they'd arrived and parked, Alice turned towards her mother. For the first time since she'd arrived in Redding, Alice noticed just how much older her mother looked, how worn down by life she seemed. Jackie Ruth looked more like a nursing home patient than the tough-talking sixty-five-year-old mother Alice pictured in her mind's eye.

Alice asked her, "You okay?"

"Don't want to do this."

"You have to, Ma."

"What did your uncle Bruce say about it?"

"He said you didn't need a lawyer because it's just routine. You have nothing to hide."

Jackie Ruth turned her head and stared out the front windshield. She didn't say anything.

"Is that true, Ma?" Alice said quietly.

Jackie Ruth said nothing.

"Because if something else is going on here, something I don't know about, you need to tell me, and you need to do it now. I can't help you otherwise."

Jackie Ruth shook her head slightly.

"You sure?"

"There's nothing left to say, Dolly."

Alice gazed at her mother a little while longer and shrugged. "Well, than I guess that's that, right?" She glanced at her watch. Ten-twenty. Almost time. "We better get moving. We still have to get in and find out where to go."

Alice followed Jackie Ruth into the smallish red-brick building that looked like Alice's elementary school. It didn't take long to figure out where to go. A deputy sat behind a reception desk and looked at them encouragingly when they walked in.

"Ah, Mrs. Wynter. And Alice. Right on time," a voice said from behind them.

Alice turned around and saw the big detective approaching. His considerable gut strained against the front of his shirt. His belt was lost somewhere underneath the giant fold of flesh, nearly hiding his badge, which was attached to his belt and poking out on the detective's left side.

He held out his hand indicating that they should follow him and said, "Please. Come this way."

They followed the big man into a bare office. Another deputy was seated at a small conference table.

The detective waved his hands at the chairs around the table and said, "Please have a seat. Can I get you anything? Coffee?"

"An ashtray," Jackie Ruth said.

"I'm sorry, Mrs. Wynter. This building is a no-smoking area. State law."

"Damn stupid law if you ask me," she said.

The big detective chuckled, reached into his shirt pocket, and removed a pack of cigarettes. He shook them and nodded his head. "You maybe right about that, Mrs. Wynter. Now, please have a seat."

They sat.

The detective took his seat. The chair groaned in protest. He said, “I take it that you’ve waived your right to counsel during this interview, Mrs. Wynter?”

Jackie Ruth nodded. She stared at the floor, clearly uncomfortable and out of her element.

“Well, that’s fine. Let me explain a little bit about what’s going on, okay?”

Nodding.

“We’ve asked you here today not because you’re a suspect or even because we think you’re a person of interest. Do you understand?”

For the first time, Jackie Ruth looked up at the detective. She nodded. Her face was deadly serious.

“The fact is that your husband was murdered, Mrs. Wynter. We hope that by speaking with you, some fact or aspect of the situation we’ve missed will come to light. It might help us to figure out what happened that night. That’s all this is. Okay?”

Jackie Ruth nodded again.

“So, how this works is, my associate, Matt Ivey, and I are going to take you to a room, set up a recorder and ask you a series of simple questions. At any time, you can stop the interview and request the advice of counsel. If you can’t afford counsel, we can arrange for a public defender. That okay?”

Jackie Ruth said, “I suppose.”

“Fine. Alice, you can wait here if you like. If you don’t mind, we’d like to speak with you as well.”

Alice shrugged and said, “Okay.”

The big detective nodded towards his associate and stood up. Jackie Ruth stood as well and gave Alice an oddly sorrowful look. And then they disappeared.

Alice imagined what sort of questions they were going to ask her mother. Where had she been the night Papa had been killed? Had he been with anyone? Had he made any new friends lately? Had anything in his life changed? Where was Chris? They would want to know the answer to that last one for sure. Alice wondered if her mother knew the answer.

About forty-five anxious minutes later, Jackie Ruth and the other detective, Matt Ivey, reappeared. Alice looked into her mother's eyes, trying to gauge her reaction. It reminded Alice of a time a few years ago when she'd had to have a second pap smear because her gyno *didn't like the looks of something*, and Alice had tried to guess the results of the second test by the look on her doctor's face when she entered her office. Her doctor's well-rehearsed poker face hadn't revealed that the test was fine, and Jackie Ruth's equally stoic expression bore no hint as to what had happened.

Matt said, "Take a seat Mrs. Wynter. We'll just be a few minutes with Alice." He looked at Alice when he said it, waiting for her to come along.

Alice followed him into another room and saw the detective deep in thought, chewing the top of a pen while staring up at the ceiling. She sat down.

"I have nothing to hide, detective."

He leaned forward and smiled. He said, "Call me Don."

"Okay, Don."

"First of all, I'd like to say how sorry I am about your father."

"Thank you."

"I know it must be hard for you."

Alice didn't say anything. She wondered if Don the detective knew about her family. He must. Everyone did.

"Do you know where your brother is, Alice?"

Alice shook her head. "No. I don't."

"Do you think your mother does?"

Alice shrugged. *Where was this going?* She said, "At this point, I have no idea what to think. It's all so—"

"We found the gun used to kill your father. Unfortunately, a couple of kids found it in a field first and started playing with it. One of them is still in the intensive care unit."

Alice's hand went reflexively to her mouth. She said, "Oh, that's terrible."

"You're not kidding. But we verified the bullet that killed your father came from that gun. We also ran the gun's serial number and traced it to a little guns-and-ammo store outside of Redding a few miles. We'll be meeting with the owner."

"You think Chris bought the gun."

Don shrugged. "Don't know. The gun was never registered in his name. Did you talk to Chris before this happened?"

"No. We . . . we don't speak much any more. Not since I left." That age-old guilt bubbled up a little in Alice's mind, and she looked at the floor.

"Okay," Don said. The top of the pen went into his mouth. "Look, I'd like to be straight with you." He leaned forward and turned off the tape recorder.

Alice looked up at him expectantly.

"We're sure your mother's lying to us. We're sure she knows where Chris is. We're beginning to think you do as well."

Anger surged in Alice. How dare he! Then, she calmed. Alice thought, *he's just trying to rattle me a little.* She said,

"Me? How? I'd tell you if I knew! I swear!"

"Really? Isn't he your twin brother? Wouldn't you want to protect him?"

"Yes, but not like this. The best thing he could do now is come forward. I'm worried sick about him. He's had some problems in the—"

"Booze?"

"I don't know what exactly. We're not close. Not any more. But yeah, he's an alcoholic."

"Like his father?"

Alice nodded. "Just like Papa."

"Uh huh. We know. I'm good friends with a bar owner. They spent a good deal of time in that bar."

"What exactly do you want from me? I was estranged from my father. Truth is, I couldn't stand him. He was a mean old man. And I'm sorry about that. But I can't help you."

"Sure you can."

"How?"

For the first time, Don's associate spoke. "By keeping an eye on your mother. You can get her to talk."

Alice shook her head. "I can't. You don't know my mother. She's angry with me. She'd never open up like that. Not to me."

Don said, "Then maybe to someone else?"

Alice shrugged.

"We think you can make that happen," Don said. "You really want to help Chris? You get Jackie Ruth to tell you where he his."

"What if I refuse?"

"Go ahead. Nothing we can do about that. But you want to do the right thing, don't you?"

Alice stared at Don and Matt for a few moments, unsure whether she should be incredulous. But it didn't take long. The other Alice broke through the madness. The Alice Dunn part of Alice. The new Alice. Of course they were right. Her father was murdered. Likely by Chris. And now he was gone. For all she knew, Chris was dead. But she'd felt this morning that there was more to this mess than she knew.

"You're right," Alice said. "I'm sorry. You're exactly right. We need to get to the bottom of this."

Don smiled and said, "Great. For what it's worth, I knew your father. And you're right. He *was* a tough old bastard. Anyway, that's all over. Let's just concentrate on getting this thing resolved." He fished around in his shirt pocket and took out a card with a Sheriff's logo printed in one corner. "You call me. Any time. With anything. Okay?"

Alice took the card and nodded. She tried to manage a grin and failed.

1984

Chris hadn't seen Ray or Vic for days. He'd kept low. Stayed home sick a couple of days. But he knew he was kidding himself, that his luck would run out. He'd even stopped talking to Alice and the rest of his family for the most part. He just couldn't bear the thought of it, of them being able to see through to what he really was: a monster. He'd also taken to sneaking down into the kitchen at night and nipping from his mother's jug wine and even a bottle of cheap vodka his father kept under the sink. It helped him to sleep, which was something he wasn't doing much of these days. He felt as though he were always on the verge of losing it and knew that he couldn't continue much longer. Something had to give.

He assumed that his mother and Alice thought he was shaken up by the murder, which was good because they left him alone. Only once had Alice stopped at his bedroom door and asked, "You okay, Chris?"

"Yeah," he'd replied. "Just got a couple of things on my mind."

Boy, if she only knew. But she'd let him be.

The murder of Randall Gartlin made the national news coast to coast, which was good for only one reason: Chris knew that the cops hadn't gotten anywhere on the case. They were calling it a random act of violence, which Chris figured was cop-talk for "we don't know what the fuck happened, okay?" Getting away with the crime was only a part of what was worrying him, however. It was the guilt that was killing him, and how what had happened had revealed something he'd thought before but never had given much credence too: that he was a bad person. A very bad person. Maybe his father was right. Papa Wynter had always called him weak willed, or, when he was into his vodka, gutless.

But he wasn't gutless. In fact, what he was thinking about doing wasn't gutless at all. He'd been thinking about nothing else for days. If he went to the cops, alone, and told them what happened, they might let him off in exchange for turning in Ray. Maybe Vic would get off as well. But Ray was his cousin. You don't do that to family. You just don't. Right?

His luck with avoiding Ray ran out after school on the Friday after what they'd done to Mr. Gartlin. Chris was walking home, jumpy, sure that the cops were going to come racing along and bust him at any moment. Someone did come racing along all right, but it wasn't the cops.

Ray's Chevy Nova thundered past him and skidded to halt. The backup lights came on and the car roared backwards and stopped in front of Chris. Ray and Vic got out. Ray leaned against the car and lit up a smoke.

"Want one?" Ray said.

Chris shook his head. Even *that* made him feel guilty nowadays. He didn't want anything to do with Ray or his cigarettes or his pot. He avoided Butt Hall, where they all went to smoke ("Like Study Hall," Ray had dubbed it). From now on, as far as Chris was concerned he was living like a monk (except for his lonely midnight visits to the fridge for the jug wine—that was okay, comforting, because it was *his* thing and not Ray's). Ray made him feel dirty.

Ray bumped himself off the car and walked towards Chris. He'd developed an unpleasant swagger, as if he really thought he was something now. He said, "Chrissy, seriously, what the fuck is wrong with you?"

"Why do you keep calling me that?" Chris said, watching Vic carefully as he walked in back of Chris.

" 'Cause it rhymes with sissy, why'd you think?" Ray said, laughing. "Seriously, man, you're starting to freak me and Vic out here. You don't hang with us in the morning. You don't hang after school. I haven't even seen you out in Butt Hall."

Vic said, "What gives? You know?"

"I just don't think it's good for us to be hanging together right now, you know? I mean maybe it'll bring heat on us or whatever," Chris said.

"Heat?" Ray said. "What the fuck are you talking about? The cops have no idea what's going on. They don't know anything, man."

"Besides," Vic added, "It would look weirder if we *weren't* hanging around than if we were, right?"

"I guess."

Ray put his arm around Chris and said, "Why don't you take a little ride with us?"

"Yeah," Vic said.

"Why?"

Ray smiled and looked down at Chris with those cold eyes. He said, "Just for old times' sake. You know what I mean?"

"Nah, I'd better not. I gotta—"

Vic grabbed his arms from behind and pushed him towards the car.

Ray said, "Get in back with him so he doesn't bolt."

Mental alarms were screaming like fire engine sirens in Chris's mind. *What was going on here? They can't just kill me. Can they?*

Chris said, "Lay off!" He tried to shake loose, but Vic held him fast. "Where are we going?"

Ray hopped into the driver's seat and said, "Don't worry about that. Me and Vic got it all planned out. Don't we, Vic?"

"You know it, boss."

Ray punched the accelerator and they were off, headed North, snaking up one endless country road after another. Somerset County, Maine, stretches all the way up through the center of the state into some very remote woods, not the kind of places you want to get stuck if you know what's good for you. But Ray seemed to know where he was going, so Chris just shut up and tried not to think about what he and Vic were going to do to him when they got to wherever they were going. Finally, after driving for what seemed like hours, Ray stopped the Nova and got out.

Chris said, "I'm not getting out."

Ray poked his head in and said, "Oh, yes you are. You're getting out right now." He reached into the car with this long arms and grabbed at Chris.

Chris shrugged away Ray's arms and pushed Vic hard against the side of the car so he could get a shot at the front seat and freedom. He even managed to kick Vic in the gut, which made Vic cough and try to catch his breath. Chris struggled with the front seat, but it was hopeless. Ray had his foot on it, which prevented Chris from pushing it forward to escape. Chris slumped in the backseat. It was pointless to fight back. He was better off letting them lead him out of the car. He'd find a way to escape when he was out.

Ray said, "Chrissy, are you going to behave? Vic, get him out here."

Chris nodded and let Vic take him by the shoulders. They got out of the car.

"Take him over there by that tree," Ray said. "Tie him with this." He threw a rope he'd retrieved from the trunk of the Nova. Ray ducked into the Chevy's trunk and came up again.

He was holding the compound bow he'd used to kill the teacher.

Chris screamed and struggled again. They were going to fucking kill him! Panic surged through his body. He punched and kicked his way free of Vic, who gave chase.

Chris ducked into the dark brush at the side of the little road. He ran completely blind, the brush tearing at his skin and occasionally threatening to poke him in the eye. His breath came in deep gasps of cold air. Winter had already settled in this far north in November. He wouldn't last long out here in these woods. Not long at all.

"Get him!" Ray said. "Vic! He went left! He went left!"

Ray and Vic split up. Chris barreled on straight ahead, blind with fear and panic.

Then, he was on the ground. He couldn't breath. Vic had come out of the dark on his right and clotheslined him, knocking the air out of his lungs with a forearm.

Vic screamed, "He's down! He's down! I got him!" And then he was on Chris, flipping him over and tying his arms behind his back. He did this quickly and efficiently while Chris was still struggling for air.

They had him. Cold.

After several minutes, Chris was breathing normally again, although his upper chest was sore. He was resigned to his fate. He was to die up here. It was pointless to struggle. Even if he did get away, his arms were tied. He wouldn't get far.

Ray walked toward him with the compound bow and pulled it taut, aiming at Chris's head. "This is what you get, you little fucker. This is what you get when you cross the Masters of Chaos."

Chris tried to say, "But I didn't. I didn't." But his throat was too dry to speak. He felt a little piss escape and wet the front of his pants. He was faint.

Ray walked closer.

Chris managed a weak, "Please. Ray. Don't."

Vic stood to one side smiling and watching with intense interest.

And then, Ray burst out laughing and dropped the bow. Vic started giggling.

Chris couldn't believe what he was seeing and hearing. They were fucking laughing. Was this a set up? A joke? Or were they just playing games with him?

Ray said, "Vic, man, untie the fucking guy?"

"We fucking got you, man. You should have seen your face. Holy shit," Vic said, reaching around back and untying him.

Ray lit up a smoke and said, "What did you think? We were going to kill you? Give us some motherfuckin' credit. Sheesh!" And then he laughed again and pointed at Chris's wet pants.

Chris went red with embarrassment and smiled. He'd believed them completely, still did in some ways. It had seemed so real. "Then why did you guys come all the way up h—"

"To get rid of this, asshole," Ray said, holding up the bow in one hand and a handful of arrows in the other. "It's a fucking murder weapon. You think I want that in hidden in my barn in the backyard?"

And so they buried the bow and arrows after carefully wiping them clean of fingerprints. The boys managed to dig a 3-foot hole, despite the frozen ground. After the snow started, they wouldn't have to worry about anyone finding it for months, if ever.

On the ride home, watching Ray and Vic pass a joint back and forth in the front seats, Chris thought that maybe what had happened here wasn't completely a joke. You know what they say: behind every joke is a kernel of truth. Chris was starting to think that maybe scaring him half to death had been meant to teach him a lesson, one that said, "We don't want to kill you, but we will if we have to."

EIGHT

The first thing Jackie Ruth did when she got home was lean against the kitchen counter and light a cigarette. She glared at Alice because Alice wouldn't let her smoke in the Mercedes.

Alice said, "I'll make us some lunch. Sandwiches okay?"

"Do whatever."

"Ma, I don't understand why you're angry with me."

"Because you don't believe me."

Alice sighed. She said, "Ma, it's not that I don't believe you, okay?"

"Then what? What is it?"

"I think you know where Chris is, and I think you know more about what happened to Papa then you let on." Alice could hardly believe she'd said it aloud, but there it was, out in the smoky kitchen air.

Jackie Ruth stared at Alice for a minute, her head shaking with rage. Her cigarette smoldered hotter with each successive drag. Finally, Jackie Ruth stubbed out the cigarette haphazardly, leaving it burning in the little black ashtray on the kitchen counter.

She said, "I don't have to listen to this. Especially from you."

"What?" Alice said.

"You think I killed him, don't you? Don't you?"

Alice said, "I don't know what to think, but no, I don't believe you killed him."

Jackie Ruth continued. "Well, I didn't. I didn't! Are you happy with that? 'Cause the police weren't. They think I did. I could see it in their eyes. Well, they don't know shit from shinola. And neither do you. This is *family* business."

"Where's Chris, Ma?"

Tears dripped from Jackie Ruth's eyes at the mention of her son. She shook her head and braced herself again on the counter. "I don't know."

But Alice saw something else in her eyes. There was more information behind them. Her mother knew something.

"Is that the truth? Ma, you're acting funny. Tell me. What's going on?"

Jackie Ruth looked up at Alice, her eyes swimming in tears. "I can't, Alice. Okay? I just don't . . ." But she stopped herself, blinking her eyes. She wiped them with her hands. "Yes," she said simply. "That's the truth." Her eyes defied Alice to challenge her.

But Alice didn't believe her, and Alice knew that her mother knew that. Alice said, "I have a right to know. He's my brother."

"No he's not! He stopped being your brother when you left your home. You decided then that he wouldn't be your brother. And that your father, God rest his soul, wouldn't be your father. And that I wouldn't be your mother. You decided that! It was you. Not us." Jackie Ruth's eyes blazed.

"That's not true!" Alice cried, but she felt like she was lying. It was true. She'd run from the truth her whole adult life. The truth about Ray. The truth about Chris. All of them.

Jackie Ruth's tears dried up, and she regarded Alice coldly. She said, "You know it is. You, with your fancy German car. That fake accent of yours. I bet you tell people you grew up in Massachusetts or Connecticut."

Alice felt stripped bare naked. Her mother had called her on her bullshit and gotten to the core of it. In one lousy sentence. The Alice Dunn part of her felt phony in that instant. It was stupid, she knew, because she was still the same Alice. She'd always been that same timid Alice waiting for the school bus out at the end of her driveway. That same Alice who'd eventually let Chris's problems in high school become her problems now. That same Alice that let *everyone* in this God forsaken shit-of-a-town do whatever they wanted because she knew she would escape one day and never come back.

But she *was* different now. She was Alice Dunn now. Alice Wynter had stopped existing the very moment she'd crossed over into New Hampshire all those years ago, and she'd never regretted it. Alice Dunn was a normal person with normal problems. Alice Wynter was something else entirely.

Calmly, Alice said, "No. That's not right. It's not fake. It's me. I'm me. There are things you can't understand about my life, things—"

"What things?" Jackie Ruth said. "Things like Ray?"

"What do you mean, 'Things like Ray'?" Alice's stomach

seemed to drop below her knees. She and her mother were treading in very deep, very dark water. And the sharks were circling.

"Well, that business doesn't make any difference now," said Jackie Ruth

Alice's voice was just barely a whisper. She said, more to herself than her mother, "But it does matter. It's all that matters."

Jackie Ruth shook her head and stared at Alice's eyes. "It shouldn't."

"But it does."

Alice felt something happening in her mother's little kitchen in Maine. Some unspoken communication between them, both knowing and not knowing, both too frightened to admit the truth about a terrible gaping bloody wound in their family. Alice felt her world slipping through her fingers. The fragile house of cards she'd constructed to hide herself began to fall apart. It was as if Alice Wynter was becoming Alice Dunn. Or the other way around. The two were merging, and it felt horrible, like she was trapped. She felt certain she would explode if she spent another minute, another second in that awful house.

"C'mere, Dolly," her mother said, her arms outstretched.

Alice shook her head. She said, "No! No, no, no, no! You're a monster!"

"You don't understand. Alice, honey, you just don't understand."

"I understand perfectly. You wanted to keep our problems quiet. It's family business, right? No one else's business."

"Alice, you—"

"And that's why you were so worried about talking to the

cops, wasn't it?"

"A little."

"Oh, my God. I can't believe this is happening." Alice no longer felt in control of her life. She felt Alice Dunn slipping further away. She felt as if she were trapped in a giant whirlpool that threatened to suck her under and drown her.

Alice said, "Did Dad know about Ray?" She was really asking two questions.

"We didn't talk about it."

"What do you mean?" Alice said.

Jackie Ruth turned her head to look outside.

Alice said again, "Ma, what do you mean?"

"Shh! You hear me? Just shush up, now."

"Ma, what—"

Alice followed her mother's gaze outside. Uncle Bruce had pulled into the dirt driveway and parked next to the Mercedes. He got out and was approaching the house.

"Alice, you keep quiet about this. About Ray. You hear me? I mean it. He's got enough to deal with without dragging all this up."

"But—"

Jackie Ruth gave Alice a look that she hadn't seen from her mother in years: panic.

Alice stopped, confused.

Uncle Bruce let himself in the kitchen door. He said, "Hiya, ladies. Colder than a witch's tit out there. Snow's coming soon. You feel how humid it is? Gonna need tire-chains after this for sure. Jackie Ruth, you—?"

He stopped talking when he saw the women's faces. He must have felt it in the air, seen it on their faces.

"Interview go okay with the police?" he said.

Jackie Ruth smiled and said, "Fine. Just like you said. Routine. Can I fix you a sandwich? Dolly and me were just talking about lunch."

Bruce nodded. He said, "So, Jackie Ruth, you got the keys to the shed? I'd best be getting those chains on before it's too late. Gonna be a helluva year this…"

But Alice didn't hear anything after that. Papa, Bruce, Chris, her mother, and especially Ray were swimming around in her head. Something was at work. Something rotten. And big.

Alice felt like she didn't know them at all.

Then she felt like she had to talk to Michael. She'd never wanted to talk to anyone more in her life.

* * *

"It's gonna be a bad one by the sounds of it," Matt Ivey said, staring out the windshield up at the sky. "Some very dark clouds rolling in."

"Yuh uh," Detective Don Lambert grunted in reply, not thinking about the weather, despite the fact that the impending storm was on everyone's mind.

The detectives were on their way to visit Daniel Hardman, a few miles north of Redding. Thanks to the National Crime Information Center, run by the FBI, they traced the gun little Ryan Crane had found in the field near his home, the gun that nearly killed Joshua McLain, to Danny, who owned a gun dealership that catered to hunters and rural homeowners. These visits were always a little tricky because men like Danny Hardman didn't usually take kindly to police officers asking a lot of questions, especially about a murder weapon.

Don had no doubt he had the right gun and the right

dealer, but the central question remained: who shot Papa Wynter?

"Want to talk things over," Don said.

"Shoot."

"Jackie Ruth clammed up."

"Sure did."

"But she didn't do it," Don said.

"What makes you say that?"

"All those years of living under Papa Wynter's boot-heel? She woulda snapped years ago. Dontcha think?"

Matt nodded. "Makes sense, yeah. And of course Alice is out of the picture."

"Right. Although . . ." His voice trailed off. Something had clicked in Don's mind, but he couldn't put his finger on it.

"What're you thinking?"

"Can't say exactly. My gut tells me that Alice isn't completely out of the picture." Don turned to look at Matt.

Matt was nodding in agreement, staring out at the road.

Don continued. "It's like every one of them knows something. A piece of something. You put it all together and bang. You got a murder."

"It's true. I guess I kind of felt that too. But Alice? You think she had something to do with it?"

Don shook his head. "No. Not directly. But there is something there. I'm not crazy, am I? You felt it too."

"Yeah, I did. So where does that leave us?"

Don stroked his chin thoughtfully. After a moment, he said, "The way I see it is that we have three possibilities."

Matt said, "One."

"Chris argues with Papa Wynter at the bar. They get into

a car, argue some more. They're drunk and mean. Chris shoots his father. Chris is scared now. He runs into the woods and dies of exposure."

"He'll turn up in the spring if that's true, what's left of him, anyway," Matt said. "Okay. Possibility two?"

"Stay with me here. I'm just throwing it out to see if anything sticks."

"Shoot."

"Okay," Don said. "Bruce Wynter killed Papa. The uncle. Papa's brother."

"Motive?"

Don's lips pursed as he thought. After a moment he said, "Don't know."

"Didn't seem too rattled when we questioned him."

"True. But he's definitely on the short list. Remember that old Jimmy Bible said Chris and Papa had been arguing about Ray, who was Bruce's son."

Matt said, "Yeah, but that could have been anything. Those two probably talk about old times every day."

"Uh yuh. That's what I was thinking too."

Matt said, "Next."

"The man I talked to outside Flynn's said Chris and Papa were talking to a third man. Maybe that man killed them both. Say he was a drifter out to make a quick couple of bucks and move on."

"Uh huh."

"So he kills Papa straight off, but Chris gets away. We just haven't found him yet."

"Not bad. I like possibilities one and three. It's Chris or a drifter."

Don nodded.

Later, Don spotted the gun dealer on the right and slowed his Crown Vic. The dealership was nothing more than a worn-out shack. It was faded blue and set back from the road perhaps a hundred feet. The words "Guns and Ammo" were written on the side of the gray building in fading white paint.

They parked the car outside and walked in. The place was warm, well lit, and stuffed with camping equipment and other supplies almost to the point that Don couldn't maneuver his giant body towards the counter. Matt had no trouble, of course.

Daniel Hardman watched them warily from behind the counter, his hands planted firmly on it. He was chewing tobacco and occasionally spit into a cup that had the words, *Your Fresh, Hot Coffee* printed on it. Underneath the glass counter on which Daniel's spit cup sat were several dozen pistols and guns. Behind him, a long row of rifles and compound bows hung neatly.

Don said, "Hiya. Looking for Daniel Hardman. You him?"

"Who wants to know?"

Matt stood behind Don, his hands on his waist as close to his gun as could be without looking threatening.

Don laid on the charm. "Aw, it's nothing like that. Names Lambert. Detective Don Lambert. Somerset County. Drove out from Madison. Tell ya, we're working on case down in Redding. Ever hear of Redding, Daniel?"

"Maybe." He spit into the cup.

"Damndest thing. Old guy gets shot in his car out on Route 6. Turns out the gun was purchased here. NCIC had you as the first owner, but nothing after that."

"You don't say."

"Well, thing of it is, we're kinda hoping you might help us ID the guy that bought the gun."

"I sell a lot of guns. What makes you think I'd remember?"

"Like I said, Daniel, we're just kinda hoping."

"I run a legal shop here. No funny business." Daniel said, spitting again into his cup, clearly not comfortable and not happy about the scrutiny. "I got papers for everything I sell."

Don smiled. "Of course you do. It's just that this gun, the gun that killed that old guy, doesn't have any record at the NCIC after you. So, technically, that makes you the owner of a murder weapon. Is that right, Matt?"

"I believe you have that right, detective."

It was a mild threat, but Don hoped it would prod Daniel into cooperating. Even if the guy could ID who bought the gun, he might be reluctant, knowing that he'd have to appear in court and finger someone. People get killed for less.

"Whaddaya got? Pictures?" Daniel said. His bravado ticked down a notch. He wanted nothing to do with being the owner of record of a murder weapon.

Don smiled again and said, "That's right, just a couple of pictures for you. He opened a manila envelope and pulled out several pictures of Chris. He placed them on the counter in front of Daniel and waited.

"I remember him."

"You're sure?" Don said, somewhat taken aback.

"Looked a little older than that, but yeah, I remember him. He was in a couple of weeks ago."

That made sense. Chris's alcohol abuse had aged him prematurely and the mug-shot was taken over a year ago.

Don said, "You got a record of the sale?"

"Lemme look."

Daniel Hardman bent down and picked up a shoe box filled with receipts. He said, “I’m sure I just forgot to file the paperwork on that particular gun. Just a mistake. You know what I’m saying, dontcha?”

Don nodded and said, “Sure do.” He motioned Matt over to help. The three men went through the receipts one by one.

After fifteen minutes, Daniel said, “Ha! Here it is right here. Yeah, this is it, see?” He held it up smiling. He said, “I don’t own that gun. See? I guess I just overlooked it. Just like I said I did.”

Don took the receipt and looked it over: *S&W Texas Hold ‘Em, $800.* Then, a little further down: *Wynter. Cash.*

Don said, “We’ll need a copy of this.”

Daniel was still grinning. “Sure thing, Detective.”

* * *

The detective called at eleven o’clock, just as small snowflakes began to fall, and asked Alice to meet him at Denny’s for an early lunch. Alice reluctantly agreed and called Michael to let him know that they’d have to put off meeting until later in the afternoon. She needed to speak with both men. The detective needed to know about her strange argument with her mother the day before. And Michael . . .Well, that was more delicate.

When she got into her black Mercedes, she had to turn on the windshield wiper to wipe away a thin layer of snow. She hoped the heavy stuff would hold off until late in the evening.

She pulled out of the driveway and drove towards the Denny’s, thinking about her relationship with Michael. Alice was beginning to feel guilty about her feelings towards him. She realized that she was using him, that in another place and time, she wouldn't need him like she did now. She'd been calling Gerald, her husband, daily since arriving in Redding, but for reasons she couldn't fully explain, she'd held back when speaking with him. She'd given him the basics but couldn't quite bring herself to tell him everything, to tell him *both* sides of the story. The Wynter side and the Dunn side. She'd simply been reassuring him that all was well, if not a little complicated. And, true to Gerald's personality, and partly because she wasn't telling him everything, what he'd offered in return were platitudes and legal advice, none of which were particularly useful. She promised herself that she would come clean. After. When all this was done.

But Michael was different. He listened to her when they talked, which was often by phone, and he seemed to care—perhaps too much. And that was something Alice needed to set straight when they met later in the day. She sensed in Michael a deep loneliness and longing to connect with someone. She didn't want to give him the wrong idea, although she was certain she already had. When this was over, however it ended, Alice would go home to New Jersey, work things out with Gerald, and resume her life as Alice Dunn, successful marketing executive and wife of a prominent Wall Street lawyer. She would become Alice Dunn forever and finally let this junk go. She had to.

Several minutes later, she parked in the Denny's parking lot and entered the restaurant, which felt hot and humid and smelled like coffee. She saw the detective immediately. It was hard to miss the enormous man squeezed behind the table at a booth in a back corner.

"How many?" a pimply teenaged boy asked.

Alice said, "I'm meeting someone. I think he's just back there."

She walked back to the detective and sat down.

"Alice. Good to see you again. Thanks for meeting me here."

"Good morning, Don."

"You ready for the snow?"

Alice shrugged. Truthfully, she hadn't thought about it much one way or the other. Snow in Maine is nothing new.

"Could be a bad one," Don said, studying her face. "Okay. No more small talk. First things first. I'm sorry about the way I spoke to you at the station. I got the feeling that maybe I was a little too . . . How do you say? Direct. I think we need to be friends here. We need to understand each other to get through this thing."

"I understand."

"Do you?"

"You have a job to do."

"I do."

"You have no reason to believe that I'm telling you the truth. You don't know me," Alice said, not quite trusting the man and his motivations.

"I know your family. They've been here a long time. I'm not out to get anybody, to prove anything. I'm too old for that. I just want to get to the bottom of this thing."

"Yeah, well—"

Don said, "Look, I may as well get to the point."

Alice nodded.

"Your brother purchased the gun that killed your father. We found it in a field just a hundred yards or so from where it happened. We had it traced to a dealer a few miles north. I saw the receipt."

"So you think he killed him?" Alice said, coldly, trying not to betray her true suspicions.

A pretty waitress walked over and stood before them. "Hi," she said. "My name's Sheila, and I'll be taking care of you this morning. You two know what you want or are you still working on it?"

Alice said, "I think we know. Don?"

"Pancakes, sausage, 2 eggs over easy, and a big glass of orange juice."

Sheila said, "You got it! And you?" She looked at Alice.

"Just a fruit cup and some coffee."

"Coffee for me too," Don added.

"Great! That'll be just a few minutes."

Alice watched her go and then turned back to Don. She said, "So, you think he killed my father?"

Don nodded. "I hate to say it, but yes, Alice, I do. We just need to find him. And for that, I need your help."

Alice said, "Believe me, I want this over as much as you do. But I don't know where he is."

"What about your mother?"

Alice sighed. She decided to give the detective a little rope. "That's a different story."

"How do you mean?"

"Listen, I'm just trying to be honest here. Full disclosure and all that?"

"Of course. I appreciate that. Like I said, no one's out to get you or your family."

"I think my mother knows more than she lets on."

"I think so too."

"We argued yesterday after we got home from the police station. I confronted her about what she knew, and she . . ." Alice stopped and stared at the table. How could she explain things to the detective without having to talk about things she couldn't bring herself to think about, let alone reveal to a stranger?

"You okay?" he said. "Alice, this conversation goes nowhere."

"Let's leave it at this: I had some trouble with Ray, and my mother seems to know about it. I don't know how, but she does. That spooked me. No. It was worse. It terrified me because those things are done forever. And then Uncle Bruce showed up and—things just got weird."

"What kind of trouble did you have with Ray?" the detective asked, mild surprise in his voice.

"Just . . . Trouble. Okay? It was a long time ago."

The waitress brought their food and began setting plates down on the table. She poured them each a cup of coffee. She said, "Free refills today, so don't forget to ask. Can I get you anything else?"

Alice shook her head.

Don said, "No, I think that'll about do it."

The waitress paused a moment, perhaps sensing the strange vibes at the table, but then walked away.

Don grabbed a fork and tucked into his plate. After a few silent minutes, he swallowed and said, "Something's been bugging me."

Alice said, "Oh?"

"Now, this is off the record."

"Okay," Alice said, curious.

"I got a feeling something else is going on here."

Alice nodded.

"You agree."

"Yes."

"What is it?"

Alice shook her head slowly. She hadn't touched her fruit cup. Her stomach felt as though it were filled with acid. She had a bad, bad feeling inside that seemed to be consuming her mind. She hadn't felt this way since she was a teenager. It was as though opening up the can of worms that was her childhood had brought her right back to that terrible place, perhaps even back to the day the worst of it happened.

Finally, Alice said, "I don't know. But it's old. And it's poison. I think that's why my mother wants you out of it. She's terrified of something, but I don't know what it is. Not exactly, anyway. And that scares me. She wants so badly to believe that Papa just shot himself out on that road. I don't think she's trying to deceive you—or me for that matter. It's just old, rotten family business."

"What happened between you and Ray?"

"I'm not going to tell you that." Alice stared up at Don defiantly.

"Okay. Fair enough. But remember. He was a bad kid, Alice. A very bad kid."

Alice nodded and said, "I know. Believe me, I know. And Chris knew it as well."

NINE

1984

"Chris, seriously, what's going on with you?"

Chris turned his head slightly and saw his twin sister Alice in the doorway, leaning against it. He turned his head back to its original position and continued to stare at the ceiling. He'd been that way since after dinner with his mother and Alice. Papa was working late.

Alice came in and closed the door. She said, "I'm not kidding. Out with it."

He and Alice had been through a lot together: his father's drunken middle-of-the-night tirades when he'd hit their mother hard enough to leave the side of her face red for a couple of days; nights when they'd come home to find both Papa and their mother too drunk to cook dinner; and some nights when they weren't there at all, passed out somewhere after league night at the bowling alley. But he'd always had Alice. They were twins, but she'd always been more like a big sister to him. She looked after him. Alice had bailed Chris out more times than he liked to admit, but his troubles with his cousin Ray and friend Vic were too big for Alice.

The past few days had been unbearable for Chris. He figured it was only a matter of time before the cops showed up at his door. The episode with Ray and Vic out in the woods had scared him half to death, but it seemed a million years away. Every day felt like that now, like it had happened years ago. He and his friends were hurdling headlong towards something terrible, he felt sure.

But what they'd done had invigorated Ray. He built up what almost certainly *was* an accident, bragging every time they were together about how he'd planned it and thought about it, even to the point of wearing gloves to keep the fingerprints off the compound bow and arrow. He positively *glowed* in it. He *knew* the cops didn't have shit on them, and he got off thinking that he'd done it, gotten away with murder. But now Ray reminded Chris of a dog rolling in his own shit. Sooner or later, everyone is going to figure out that the dog stinks and know why. And now Ray was talking about bigger and better things, becoming hit men, selling drugs. All kinds of crap Chris could hardly stand to listen to any more because he knew it was just stupid macho bullshit.

But he couldn't think of a way out. There was nowhere to go.

To Alice, he said, "Don't want to talk about it."

Alice sighed. She said, "Are you upset about Mr. Gartlin?"

A wicked bolt of nerves squeezed his gut. He wanted to tell Alice everything, but he couldn't. He wouldn't. Not yet. Maybe not ever. He said, "Something like that."

"We all are."

Not like me, Chris thought, struggling like hell to keep from bawling in front of Alice. *How he longed to tell her everything!*

"Just tell me this, Chris. Are you okay?"

"I'm fine," Chris lied.

"Okay, then." Alice stood up and looked down at her brother. She said, "You can talk to me about it."

"I know."

And then she left.

When the door closed, Chris rolled over and cried into his pillow for a long time, hours it seemed. No one could understand. Not Alice, not Ray, not . . . *What about Vic?* Chris thought.

He wiped his tears on his sleeve and sat up. For sure, Vic seemed just as nutty as Ray about this thing lately. But Vic wasn't Ray. Vic just worshipped Ray and looked up to him like an older brother, like Chris did. Vic had to be scared like Chris. Vic was crazy, but he was no criminal. He was the clown, the one of them who always ended up getting busted for the crazy things they thought of. The kid with the goofy grin who'd try anything once—even murder. Vic must be thinking about this stuff, right?

Chris thought about the days since the murder. He hadn't talked to Vic alone since. They'd always been together, Vic and Ray. Was that intentional? What if Chris could talk to Vic alone? Maybe talk some sense into him?

If Vic and Chris put up a united front, the cops would definitely give them a break, right? After all, they'd only thought Ray was going to *egg* Gartlin, not fucking kill the guy, for Christ's sake. If they both said Ray was the one who planned and did the thing, that he *bragged* about it afterward even . . . Hell, it was like the cop shows on TV! They always gave the guys who talked a free pass—well, maybe not free, but at least *something*.

Chris felt better. He glanced at the clock: 9:45 PM. Vic would still be up. For sure. He was an only child and had his own line.

Chris picked up the phone and dialed. It rang twice before Vic picked up.

Chris said into the phone, "I can't sleep. You want to smoke a joint?"

"Yeah. Lemme call Ray."

Chris shook his head. "No, fuck Ray, he said he was crapping out early tonight," Chris lied. "Besides, we gotta talk about something."

"Yeah? What?" Vic said suspiciously.

"C'mon. Not on the phone. In person."

"Fine."

"Meet you behind the school, like usual?"

"When?"

"I don't know, like fifteen minutes?"

"Okay. I'll see you there."

"Okay, cool. Later."

Chris hung up the phone and sat up. He felt better. He was sure Vic would come around. He was also sure that he'd sleep the whole night through tonight after he got home, something he hadn't done since the night on Gartlin's porch.

Detective Don Lambert was unnerved after his meeting with Alice at the diner. He'd gone about his duties that afternoon mechanically. Maybe it was just the weather, but he felt like all the pieces to the Papa Wynter puzzle were floating around in the air, just waiting for his brain to catch up and put them in the right order.

A quick glance at his Timex told him it was just past six o'clock. Matt Ivey had already left. Don realized he'd never make dinner. He picked up the phone and dialed Gaye.

"Don? Is that you? Everything all right?"

Don leaned back in his chair. "Everything's fine. How's everything with you?"

"Nothing to speak of."

"Good," Don said. "Listen, I'm not going to make it for dinner. This case, it's—"

"Papa?"

"Exactly. It's driving me crazy."

"You want to talk about it?"

"You know I can't."

"Can't blame a girl for trying. Hey, why don't I come in, maybe drop something off for you? It's already on the stove. Be ready in a half hour or so."

Don smiled. "Nah. You sit tight. I'll be home later. I got some thinking to do."

"You sure? It's no trouble."

"You enjoy yourself. I'll be home before too long."

A beat of silence passed.

Gaye said, "Well, listen here, mister. Don't go off eating junk. Get yourself something decent."

"Yes, ma'am. You can trust me."

"Hmm, well . . ."

"Gaye, c'mon, now. I gotta get moving."

"I love you."

"Love you back," Don said and placed the phone in the cradle. He hated lying to his wife, but he figured they both knew he'd end up in the Wendy's drive-thru lane, and it was better not to have her worrying.

He pushed himself from out behind his desk and grabbed the keys to the Crown Victoria. He thought better when he drove. He stepped outside to a face full of cold air and blowing snow. He thought about the chains he hadn't put on the tires and swore.

He drove, thinking.

It seemed like everywhere he turned in the course of this investigation, that damned Ray Wynter kept coming up. Alice and Chris's cousin. Bruce Wynter's boy. Papa's brother.

He'd been just a patrolman when Ray'd gone missing in the winter of . . . *what was it now?* Sure. 1984. That had been a hell of a year around these parts. Fires. Vandalism. And the murder. High school teacher. Gaitman? Garland? Something like that. Ray'd been brought in for questioning in late '84. Don hadn't been there, but he talked plenty with those who had been. They said the kid was like ice. No emotion. Could see it in his cold, dark eyes. Didn't respond to threats, physical violence (well, *pretend* physical violence, anyway—that's what Wesley Nimmons, a detective on staff then, told him), good-cop-bad-cop routines, nothing. They'd all thought he'd done it. Hell, they just *knew* it, but that kind of truth won't hold up in a murder case. Not even close.

Then, the snowmobile accident. The boys had been rat-racing, like they do, not thinking. That was the theory, anyway. And Ray never came back. Happens all the time in Maine. Kid races out onto a lake that isn't quite hard enough yet and *ploop!* In he goes.

But what of it? What did all that have to do with Chris and Papa Wynter? That was twenty-five years ago. Something told Don that it had *plenty* to do with it. Just intuition. Instinct. You get that after so many years in the business, just like anything else.

Alice had nothing to do with what happened to Papa out on Route 6. No way. His gut also told him that, but she wasn't just another piece of the puzzle. She was more. Perhaps Alice Wynter held the key to unlock this mystery, perhaps not.

Speaking of his gut, Don's was rumbling. He pulled into the Wendy's drive thru and picked up a burger, fries, and a shake. He parked and ate, feeling a little guilty, wondering how something that tastes so good could be so wrong. He watched the flakes falling on the windshield. It was starting to blow a little now, gathering on the roads, swirling like lost, restless ghosts.

When he was done, he headed back to the office, deciding to pull the incident reports, read the investigation notes, go over the autopsy photos. Put some faces with names. Read anything and everything he could get his hands on.

Case files nowadays were on a computer, but without the budget to do it, the old stuff (and this was *definitely* in that category) was archived in the basement in boxes on long shelves, like a library. Each file box was marked by year and a letter or two. It didn't take him long to find the murder file. Cold case.

Gartlin. Randall Gartlin. That had been the teacher's name. Shot through the neck with a hunting arrow. Bled to death on his front porch early one evening. No witnesses. The only piece of physical evidence had been the arrow. His wife had mentioned that the perps rang the doorbell, but that only led to a partial print. A *very* partial print by the looks of it. Useless.

A perfect crime in many ways. Random, little evidence, no motive to speak of, at least none that the police were aware of. Finding a suspect was like finding the proverbial needle in the haystack. No chance in hell.

Leafing through the report, Don saw a flurry of tips that had come in during the weeks that followed the murder, but there had been nothing substantial.

Almost nothing. A note had been paper-clipped to the report in what seemed like an offhand or second-thought sort of way. Don read the note with increasing interest. A patrolman in 1984 named Timothy Dennison had been stricken with his own strong sense of intuition—no surprise that Don recognized the name and knew he'd made detective and retired only five or so years before—and noted an odd confluence of events that had led to Ray's being brought in for questioning. And from that came a new name: Victor Acree.

After years in police work, Don had learned about the power of possibilities and the magical phrase: *what if*? *What if* gave you power. And Don performed this mental trick every day and did now, staring down at the unsolved murder report, thinking about Ray and Chris and Alice and the myriad of *what if's*. What if Ray Wynter wasn't really dead? What if Alice Wynter had killed her father? What if Chris Wynter had killed his father? What if Jackie Ruth knew where Chris was because she *knew* that Chris had killed

Papa? What if she was protecting him? What if Jackie Ruth herself had killed Papa? These questions swirled around in his mind. Some made sense, others not.

And then, in the cold January darkness of the basement archives, a most logical *what if* clicked into place like a good chess move. He saw other *what-ifs* all leading towards the same conclusion: a checkmate. It was just a hunch, but he needed more information.

He thrust the report back into the box hastily, suddenly excited and focused, knowing that he only needed a little more to make it work. He didn't have that checkmate yet. Something was missing, but he knew he could have it in a few more moves and with just a little more information about this Victor Acree.

For a huge man, Don Lambert could move quickly when he had to. He bounded up the stairs, lungs heaving for air. Halfway to the first floor, he felt a twinge in his chest and stopped, breathing heavily, holding a hand to his heart. He shrugged it off and moved on.

Deputy Jay Topp, glanced up in alarm seeing his boss slam through the emergency stairwell. He said, "Everything okay, Don?"

"Get Ivey on the phone," Don said. "Tell him to meet me at Bruce Wynter's. He'll know where it is."

"You got it, boss!"

"And, while you're at it, run a background check on a guy named Victor Acree. I want to know what he's been up to since high school."

Don ran outside. The snow was really coming down now. Damn.

On the way to Michael's house for dinner, Alice was apprehensive. She couldn't shake her guilt. She hadn't told Gerald about running into her old high-school flame and knew perfectly well why. Gerald may or may not be having an affair—after all, she didn't really know, not for sure—but he was her husband, and that meant something to her.

But Gerald wasn't here to support her. Wasn't even interested in offering to come up to help her. And that also meant something. But she knew that going in. Gerald could be a real selfish bastard when he wanted to be. Alice thought of that night he'd taken her out and told her with a shit-eating grin about his ex-crony and only competition for partner, Eddie Sasso, who'd confided in Gerald that his son had been diagnosed with leukemia a week earlier. Gerald had somehow let the news slip in a partner's meeting and expressed concern that the stress on poor, poor Eddie might make it too hard for him to be an effective lead counsel on an environmental case they were fighting with Allenbach Chemical. Of course, he'd told an unbelieving Alice that he was only doing what was right for Eddie, who conveniently never made partner (unlike Gerald) and eventually left the firm altogether. Needless to say, they'd stopped receiving Christmas cards from the Sassos and Alice never found out what became of Eddie's boy.

She wasn't proud of that kind of thing, but it probably wasn't possible to be a good Wall Street lawyer without being at least partly that way: macho, arrogant, selfish, pushy. It was just how things worked, right? After all, when Gerald wasn't playing that part, he was a good man with a good heart. But like all men, he was flawed.

So why was she going to Michael's? Was she hoping to reconnect with her impossibly handsome former boyfriend, who was obviously lonesome and vulnerable after the death of his wife? That wasn't it exactly. No, it was more like grasping at a life preserver after being thrown into a violent ocean. Michael was sanity in all this insanity. A good memory mixed among the worst of her life. Alice promised herself that she would tell Michael that she wasn't interested in him romantically—lie, in other words.

She turned her black Merc into Michael's driveway for the second time in so many days and wondered what it would be like living here with him. His warm bed, watching TV in the evenings with a glass of wine, snowy Sunday afternoons . . .

Stop it! Alice thought. *Good lord, you're going off the deep end. Tell him, Alice. Tell him the truth.*

She walked up his front porch steps, making footsteps in the inch or so of snow that had fallen. She pushed the doorbell and heard a faint chime. A moment later Michael opened the door. He was wearing a woman's apron with frills on it and was holding oven mitts.

"Interesting choice of wardrobe," Alice said, smiling. The conversation she'd had with herself on the way over seemed a distant memory. He was adorable.

"Ah! Oh, Christ! I meant to take this off. It was Kerri's. I never bothered to get another one."

"Well, I did see a lovely pink one with stripes the other day."

Michael laughed. "C'mon in." He stepped aside.

Alice brushed by him, taking off her coat. His place was warm and cozy, just like last time. Picture perfect, really, especially with the snow and fire in the fireplace. She plopped down on the sofa and stared into the fire.

Michael went into the kitchen. From within, he said, "You're in for a surprise. I've been saving this for a while. It's not expensive, but it's a damn good bottle of chardonnay. Chilean, I think. I love Chilean wines. You?"

"No idea. Truth is, I don't drink much. Well, at least I don't when I'm not here in Maine."

"No?" Michael said, back from the kitchen with two glasses. "Why not? Wine is so good for the soul."

"In my family, it lives in the fridge in a gallon jug. It's not quite the same thing."

Michael nodded. "Good point. Well, enjoy this. This didn't come from a jug in the fridge. Or a box."

Alice sipped. It was good. It reminded her of dinners in fancy overpriced New York City restaurants.

"So, anything new? With your father, I mean? Chris?"

Alice shook her head. "Well, I guess this is no surprise, but they found the murder weapon. The gun. They identified that it was Chris's. And also that it was used to kill my father. My mother's a wreck, of course. They brought her in for questioning. This is all so unreal, Michael. But, in some ways it feels like it's supposed to happen this way. I don't know, I can't explain. I feel bad all the time. I just—"

Michael nodded, listening.

"—I don't know. My mother's been acting funny, but not like you'd think. I mean, it's so hard to describe. I know there's more going on here." Alice felt her chest tightening with anxiety and was a little short of breath. She felt an incredible sense of badness. About everything. Like something was coming. At any second.

She'd never had a panic attack in her life, but she felt close to whatever that might be now. Something was stirring inside her, something foul. She willed herself to calm down, to stop the thoughts that were screaming to get out of her subconscious. It was clear that talking about it triggered her feelings.

How much did her mother know? Alice thought. Her mother likely knew about Chris, where he was, but what about the other thing? The awful thing that only Chris knew. Her secret. Her terrible secret. A secret she'd kept for 20 years.

Where was all this coming from? And why now? Her breathing quickened. She remembered the figure that looked like Ray that day she was in the phone booth. Then again: the man leaning against the light post at the end of the driveway. But it wasn't Ray. It couldn't be. Ray died. But he was here, in spirit, torturing her all these years later. Torturing her family. Those ancient memories were connected to what Chris had done to her father somehow, out on that dark road. Damn him! But she loved her brother.

"Alice?"

If they catch him, everything will come out. Everyone will know. Gerald *will know. Their neighbors. Everyone will know the terrible truth about my family*, Alice thought. She was breathing hard now, trying not to let her rising panic get the best of her. She felt like driving through the snow all the way back to her house in New Jersey and burying herself in her comfortable bed and never answering the damn phone again, about running away, maybe to the Florida Keys or Hawaii. Or maybe she'd be better off jumping off a bridge. She had no children. What would it matter? Who would care?

She was screaming in her head now: *How can I possibly ever be okay again, like I was?* And then she was guilty. Guilty for not helping Chris and for running away. Guilty for something that was well beyond her control, beyond her fault.

"Alice? Are you okay?" Michael said. His face was creased with concern. He snapped his fingers.

Alice took a deep sip of wine. Her hands shook. There was so much she wanted to say, to tell. She longed to remove this terrible weight from her shoulders.

Michael said, "You're shaking." He took her wine glass and set it down on the coffee table in front of them. He slid his hands over hers and squeezed gently.

Alice began to cry then. Big, sobby wet tears flowed from her eyes and down her cheeks.

"Shh." Michael brought her towards him and held her, saying, "Shh. It'll be okay. It's okay."

She wanted to confide in him. Tell him everything. About Chris, about her senior year in high school, about Ray, about after. Everything. But she couldn't. She wasn't even able to admit to herself that any of it had really happened. But all of it was real and had happened. Every terrible minute of it. And she hated herself and her family because of it.

Alice pulled herself away and wiped her eyes the best she could. "I'm sorry. I don't know why I—"

"It's all right. You're under a lot of stress."

Alice nodded. "It's more than that. There's so much more." Her tears stopped flowing. She looked down at the ground. She felt pale and sick.

"Like what?"

"No."

"You can talk to me, Alice. We were close once."

If only Michael had known about it then. About any of it. He would be angry that she hadn't told him, even all these years later. Of that, she was sure. So would her mother.

They moved closer.

"It's okay," he said again. His voice was soft, comforting, warm.

They were inches apart.

Alice shook her head. She said, "It's not okay. It never was."

"Shh."

Then, inexplicably, she was filled with an overpowering and immediate desire to make love to Michael, like they'd wanted to as teenagers but never did—hot, desperate, almost animal. She felt her insides turn to liquid. She was hot. Very hot. She kissed him passionately, almost violently.

He hesitated at first, unsure, and then gave into it, pulling her towards him, groping and kneading with strong, determined hands. She groaned at his touch and found her hands grazing over his body, his crotch. He was raging and hard as the firewood he used to fuel the fire. She wanted him inside her now. Immediately.

She felt his tongue exploring her mouth and groaned again, pushing her hands through his hair, down his neck, and finally up his shirt, running her hands through his coarse chest hair. His hands ran urgently across her body in return. He cupped her breasts. Her nipples hardened and she longed to feel his mouth on them.

She wanted to be close to him, to feel his bare skin on hers, rubbing and pressing. Her breathing was quick and hot. Slowly, she leaned back, pulling him on top of her, desperate to feel him inside her, to thrust with him, thinking about how they could get their pants off without destroying the mood, the—

NO!

Alice pushed him away. She couldn't. It wasn't right. She'd promised herself. This wasn't right. Even if Gerald was cheating on her, it didn't make this right. Even if she was vulnerable and longing for contact, for comfort, for love, for understanding, this wasn't right. She was married.

He leaned in for her again, his face lost in his lustful desire to be near her.

"Michael, I can't!"

He pulled back, embarrassed, surprised. "Please, Alice. You feel it. I know you do. Like me. There's nothing wrong with—"

"I'm married. This isn't right."

He held her arms tightly with his strong hands. "I know you feel it too. You must!"

Alice stood. "Don't," she said. "It will make this harder. You don't know me, Michael. You don't know me." Tears welled up again. She stood up and shook herself free of his grasp. "I don't even know me."

Then she was on her way out the door, out in the cold, sober air of her real life. She ran to her Mercedes and got in. Michael was at the doorway and then on the front steps. Heavy snow frosted his hair, which was a mess. His shirt hung out below his sweater. His face was flush with desire.

She rolled down the passenger side window and said, "I'm sorry, Michael. I'm so sorry."

"Alice, wait! I—"

She was out of driveway before she heard the rest.

TEN

Don carefully guided the Crown Victoria towards Bruce Wynter's house through the heavily falling snow. The flakes seemed to come at the windshield horizontally like little white daggers. His visibility was terrible. For shit, as the kids would say.

Shoulda put the damn chains on this afternoon, Don thought. *Too late now.*

He thought about Ray Wynter and the possibility which had occurred to him in the basement archives. What if Ray Wynter hadn't been in a snowmobile accident at all? Oh, how the possibilities stacked up when you asked simple questions.

Bruce Wynter had been alone for a long time now after his wife had died of cervical cancer years ago. Loneliness can do strange things to a man. Maybe he gets to thinking about Ray and comes up with a little theory about how Papa Wynter, Bruce's brother, was desperate to help his son get away from Ray's bad influence. Maybe something went bad all those years ago.

Or maybe the third boy in the group, Victor Acree, "Vic" to his friends, had come back. And just maybe things went bad when he did. Don couldn't think of an obvious motive, but what the hell? Stranger things have happened.

After all, old Jimmy Bible had said Chris and Papa had been arguing about Ray. What's to argue about all these years later? Something started the argument. Could have been Bruce or maybe Vic. Then there was the man Chris and Papa had been seen with. It could have been Bruce.

Either way, something was positively itching Don's instincts as a cop now. He needed to find out what Bruce Wynter knew about Ray and Chris and their strained relationship that had ended badly, at least according to the note paper-clipped in the murder file. And what of that? Surely all this had something to do with the unsolved Gartlin murder. Don would have bet his life on it.

Regardless of whether his what-ifs amounted to a hill of beans or the grand prize, he thought it would be a damn good idea to talk to Bruce again and push him a little on Ray. The sooner the better. Don wanted this case over and done with. He felt sure he'd see something in Bruce's eyes, innocent or guilty.

Don's cell phone rang, and he pushed the answer button on the dashboard to answer. Man, that Bluetooth technology was cool.

"Don? It's Ivey. What's up? Dispatch called and said you wanted to talk?"

"Matt, glad you called. Listen, I'm on my way to Bruce Wynter's house. Papa's brother."

"What gives? Something come up?"

"Nothing I can put my finger on, but something's cooking. Been thinking a lot about Ray Wynter and that Gartlin case. Took a look at the old murder file on it."

"They're connected?" Matt sounded skeptical.

"I'm sure of it. Don't know how."

The line crackled and Don heard Matt's muffled voice talking to someone else with his hand over the microphone. A moment later he was back on the line. He said, "Shit. Don. This snow. Traffic problems are starting to stack up. Looks like one of our cruisers was in a fender-bender. I gotta head into the station and help sort this out."

"It's okay. I can handle it alone. Just come out when you can."

"You got it, boss."

Just as he pushed the "end" button on the dashboard, the steering wheel seemed to lose all function. The Ford began to slide. Black ice. Don took his foot off the accelerator and turned with the skid, eventually straightening out the heavy car. He would have to be more careful. There was no emergency here, no reason to get into an accident. Some weather.

Minutes later, he pulled into Bruce Wynter's driveway. The house was dark.

Shit. No one home, Don thought.

He decided he'd had enough of the weather and made a wide turn in the driveway. No sense in busting his ass on some wild goose chase on a night like this.

Besides, they'll need me down at the station before too long if this storm is half as bad as it looks like it's setting up to be.

Out of the corner of his eye, he saw something that chilled his blood cold. Bruce's front door was wide open. Snow was blowing into the foyer and drifting a couple of feet high inside the house. A car was in the driveway. Probably Bruce's.

Could be he got a lift somewhere and didn't close the door tightly enough. Anything's possible. But Don felt like something wasn't right.

Against his better judgment, he put the Crown Vic in park, trained the powerful searchlight on the side of the car at the front door, checked his sidearm and got out. The wind was howling something awful and the flakes stung his face.

He approached the front door, gun drawn.

"Bruce Wynter! This is Somerset County Detective Don Lambert! Are you inside?"

Nothing. His skin was crawling with goose pimples and the hair stood up on the back of his neck. Everything about this situation was screaming *wrong* to him.

"Bruce Wynter! This is Somerset County Detective Don Lambert! I have my gun drawn. Are you inside?"

Again, nothing.

When he reached the start of the front walk, he reached over his left shoulder and depressed the talk button on his radio.

"Dispatch, Unit 3. Send some backup. Two-seven-eight Crescent Hill Road. Got a possible four fifty-nine. I'm going to check it out and then back off."

"Roger that, Don. Might be a while, though. This weather's wreaking havoc on the roads. Even got an overturned salter."

"Anyone hurt?"

"Not yet, thank God. Hold tight, Don, we'll get somebody out there."

"I'm going in for a look."

Silence from dispatch. They didn't agree, but they didn't argue.

He felt the house was empty. He heard nothing except the wind screaming through the pines. He shouldn't go in, but he was sure whoever had been in the house was gone. It would be just too obvious to leave a front door open in this weather otherwise. He saw no flashlight beams from within the house either. One more sign.

He walked up the front walkway slowly, his senses tuned for any unusual movement, an unusual sound. Nothing.

Closer.

When he reached the front door, he stepped inside. He saw that the door had blown open because someone had broken it getting in. The door frame was shattered around the lock, so it couldn't close properly.

He didn't want whoever was in here, *if* there even *was* anybody in here, to know he was inside the house. The oil furnace was blaring in the basement. It sounded like a jet engine. It must've been running for hours, trying fruitlessly to heat the house.

Don found Bruce Wynter in the kitchen, slumped over the table, a lake of drying blood pooled on top and on the floor. A river of it had run down one of the legs and onto the linoleum. But it wasn't flowing now. The back of Bruce's head was missing. He was shot from behind, up close by the looks of it. This was murder. So much for what-if number one.

He inched closer and touched the pool gently with his finger. Very tacky. An hour old. Maybe.

Don crept around the house as quietly as he could, searching, glad that the blazing furnace was masking his noise. The corpse in the kitchen had spooked Don, no doubt, but not nearly as much as the empty, busted-open gun case he'd found on the floor in the mud room at the back of the house.

Minutes later and Don was in his warm car again, feeling anxious. Whoever did this had been careless and had left the house in a hurry. The broken door and gun case suggested anger, passion. Alice and Jackie Ruth could be in grave danger.

No time for procedure. He had to get to Jackie Ruth's and get her and Alice safe before it was too late.

1984

Vic told Chris he'd think about it—going in together against Ray to the cops. And he'd apparently been thinking about it for a couple of days. Chris had reached a decision since then. If Vic agreed, they'd talk. If not, Chris would shut up about this and tell no one. Ever. Not even Alice.

He'd played nice with Ray and Vic in school, hanging out in Butt Hall, cruising at lunch, smoking joints. The school had more-or-less gotten back to normal. There was a sub for Mr. Gartlin now, an older woman who was a regular at Redding Regional High School. Chris had seen her plenty of times but never met her. Seemed nice enough for a sub. Chris's guilt and fear hadn't subsided much, however. Ray and Vic seemed to go on like usual. But Chris saw differences in both of them. Especially in Ray.

He was arrogant now. Took more chances. He'd started bullying younger kids, something Ray never did before.

Mostly he'd stuck with his friends. But weirder was what was happening with guys like Sean Wayman and Billy Cate, the two jocks who'd made Ray lick the floor in front of Nora Strawser at the bowling alley on a night that seemed like it happened 10,000 years ago, when Chris had still felt like a kid.

Yesterday, after gym, everyone was in the locker room changing, and Wayman was giving Ray a hard time after their shower. Chris had been sitting on the bench that ran down the middle of the lockers, just trying to concentrate on getting dressed and getting the hell out of there. Lately, it seemed like all he wanted to do was be by himself.

"Hey, Ray, you ever gonna get that boil you call a dick lanced?" Sean had said, laughing to his friends and pretending to shake his thing in front of Ray.

Ray had smiled and cocked his head a little as if deciding what to do. And then he was on him, pushing Sean hard up against the locker with his forearm in his throat, choking him. Chris didn't think he'd ever forget what Ray said to Sean that afternoon: "You say that again, and I *will* kill you."

Big deal, right? Just more bullshit macho crap from Ray? But Sean Wayman must have seen something in Ray's eyes, something bad, because he started crying. Sean Wayman started fucking crying right there in front of everybody. Chris could hardly believe it. Then Sean'd said, "Okay, man. Chill out. It's cool." And Ray let him down and went back to his locker.

And then there was Vic. Vic was always a little bit of the clown, and maybe a little out-of-whack in the head, but he'd changed too. Now he'd hardly look you (or anyone) in the eye. He had a creepy, dead look to him now that Chris didn't care for at all. It was as if all his happiness was gone.

He supposed that was true for all three boys, who had done a very stupid and very grownup thing. Chris seemed to be the only one of them who understood that they would all pay for what they had done in the end, whether it be jail or in their nightmares.

But Vic was his lifeline out of this. If Vic said no, Chris wasn't sure how he was going to get by the rest of his life knowing what they did that night. But he'd have to live with it because he had no other choice, and as far as he was concerned he was as guilty of killing Gartlin on his own front porch in front of his wife—

(Honey? Who's that at the door? Is everything okay?)

—as any of them were.

And so, on this sunny afternoon in early December while walking home from school, Chris, deep in these thoughts, turned left onto a dirt footpath just after going under a bridge and failed to see Ray and Vic blocking the way ahead of him, smoking cigarettes and laughing—until they saw Chris, that is.

By the time Chris looked up, it was too late.

"Hey, faggot," Ray said, smiling.

Chris's stomach clenched tight. He knew right away what had happened. He could see it in Ray's face. Vic had told him everything. Should he deny it? Say that Vic was making it up?

"I hear you and Vic have been talking."

Chris smiled nervously and said, "I don't know what—"

"Don't fucking lie to me, Chrissy, you little piece of faggot crap. You *can't* lie to me. We're family. Or, we were until you talked. What were you gonna do, Chrissy, get me put away for it while you and Vic here got married and moved in together?"

"C'mon, Ray." It was all that Chris could manage, and his voice had taken on an unpleasant desperation. He held out his hands and backed up, instinctively trying to keep Ray away from him.

Ray walked closer and threw his cigarette in the dirt. He crushed it under his boot heel. "Why are you making me do this? Huh, Chris? I thought you were a man."

"C'mon, Ray," Chris said again. "I was just feeling bad. I wasn't serious."

"You were serious," Vic said.

"See?" Ray said. "Even Vic thinks so. Now, what are we going to do about this?"

"Jesus, Ray. C'mon. I'm your cousin. You know I wouldn't say anything. I was just testing Vic for you."

Vic said, "That's bullshit."

"How the fuck do you know?" Chris said to Vic. Again, his voice cracked in desperation. "And what do you know about it, anyway?" Tears came streaming down Chris's face. It seemed that the world was against him now, or that he had his back up against it.

"Vic says it's bullshit, Chris." Ray's voice was calm, and he kept coming.

The boys weren't close enough to the road for Chris to run, but what good would that do anyway? His was a problem that running from wouldn't help. You can't outrun your own mind, your own guilt, two guys you used to call friends who you see every day.

Chris said, "So what? What now?"

"We're going to teach you something, Chrissy. You know, like detention. You fuck with the rules, *my* rules, and you gotta stay after class. Learn something. Up close. Right up close."

Ray signaled to Vic and then ran behind Chris, looping his arms through Chris's and holding him fast against his big body. Chris started peddling his legs, trying to kick Vic or Ray or at least keep Vic off him. Vic came in, staring sidelong like an inbred dog on the attack. He punched Chris in the gut and then the face. Again and again.

All the while, through the loud, white explosions going off in his head with every punch, he could hear Ray laughing in his ear and saying quietly, "You like that, you little faggot? Huh? You like that?"

Chris realized with growing horror that Ray actually had a hard-on and was rubbing it against Chris. He was *getting off* on it. Before Chris blacked out, he thought: *Ray is fucking crazy. I mean really kill-me-in-my-sleep horror-movie crazy. He's getting off on Vic beating the ever-loving shit out of me.*

Chris awoke several minutes later on the ground and felt himself being lifted up by a pair of strong arms. He smelled Old Spice and looked down to see a pair of polished shoes and creased blue pants with a yellow stripe down the side. Then, he was vaguely aware (through his blurred vision) of flashing police lights.

The conversation he heard then was ridiculous, but he couldn't quite work up the words to argue. His mouth and tongue wouldn't cooperate.

"I don't know. We found him like that. Whoever did it must've run off."

"Uh huh, possible. But I'm wondering if it wasn't you two boys right here that worked over this fella."

"Oh, no. He's our best friend, officer. I'm his cousin."

"I see. You wouldn't be lying to me now, would you?"

"No way! I think I mighta seen them even, running down that way."

The cop turned Chris's face towards his own and looked into his eyes. Chris blinked a few times and the blurriness eased some. His head felt like a swollen, infected tooth and throbbed with every heartbeat.

The cop said, "You okay, son? You want paramedics so they can look you over?"

"Hmmph fime," Chris said, working his jaw. He was coming around now. He said again, more clearly, "I'm fine."

"This your cousin?"

Ray leveled his eyes at Chris and arched one brow.

"Yeah."

"These boys. Are they the ones who did this?"

Chris shook his head.

"You're sure."

Chris nodded.

The cop stared for a while at the three boys. He said finally, "I don't like this. Not at all. I'm not going to take you in, but I am going to take your names and write an incident report. Your parents will be getting a call from us this evening, so you'd best tell them what happened."

The three boys nodded.

After a few minutes of writing in his patrol car, the cop came out and handed all three boys a business card. Chris looked down at his and read:

Deputy Timothy Dennison, Somerset County Sheriff's Department

Then the cop left.

Thinking they'd taught him his lesson, Ray and Vic left Chris standing alone on the dirt foot path. His school books were by now strewn all over the place, and he bent painfully to gather them up. He was angry and scared and didn't know what to do and he couldn't stop crying.

After he picked up this things, he shuffled home, holding the cop's business card in his right hand, turning it over and over, reading the words on it. He had to make this right. Somehow.

An idea crossed his mind then as he walked up his driveway. Ray and Vic could turn against *him* if they felt like they were backed into a corner. Maybe they too were holding the business cards and talking about it. Chris felt bad enough about what the boys had done, terrible even, but he wasn't about to take the blame for something that had been Ray all along. *Chris* hadn't shot Gartlin. The thought had never entered his mind that night, and yet Ray had roped them all in together to protect himself. And it wasn't fair. It made him angry. Very angry.

But what if someone *did* see something that night? What if some random neighbor of Gartlin's had been unable to sleep and peeked out his window to look at the moon or spy on the neighbor next door with the teenaged daughter who always forgot to close her shade when she changed? It could happen, right? What if that person was so scared by what he saw that he didn't want to come forward right away? That *could* easily happen. Maybe it already did. Maybe Chris could *make* that happen.

Perhaps with some part of him knowing that what he was about to write would be the undoing of them all, Chris went into his room and shut the door, carefully avoiding his family (who was by now used to his isolating ways). He put his book bag on his bed and sat down at his desk, pulling a brand new piece of college-ruled paper from the upper right-hand drawer. He grabbed a ball-point pen. In his best handwriting, Chris added the date to the top and then started with a salutation: *To Whom It May Concern*.

When her car went into another skid, Alice swore and said aloud to herself, only half joking, "Jesus, I don't want to die out here. Not tonight. Not tonight." The roads were terrible, and Alice was beginning to think she'd made the right choice in leaving Michael's house when she did, and not just for the sake of her marriage. If she'd stayed much longer, she would have been snowed in and then had every excuse to stay. She'd wanted Michael badly enough that it scared her. She hadn't felt sexual desire like that in years, not since she and Gerald had fallen in love when she was little more than a teenager. She kept telling herself that she'd made the right choice in leaving, that it could never work between her and Michael. Even if Gerald were not in the picture, she couldn't (and wouldn't) move back to Maine and felt sure that Michael wouldn't move south. She chastised herself for having ridiculous fantasies. But the look of lust on his face and the thought of his strong, working-man hands roaming over her naked body made her blood boil.

"Shit! Shit, shit, shit!" she said, taking her foot off the accelerator yet again. She had to pay attention in this weather.

Her black Merc just didn't want to behave on these roads and had started to spin its wheels on a little hill.

As one often does in snow storms, Alice began to feel a subtle kind of panic rising in her mind. The weather was deteriorating rapidly, more rapidly than she'd originally judged, and she still had a ways to go. She wondered whether she might not make it home at all and be forced to ditch her car and go the rest on foot. Or worse, that perhaps she'd skid off the road and into a tree.

She edged forward at no more than twenty miles per hour, hands white-knuckled and clutching the worn leather steering wheel at good ol' 10 and 2. Her face was inches from the top of the steering wheel, and she peered out into the blinding light of the headlights reflecting off the falling snow. She'd seen worse growing up in Maine. But not by much.

Concentrating on the snow and her steady progress home, she began to realize that something was wrong, seriously wrong at home only when she was almost on top of it. When she *(finally, thank the good lord, finally)* turned into her driveway, she saw the large black car, an unmarked police car, idling in the driveway and sending up a constant puff of exhaust from its tail pipe.

But what—? She thought, confused, not quite putting together that something might have happened to her mother, or that maybe they'd found Chris.

She came to her senses and parked the Merc hastily next to the idling car. She dashed out into the silent snowfall and was struck by the awful peacefulness of it that made for an unpleasant and foreboding contrast with the selfish terror that was threatening to overtake her as she thought about what they might now know about her.

She burst into the kitchen and saw the hulking figure of the detective bent over someone laying on the ground. He spun around in surprise, and Alice saw his hand move for his gun before he realized who was standing there. His face was pale and his eyes wide. He was clearly scared.

"Alice!" he cried. "You scared me."

"Detective, what's—?"

It was then that Alice saw what the detective was hunched over. It was her mother, Jackie Ruth. Her face was battered. Her right eye was swollen shut and a disturbing shiny purple color. The left side of her mouth was split, swollen, and bleeding. Her hair was matted with blood above her left ear.

"Ma!" Alice bent down and took her mother's head in her hand. "What happened?" Alice asked the big Detective.

"Don't know, I just got here myself. I found her like this, bleeding. She's been shot. Lost a lot of blood."

Then Alice noticed that her mother's shirt had been ripped open. The detective's hand was applying pressure to a wound on her mother's upper chest. Alice saw then that her mother was lying in a pool of her own blood.

Alice shook her head in confusion and stared into the detective's face. Something was wrong. He was nervous and distracted and so unlike his normally calm self. She said, "But why—?"

"Alice, your uncle is dead. I came here to warn you. You're in danger. But I was too late. You're lucky you weren't here. God knows what might—"

"What?" Alice said, suddenly feeling panicked and terrible and scared.

"Your uncle is dead."

"Bruce?" Alice said stupidly. She thought of all those nights when Papa had come home drunk and her mother had sent them to Bruce's, how he'd protected them when they were little. But that only made her think of Ray again. She began to sob.

"Who did this?" Alice said to her mother, through her tears. "Was it Chris?"

But Jackie Ruth was unconscious. Her breathing was unpleasantly ragged and erratic.

"Ma!" Alice said, louder. "Ma! Can you hear me?"

Her mother's eyes opened slightly. "Ray," Jackie Ruth said plainly, her voice just a whisper.

Immediately, Alice thought of the man she'd seen at the foot of her driveway and outside the CVS. Damn ghosts. The result of her stress, of all their stress. It was as if Ray were haunting them. Maybe he was. Maybe he was.

Alice said, "Ma? Can you hear me?"

Jackie Ruth nodded slightly and moaned a little with the effort.

The detective said, "Paramedics are on their way, but it's a doozy out there. They might be awhile."

"Ma. Stay with us here. Who did this?"

"Ray."

"But, Ma, Ray's dead!" Alice screamed, suddenly terrified at the prospect that Ray wasn't dead at all, that maybe that snowmobile accident wasn't really an accident. That maybe she'd have to face him again and worse, face what he'd done to her. Reality seemed to be slipping from her grasp and she felt dizzy.

Alice turned to the detective and said, "What's happening?"

He could only shake his head. He said, "She's delusional. Ignore it. But whoever did this likely killed your uncle."

Bruce.

Suddenly, Jackie Ruth began to choke violently. The detective rolled her over and she vomited blood. Alice screamed. Jackie Ruth reached up and grabbed the detective's sizable shoulder to pull herself on her back again. Her old, gnarled hands shook with the effort, as if she'd developed a severe palsy. Then, she whispered, "Your brother. He needs you now." Her mother's eyes burned, angry, defiant, for a moment staring at Alice and then faded.

For one brief terrifying moment, Alice thought her mother was dying right there on the kitchen floor in her arms, but the detective pursed his lips a little and shook his head. She'd just fainted.

1984

Ray and Vic stopped talking to Chris altogether the day after they beat him up, which was fine with Chris. At least now he didn't need to worry so much when he was at school. But he was still angry at them both and didn't regret sending the anonymous note he'd written to the police. He hadn't said much, just that it had been Ray's idea and only Ray's idea. He figured his part in it would come out eventually, but by then Ray would already be in jail.

In the end, when he'd been standing in front of the mail box, thinking about what he was about to do, he decided that he wasn't doing it just to get back at Ray, although that was why he'd written it in the first place. No, he was doing it because what Ray had done was wrong, and Chris was angry with Ray because it was his fault that Chris felt guilty. Sending the note was the right thing to do.

All of this flitted through Chris's mind in the moments before he picked up the phone after hearing his mother call upstairs, "Chris! Phone! It's Ray!"

He picked up the phone and placed it to his ear. He was nervous and sure that Ray was calling because of the note, even though there was no way he could know that Chris had sent anything to the police. He said into it, "Ma, I got it. Ray?"

Nothing.

Chris said again, "Ma! I got it!"

The phone clicked.

As soon as it did, Chris heard Ray say from the other end of the line, "The cops came to my house today to talk about Gartlin. Watch your back, motherfucker, because you're dead."

ELEVEN

Michael stood on his front steps and watched Alice's black Mercedes roll down his driveway in the snow and then fishtail a little as Alice accelerated away. His heart was heavy. What had happened between them was undeniable and positively electric. He was sure she felt that way as well.

Michael suddenly realized that he was freezing and turned to go inside, thinking that it was pointless to have these feelings. He couldn't betray Kerri's memory like that. Not yet. It was too soon. Wasn't it? As he had a million times before, he felt her with him here in their old house. That didn't make things any better.

He closed the door gently and sat down on his sofa. He glanced at the wine glasses and considered having a glass. No.

He stood up and walked into the kitchen, thinking that he'd make himself something to eat. No, that wasn't it either. He walked back into the living room and stared at the dying fire. He considered throwing another log on and then decided against it. Maybe he should just go to bed. Nah. Read? No.

He sighed loudly, frustrated. He thought about what his old granny used to say, *Michael LaPage! You've got ants in your pants.*

He couldn't stop thinking about Alice and about all the feelings he was having. She was guilty about her husband. He was guilty about Kerri. He stared into the smoldering fire. Maybe it wasn't right, what they'd done here tonight. Sure, he'd give her that. It wasn't fair to her husband. But why wasn't he here, anyway? What was the deal with that? How happy could she be with a guy who wouldn't even take the time to come up and support his wife? And Kerri has been gone now for over a year. He couldn't grieve forever, and he'd gotten damn tired of his lonely lifestyle. It was time to move on. Right?

Now he felt like he was rationalizing things, turning something maybe not-so-appropriate, not right now at least, into something else. The truth was that Alice was having a tough time right now. Had he taken advantage of that? Maybe, but she'd been right there with him. It takes two to tango, as the old saying goes.

Michael said aloud to himself, "Man, you really fucked things up here tonight."

A minute later, Michael grabbed his jacket and was out the door against his better judgment. They would talk, and things would be all right.

"Alice?" the detective said, gazing at Alice's face.

But Alice hardly heard the man. She was staring down

at her mother, in shock. Jackie Ruth's face was pale and drawn, but she was breathing steadily. She was asleep.

Chris is at camp. He's at camp. Alice thought.

The camp. Of course. The camp! It had been years since she'd thought of it. What had the sign read above the little doorway? Camp Venie, named after a huge, perhaps mythical turtle that lived in the lake.

She said, "He's at camp."

"Alice, what camp?" the detective said. "Alice!" He was still holding Jackie Ruth in his big arms.

Alice shook her head, trying to rid her mind of confusion, to clear her thoughts. She said, "The camp. I should have thought of it before! For a few summers when I was a kid, we rented a little camp. It was a few miles north on Lake Magaskawee. We had such a good time. Like a normal family. We never talked about it, you know, how we all felt those summers? I don't even remember why we stopped going. Money, I guess. We weren't like we used to be here when we were there. Papa didn't drink so much, wasn't so angry. We didn't fight. Of course Chris would go there. He and my mother must've talked about it. The camp is probably still there and empty now."

Alice stood up, excited, thinking about the snowmobile in the shed in the back. She could make it. She could get on Chris's old snowmobile and be there in an hour, maybe less.

The detective nodded a little and said, "But Route 6 isn't passable. Not tonight."

Alice's eyes flashed. "I know."

She stood and grabbed her jacket. She could reach Chris, help him, if it wasn't already too late. He wasn't in his right mind if he'd done this, or God forbid, killed Uncle Bruce.

Alice paused for a moment, realizing the gravity of what the detective had discovered this snowy night. Her Uncle Bruce was gone. Forever. But Chris couldn't have, could he? He wouldn't do that. He wasn't a murderer. Alice believed that with all her heart. Chris had a kind heart. He had since he was a kid. But he hasn't been well.

She said, "Chris couldn't have done this. I know that."

The detective just stared at her for a minute and then said calmly, as if he were about to tell a child that there is no Santa Claus, "Alice . . ."

Alice was suddenly overcome with emotion. Angry with the detective for believing what he did about Chris, angry with herself for not being there for him all these years, guilty about what had happened with Ray. She sobbed and began wrapping her scarf around her neck. The trip to the camp would be cold.

But could she leave her mother?

The paramedics would be here soon. Despite the snow. And the detective wouldn't leave her here. She'll be okay. And she'd said it herself. Chris needs help. Now more than ever. God knows what he'll do to himself up there in that cold cabin. He could already be—

—no he wasn't. She was sure of that. It was her chance to finally set things right.

The detective said, "Alice. Wait. You can't go up there. You'll never make it. Route 6. You'll never—"

"I'm not taking a car."

The detective's eyebrows furrowed. "I don't get it."

"I'm taking Chris's snowmobile."

The detective shook his head. He said, "Alice, that's crazy. I can't let you do that."

"Try and stop me. Chris needs my help. It may already be too late. Besides, you need to stay with my mother."

The detective shook his head a little and stared at the ground. He looked unsure of what to say next.

Alice's face reddened with anger. She said, "I have to help him!" She was near hysterically crying now and perhaps trying to convince herself as much as the detective that against impossible odds it *wasn't* Chris who did this. But if not Chris, who?

She pulled on her gloves and buttoned up her coat.

Before the kitchen door slammed shut, she heard the detective say, "Alice! Don't—"

The wind howled outside and the snow hit her face hard. She trudged out to the shed at the back of the driveway, trying to remember how they'd gone in the past. There was a short-cut, but now, out here in the storm, Alice decided it would be a terrible idea to try and find that short-cut up through the woods in this weather, at night. The roads would do just fine.

She opened up the shed and clicked on the little overhead light, which cast a pale orange glow. The snowmobile was on a trailer and covered with a dirty grey tarp. She hadn't forgotten anything since those long ago days when she could ride it as well as her brother. She topped off the tank with gasoline from an old red container and found the key. It started right up.

Soon, Alice was on the road, the snow stinging her face, winding up towards Route 6, thinking about how bizarre life can be, about all the things that brought her here to this moment, doing something that defied all good sense, hoping to save a brother she feared was already lost and lost long ago.

1984

It was 4:30 on an afternoon in mid December. Chris was suffering from a terrible and imaginary stomach flu that had kept him home for a week after receiving Ray's threatening phone call. He was afraid to go to school, afraid to leave the house even. His face and body had healed for the most part since his last encounter with Ray and Vic, but he felt sure that the beating he'd received then would be nothing compared to what he had in store for him now, if that was *all* they did to him.

But this had to stop. He thought day and night about running away but knew in the end that he wouldn't. The worse part of it was, Ray's questioning by the police went nowhere. Chris had risked his life by taking a chance that an anonymous note would lead them right to Gartlin's killer, but nothing had happened. Chris had spent the last few days convinced that the cops were going to show up at his front door any minute. But they never came, and somehow he knew they never would.

Chris could only conclude that what was coming was far worse, which meant that he had to figure a way out of this on his own.

When he heard the front door bang downstairs he jumped a little and scooted under the covers in case his mother came by. He heard slow footsteps on the stairs and recognized them as Alice's. Something was wrong, he could hear it and feel it.

He waited a moment and then saw Alice walk by his open bedroom door. She was crying. Hard.

"Alice!" he said, but she walked right on by and into her room, slamming the door.

Chris got out of bed and went to her door. He knocked gently. "Alice?" he said. "Alice? Are you okay?"

From within: "Fuck you! Go away!"

The savageness of her words and voice made Chris pause. But he tried again. "Alice? C'mon. What's wrong?"

Nothing.

Chris tried the doorknob. It turned in his hands and he opened the door a little. Alice sat on her pink bed, surrounded by what looked like a billion little stuffed animals. Her face was buried in her hands, and she was crying.

Chris stuck his head in a little further. Softly, he said, "Alice? What's wrong?"

She stood up then and raced towards the door, her face swollen and wet with tears. "Get-the-fuck-outta-here!" She yelled.

But before the door slammed, he saw that Alice's lip was swollen and split. Her right eye was purple and swollen as well.

Ray. They got to Alice. When they couldn't get me, they went for Alice, Chris thought.

He wondered how much they'd told her. Did it matter? He suddenly felt a guilty wave of relief. Maybe this was it. Maybe that was the price he had to pay. Alice just took a little beating. He'd talk to her later and they'd smooth things out. He'd tell her that it was just a thing between Ray and Vic. No big deal. That he was sorry this had to happen to her. What's a few punches?

But later, when he did try to talk to her to smooth things over, she'd shut him off again. He hadn't even gotten into her room. What was her problem?

The phone rang late as Chris was falling asleep that night. He grabbed it on the first ring, hoping that it didn't wake Papa, who, depending on how much he'd had to drink, might not take too kindly to being awakened in the night.

"Hello?" Chris said.

"I told you not to fuck with the Masters of Chaos, asshole," a voice said.

It was Ray, but his voice was thick and slurry, like he'd been drinking. He was breathing right into the phone as well, almost like he was falling asleep.

"Nighty night, fucker," the voice said.

And then the phone clicked and went dead.

For a long while, Chris stared up at the ceiling, thinking about Alice and about Ray and how he could have hit her like he did. He wondered again what he told her, how much she knew. It didn't matter, he supposed, because he knew the truth, and the truth was that this was Ray's thing. No matter how much he tried to make it different, he couldn't. In the end, Ray had killed a man, and that was all that mattered as far as Chris was concerned. That was bad fucking karma. The worst kind. Ray would get his in the end.

Michael's Subaru Outback spun and slid on the black ice beneath the snow. The weather was positively terrible. He couldn't remember a worse storm and felt simultaneous pangs of worry for Alice and a vague sense of danger for himself. Neither one of them should be out on a night like this. Every Mainer knows you don't mess around with a blizzard.

At the top of a small hill, his car began to spin its wheels and stopped moving forward. Then, it slid left. He wouldn't be able to make it over the hill. He gently eased the car into the skid, hoping he could recover his traction. He finally did, but not until he was perpendicular to the road and blocking it. If a fast-moving sand truck were to crest that hill . . .

Michael lurched the car forward, and it spun into the wrong side of the road. Fortunately, there was no one out here. The roads were empty.

Anyone with a shred of common sense would be inside in front of a fire, he thought.

After finally getting the car pointing in the right direction, he eased the Outback downhill and decided to take a longer way to the Wynters, one with fewer lights and therefore fewer stops. Michael figured that the last thing on earth he needed right now was to get stranded.

The wind rocked his car, and occasional, angry tornados of swirling fallen snow blocked his view. Through his windshield, Michael squinted at what he hoped was the road. With no other cars out, he had no tire tracks to follow. Instead he watched the right-hand side of the road, following the line of trees, trusting his instinct. He grew up here on these old roads and more-or-less just guessed at where he should be.

After what seemed like fourteen hours, but was in reality only about fifteen minutes, he pulled into the Wynter's driveway and spotted the unmarked black police car immediately, and, thank God, Alice's Mercedes. She'd made it home.

He felt foolish for following her now, especially in this weather, and especially after realizing that he'd never be able to make it home, unless the snow stopped, which didn't seem possible now. But it was too late for that. He was here, and he'd make things right.

Michael parked his Outback and stepped outside, not quite prepared for the stinging blow of the blizzard. The wind and snow crawled down the front of his jacket and set off an almost painful case of goose pimples. He zipped up tight. He was so entirely focused on the weather that he realized with sudden alarm that it wasn't a good thing that an unmarked, idling police car was parked here. Something was wrong.

He trudged as fast as he could through the snow towards the house. The snow was easily at six inches now, maybe more, and certainly more in the drifts, which, by the looks of them, were climbing towards six *feet*.

Michael noticed the shed at the back of the driveway. The doors were open and the little light was on. He made his way to the shed, turned out the light, and struggled to push the doors shut through the snow. He felt sure now that something was wrong.

"Alice?" Michael yelled. "Alice?" She wasn't out here.

He reached the front porch. The front door was partially open. He pushed it open and stepped into the kitchen. A large man in a parka reached for a gun and drew, pointing it at Michael. Michael saw a badge poking out from a roll of fat at his waistline. A cop.

"Freeze!" the cop yelled.

Michael threw up his hands instinctively. He said, "I'm looking for Alice." Then he noticed the old woman on the floor and the blood. Alice's mother?

"Who are you?" the cop said, stepping in closer. "Turn around. Hands up on the wall."

Michael did as he was told. He felt the cop's large hands frisking, checking for a weapon. Michael said, "You don't understand. I'm a friend of Alice's. We had dinner tonight. She left in a hurry, and I was worried so—"

"—so you came chasing after her in this blizzard?"

"Look, I know it sounds weird, but we're friends. We dated in high school. We ran into each other a couple of days ago. I'm worried about her. It's complicated."

The cop finished frisking Michael and turned him around. He said, "I'll bet. What's your name?"

"Michael LaPage."

The cop pulled a notebook out of his pocket and wrote the name down.

Michael said, "What happened here?"

The detective returned to the old woman and placed his hand on top of a blood-soaked folded dish towel that rested on the old woman's chest. "She's been shot. I'm waiting on the paramedics. See any on the way here?"

"No."

"Damn."

"I-is she all right?"

The cop nodded and looked down at Jackie Ruth. "Don't know. Seems to be for now."

"Shouldn't we put her on a bed or something?"

The cop shook his head. "Not when we don't know what's wrong with her. Might make things worse."

"Where's Alice?" Michael said. "I'm worried about her."

"I tried to stop her, but in the end there was nothing—"

"What do you mean?"

"She took off on a snowmobile. After her brother. I couldn't leave her mother here. Not in good conscience, and the damn paramedics are probably stuck somewhere in the snow."

"You let Alice take off in this snowstorm?" Michael said incredulously.

"Look, I didn't have any other choice. She's a big girl. She grew up in Maine. Sooner or later, she'll come to her senses and turn around. Come home. It's as simple as that."

Michael turned and grabbed the kitchen door. He said, "I'm going after her."

Calmly, the cop said, "No, you're not. I am. Just as soon as the paramedics or my partner get here. You won't be able to follow her in this snow."

Michael had to admit that the large cop was right. The snow would cover her tracks. He had no way of following Alice. What had she been thinking?

He said, "So where did she go?"

"To find her brother. He killed her uncle tonight and then attacked his mother. The guy's messed up nine ways to Sunday and always has been."

"Jesus," Michael said and sat down hard on a kitchen chair. He couldn't imagine her life, living with all this conflict and pain. She hadn't talked about it much when they'd dated in high school. Was it this bad for her then? He only vaguely remembered her twin brother Chris. He was a pudgy kid with greasy hair. Always wore an army jacket.

The cop and Michael remained in the kitchen for nearly fifteen minutes, the cop bent over Alice's mother, who seemed to be peacefully sleeping. But for all Michael knew, she could be in a coma.

The paramedics finally arrived. Michael saw the red and blue lights through the snow.

The cop grabbed his heavy jacket, zipped it up to the stop, and pulled the hood up over his head.

Michael made a move to go with him.

The cop said, "You stay. Or go home. I don't care which, but you're not going with me." Then he added, half-heartedly, "For all I know you're involved in all this."

"Gimme a break, huh?"

"Yeah, okay, okay."

"Where you going?" Michael asked, fully intending to follow the cop in his Outback if it came right down to it.

The cop sighed. "Magaskawee. To the camps up there."

"Lake Magaskawee," Michael said.

"You know it?"

"Who doesn't? Been fishing up there since I was a kid."

The cop looked out towards his car and then back at Michael, hesitating.

Michael said, "You can't go there alone. That's crazy."

The cop stood nodding for a moment and then said, "I'll probably get canned for this, but since you know her better than I do, let's go. I'll fill you in on the way. And you can do the same."

"We should take my car," Michael said. "Four-wheel drive."

"You have a CB?"

Michael shook his head.

The cop said, "Then we're taking mine."

And then they were off into the cop's waiting car.

TWELVE

1984

It was the week after Christmas, and Chris was pulling his snowmobile out of the shed in back, planning to go for a long ride to clear his head. It was early, just after 9 o'clock in the morning. He was headed up to camp where his family had stayed summers in better times. There was a little lake there, Lake Magaskawee. It was more of a pond really, but it was a smaller shallower version of several lakes that dotted Redding. It froze early and stayed frozen. It was perfect for racing. Everyone knew about it.

If Ray and Vic had any ideas about Chris, they kept it to themselves. Alice had been unusually quiet and hadn't spoken to Chris since the night she'd come home, beaten and bruised. But, as far as Chris was concerned, it was over for now. Chris didn't like the idea of having gotten Alice involved in his mess, but it was too late now. Apart from the silent treatment he was receiving from Alice, things weren't too bad. He still felt terrible. Every day. And now, it wasn't just Gartlin. He thought about the Orange Products fire, about watching the place burn to the ground and how excited that had made him. It was wrong. All of it was so horribly wrong. But he didn't know how to make it right. Chris felt like there was a hole in his life he couldn't fill.

He pulled the snowmobile off the trailer, took a seat, and started it up. He revved it a few times to warm up the engine and then was off. He planned to be free of his troubles, if only for a few hours. The cold December air whipped his face as he sped off through the trees in the backyard, pushing the machine faster and faster.

He leaned to the left and to the right, avoiding rocks and fallen branches. The day was clear and bright—the kind of day when the sun reflecting off the snow is nearly blinding and the world seems white. It was a trail he'd followed many times, but even Chris wasn't immune to the optical illusions a field of bright snow can create.

As he raced along, lost in thought, perhaps not quite paying as much attention as he should have, he felt the machine grind across some rocks and realized with horror that he was skirting alongside the edge of a ravine. The snow had drifted thanks to a couple of fallen trees and created the illusion of solid ground. And he'd barreled down the path blindly in his stupidity, not quite recognizing what had happened until it was too late. His mind began immediately ticking off the countless stories he'd read over the years about missing snowmobilers: kids who'd crashed through a supposedly frozen lake, not realizing they weren't on land; others who'd hit trees head on; or many who'd gotten hit by cars, or other snowmobilers. He wondered what his story would be and began to panic.

He turned the handlebars and leaned hard, but the machine wouldn't obey. Instead of fighting it, he slowed and tried to suppress the bubble of panic rising as he felt the snowmobile begin to slide. He still had time to jump for it if it came to that. Instead, he waited for the heavier back end to dip down the ravine and then gunned it, launching himself from the trouble.

Chris cursed himself for not paying better attention and stopped to take several long, deep breaths. He would be more careful next time.

A moment later, his near-accident forgotten, he was racing on towards the camp, a place he often came to for reasons he didn't fully understand other than that he found it comforting.

After twenty minutes or maybe a full half hour, Chris raced into a clearing and saw the little red camp. The owners had boarded it up for the winter. Even the front steps had been pulled up and leaned against the little cabin with the picnic table. Snow covered the roof. Chris gunned through the open yard, swerving sharply to the left and right for the hell of it, enjoying the freedom and wind in his face.

He saw them after it was too late. Ray, Vic, and another couple of kids from school were hanging out on the frozen Lake Magaskawee. They were in the middle, probably drag racing. Chris thought about turning, but it was too late. Ray was waving him over. Ray would only give chase if Chris turned around now.

When Chris got close enough, he recognized one kid as Justin Dodd and the other as Pete Mayer. They were all on snowmobiles, like Chris. They'd probably all just met up there. It was a popular spot, although it was usually empty in the morning. So much for that.

For a brief moment, Chris remembered the old days, when they were younger and still friends, before they'd become teenagers. The families used to rent the little camp and stay for the summer. It was close enough that they could come whenever the mood struck them. They fished, swam on the lake, played Ghost in the Graveyard or Kick the Can or whatever. Things had been much simpler then, and Chris longed for those days.

Chris stopped his snowmobile short of Ray's. "What's up?" Chris said timidly, looking at the ground.

"Heya Chrissy. We were just talking about your sister. How's she doing?"

"Fine."

"Heard she had a little trouble at school," Vic said, smiling. "Or something like that."

Chris looked up at Vic but didn't say anything. There was nothing left to say. He wondered when he'd finally get the courage to go the cops and tell them everything—everything including the dumpsters and the bowling alley and the broken windows and Orange Products. Maybe never. Maybe tomorrow. It was driving him crazy. He hoped Ray couldn't see that in his eyes.

Finally Chris said, "You should've left Alice out of it."

"Too late for that, Chrissy. You know what I'm talking about?"

"Fuck you, Ray," Chris said and throttled his snowmobile, wanting to be anywhere but here talking with his cousin and Vic.

But Ray hopped off his own snowmobile and held him fast by the handlebars. "Where you going, faggot?"

Justin and Pete laughed, unaware of what was really going on. Chris thought that maybe Ray was getting off again on having that secret, knowing something everyone else didn't. Maybe he thought it gave him power. Chris thought he'd just turned into an unbelievable asshole.

Chris hit Ray's hands and turned the handlebars, increasing his speed. Ray slid off and fell into the snow. Chris raced out onto the lake, giving his machine all it had on the relatively smooth surface. A few moments later, he turned and saw Ray and Vic behind him to the left and Pete and Justin to his right, flanking him. Chris raced on, turning left to increase the distance between him and Pete and Justin. A moment later, Ray and Vic were closing the gap, forcing Chris forward, fortunately towards the long end of the pond. Chris would have a better chance of outrunning them that way.

But they kept gaining. Soon, Chris saw Pete and Justin laughing just alongside him, bumping him, forcing him towards Ray. Vic was behind him now. Ray was signaling to Pete and Justin. They were all looking at each other and laughing.

Chris began to sense that there was more to this than a race. There were forcing him forward, forcing him towards—

Chris never had a chance. He hit the snow covered log at full speed and was thrown off his snowmobile. He heard a bang and then hit the snow-covered ice after flying over his handlebars. He felt his chin hit the ice with a crack and immediately tasted blood. He skidded on his hands for 20 feet or so. Finally, he came to a stop and rolled over on his back. His head was swimming and blurry. He reached out to help himself up but found his arms wobbly and achy. He spat blood and felt a sharp stump of an upper canine tooth wobble underneath his tongue. A quick inventory told him that it felt like that was the only one broken, thank God.

The other boys pulled up alongside him, blocking him in (as if he could get up and run away).

Pete said, "Holy fucking shit, Chris! You flew like 30 feet! Are you okay?"

Justin laughed. They were all laughing.

Ray said, "Chrissy, you really gotta be more careful out here. Sometimes the old timers drag logs out here to sit on when they're ice fishing, you know."

Chris only lay on the ground, staring up at the blue sky.

Then Ray got off his snowmobile and walked over to Chris, kneeling down. He said to Justin and Pete, "Why don't you guys let me have a word alone with Chrissy."

Pete smiled and said, "Sure, Ray. We're supposed to meet Carl and those guys anyway. C'mon, Justin."

Justin waved at Chris and said, "It's been real."

They shrugged and sped off, laughing, back where they'd come from.

Vic stayed put, watching Ray closely. Chris could hear only the soft sound of their snowmobile engines idling.

Ray kneeled down and reached into his jacket. He said, "The next time you pull a stunt like going to the cops—because I know you're thinking about it, believe me, I know—you better think about your family. You got fucking lucky this time, cousin. And so did your sister. I'm not fucking kidding. You hear me?"

Chris was angry at Ray, angry at Vic, but mostly angry at himself. He hated himself, in fact. He hated everything about his life and about what he'd made of it.

But Ray was about to make it much worse. In the end, it would cost him everything, but he didn't know it then.

Ray stood to go, pulling his hand out of his jacket. He tossed a pair of ripped panties onto Chris's chest. He laughed at Vic, then turned to Chris, and said, "Tell your whore sister that she left these at my house."

Chris watched Ray walk back to his snowmobile and race off. Vic followed for a bit and then veered off in a different direction. Soon he was alone on the ice, crying. He took Alice's underwear off his chest and threw it in anger. His eyes burned with tears and frustration. He couldn't imagine what they'd done to her. He couldn't live with himself knowing that it was his fault, if it was real. But she hadn't said anything. She would have said something if they'd done anything more than hit her. Wouldn't she? Ray was just fucking with him. They weren't Alice's panties. Couldn't be.

He didn't know what to do or where to turn. Chris Wynter had never felt lonelier, and he lay on the ice for an hour, hoping that he'd just die and end the living nightmare his life had become.

Alice raced on through the blinding snow that pelted her face. The snowmobile's headlight cast a meager yellow glow on the fallen snow ahead. She hadn't forgotten at all how to ride after all these years. Some things never leave you.

She thought about her neighbors and coworkers back home and wondered what they'd think of her now, racing through the night on a snowmobile during a fearsome Maine blizzard. They'd think she was nuts, and Alice was beginning to wonder herself.

Then she thought about Chris and about how bad he'd gotten in the years after high school, after Ray had died, about the rehab in Portland, and the drunken fellowship he and Papa had formed. Chris was a pale reflection of Papa, a brutish alpha-dog of a man, a man whom Chris hated and yet aspired to be like, coming up short again and again.

And Alice wasn't there. Not for years. Maybe her mother was right about her.

But she could make things right tonight and find Chris. Help him. Help him turn himself in and come clean about whatever had haunted him all these years and prevented him from living a real life. She had to. Alice Wynter wasn't much for spiritual guidance and guardian angels and all that jazz, but now, here, this was a time when she felt like she was doing exactly what needed doing.

Alice's eyes burned from the cold and her tears weren't helping. She realized that she'd better take it easy on herself or *she'd* be the one to come up missing after all this was said and done.

But she couldn't shake the guilt she still held about abandoning her lost brother. She could have been stronger. There was a seed of truth to that guilt because if she *had* been strong and *had* come out swinging after what had happened with Ray, maybe…

Don't. Not here. Not now. Focus on what's in front of you, Alice thought.

But the memory bubbled up anyway, a little bit of it at least. Often, Alice would think about her life, mostly her new life. There was her life before Friday, December 14th and then in Alice's mind there was simply a black smudge, like a blacked-out sentence in a redacted government document. There were bad things under there, but she'd learned to hide from all those dark days and months like a child who learns not to think about scary spiders or the axe murderer that *just might* be lurking around downstairs while she slept. There were things she simply didn't think about.

But her snowmobile wasn't the only thing racing this night. Being back home with Papa murdered and seeing what she was now really starting to believe was Ray's ghost had started a terrible chain of emotions and thoughts and guesses too horrible to think could possibly be real. In some ways, finding Chris and finally finding out what really happened to Papa out on that cold road would put an end to her silly guesses. Chris *had* to have killed Papa, *must have*, because if he didn't, well, the possibilities were too horrific to imagine. But Alice's worried, anxious mind hadn't quite come to any of those alternatives. Not yet.

She gripped the handlebars tightly and tried not to think about that little bubble of a memory in which she was walking home from school and saw Ray and his friend Vic. Ray wanted her to stop by to pick something up to bring to Chris, which should have made Alice wonder, but she didn't. Not when it was family. So she'd followed the boys amiably enough to Ray's house . . .

"Where's Uncle Bruce?" Alice said when they reached the little white house.

"He works late on Fridays," Ray said, opening the back door with a key he kept on a chain in his pocket. "Come on in."

Alice caught a look between the two boys. Like a kid who's playing a prank on another.

They sat in the kitchen.

"Want a Coke?" Ray said.

"Can't. I really gotta get going," Alice said. "What do you want me to take home?"

"Aw, c'mon, split a Coke with me and Vic."

"No, really, I gotta go."

Ray popped the top of the Coke anyway and poured some in a glass for Alice. He slid it towards her.

She gave him a gimme-a-break look and ignored the glass. What was going on here? *She thought.* Vic is acting kind of funny. They both are.

"You like Coke, Alice?" Vic said.

"I guess," Alice said.

"I love it," Vic said, looking at the floor.

Alice said, "Yeah, well, that's great Vic, I'm real happy for you. Okay, Ray, I gotta go so . . ."

Ray nodded and said, "Can you give me a hand? The thing is in the basement." He walked to the basement, opened the door, clicked on an overhead light, and walked downstairs. When he reached the bottom he said, "Vic! C'mere! You gotta see this."

Vic shuffled down after Ray.

Alice felt indescribably weird. She felt like she should go, but Ray was family. And Uncle Bruce was like a surrogate father to her and Chris. They'd spent countless hours over at the house.

Then Alice remembered something that gave her pause. That Halloween night out on the porch. She'd forgotten all about that night. Neither she nor Ray had ever talked about it, about what happened out on the porch, when Ray had touched her in her princess costume. But she guessed she'd forgotten be-

cause it wasn't that big of a deal to her then. But now it seemed like maybe it had been a bigger deal than she'd thought.

"Alice!" Ray called up from the basement. "Come down!"

And like a fool, she did.

Alice screamed and swerved her snowmobile, narrowly missing what looked like a rock, but may have been nothing more than a drift in the snow. She cursed herself for not paying better attention and wondered if that's how it had been for Ray in the end. One second cruising along and dead the next, maybe fallen through ice, maybe a broken neck and eaten by animals. She was glad when he'd gone missing. She'd felt as if God himself had taken the time to enact some karmic justice in her life and had prayed that they'd never find him.

About that, she'd never felt guilty. Not after what he and his friend had done to her.

"Roads are a lot worse," Michael said. "When I drove to Alice's they were bad, but this is ridiculous."

Detective Don Lambert nodded absent-mindedly. He was focused on the road, on the storm, and Chris Wynter. Don was trusting Alice's instinct that Chris was hiding out at the camp. Sometimes it happens that way with twins. Besides, it made perfect sense. He had a gut feeling about it.

He cursed the weather. Because of this damn snow, his unofficial partner, Matt Ivey, was tied up. The whole damn office was hopping with accidents, power outages, and, well, you name it. He was on his own now, but glad to have Michael as company. The guy seemed nice enough, smart.

But his mind kept returning to the single word Jackie Ruth had said before the paramedics had arrived: *Ray.*

Did Jackie Ruth really believe that Ray Wynter had attacked her? What could it possibly mean? Jackie Ruth couldn't mistake her own son with Ray. From what he remembered, Ray had been a tall kid with dark skin and greasy jet-black hair. Chris Wynter was shorter, pudgy, and . . . well, there was just no mistaking them.

And then Don thought about Chris buying that gun. What if he bought the gun for protection and not to kill? What if he and Papa had been arguing that night at Flynn's because Chris said he'd seen Ray?

No. It was crazy. Ray was gone.

Michael said, "What should I call you, anyway?" He was staring out into the white intensely.

"Call me Don. I'm a detective." A moment passed. "You knew Alice in high school, right?"

"We dated for a while. It ended a few months before we graduated. Christmas or so. Alice got weird. Stopped calling me. I was hurt, but I haven't really thought about it in a long, long while. I started dating my wife Kerri a few months later."

"Did you know Ray?"

Michael shook his head no. "I knew *of* him. I knew him that much. He wasn't really on my radar, you know? He was kind of a loser. So was Chris, for that matter."

"Uh yuh. What about a history teacher? Gartlin."

"Gartlin. Yeah." Michael let out a long breath. "Haven't thought about that in a long time. He was killed halfway through my senior year. Or around then anyway. Some bad business. Never caught the guy that did it, right? But what has that got to do with anything?"

"Don't have any idea. Maybe nothing. What do you remember about that?"

"Well, I remember feeling really bad about it now that you mention it. We all felt bad. And scared. For something like that to happen here, in Redding. I mean, it was crazy. I never had him as a teacher, so I didn't really know him, but man, that was something else. Hey, I didn't realize it until now but, Alice and I broke up or whatever right about when—"

Don said, "Yeah, that's just it. Alice started acting funny right around that time. You said it yourself."

"Jesus, Don, you don't think she could be involved in all this, do you? And Gartlin?"

"That's exactly what I think."

"Nah, not Alice. I'd know. She's not a liar. She wasn't even here when Papa was murdered."

"No, that's not what I mean."

"But how then?"

"I don't know. Not yet. But something tells me that we're going to find out tonight. Now, you're sure you know where this camp of theirs is or was? I haven't been there in years."

"Oh, I know it's still there. There's a bunch of them next to Lake Magaskawee. Alice mentioned it to me way back when, that she used to go there with her family. I knew right where it was because I used to fish there sometimes in the summer. Winter too. Have since I was a kid. Not much in it. Pike mostly, but hell, fishing's not really about the fish, is it?"

Don steered the car, slow as molasses, up the winding Route 6, finding it near impossible to imagine the summer out here in the middle of blizzard hell. The car was sliding all over the place.

A few minutes later, Michael said, "Okay, there's a turn-off up here on the left somewhere. It's hard enough to spot it in the middle of the day, let alone during a blizzard and at night."

The car nudged forward, occasionally spinning the front wheels to gain traction.

"There!" Michael cried. "It's there. Just up on the left. You see it?"

Don didn't. Not at first. He edged the car closer. Finally, he thought he saw it, a little patch of snow that looked vaguely like the entrance to a road. A dirt road. That was good. Better traction. He turned slowly onto the road, praying the car wouldn't start sliding, and took a deep breath when the car started down the steep little hill. He shifted into low and took his foot off the brake, letting the transmission slow them down. The car reached the bottom of the hill and Don gave it a little gas.

He said, "How much further, you think?"

Michael said, "Not long. It's maybe a mile and a half down the road. We'll see the first camps there. Just take her easy here, this road is rough in the best of times."

He wasn't kidding. Don felt the car rock and roll over rocks and through pot holes. Slowly, he crept along the road, struggling to even see it. And then the car started to get away from him. It was slow at first, just a spinning wheel on the passenger side. Then, a moment later, it lurched right, and Don realized with growing alarm that what he'd feared was actually happening: he'd steered the car off the road.

Michael said, "Left! Go left! We're right on the edge over here."

But it was too late. Don hadn't seen it. He frantically spun the steering wheel to the left, but the car had already started down the side of the road, a good 10- or 15-foot drop. They slid down to the right. The car was leaning much too far. For a brief moment, Don thought the whole shebang was going to turn over, but it held.

"Hang on!" he said.

Don finally managed to gain control but the car hit a tree head on and stopped. Michael slammed into the dashboard with a bang.

Then it was silent. The car's engine had stopped. The passenger side headlight was out. The windshield wipers worked silently on the windshield until Don turned them off.

Don said, "Damn. You okay?"

"Fine."

"Engine's dead. We'll have to go the rest of the way on foot."

Alice broke through the trees and into the wide clearing in front of the old camp. She saw the dark outlines of the small red building in the dark through the raging snow.

Not wanting to scare Chris out, she stopped the snowmobile and turned off the engine. She stepped off and lifted up the seat to retrieve her flashlight. She turned it on and walked through the snow towards the camp. It was tough going. She suspected the snow was now close to a foot deep.

Without the snowmobile's headlight to guide her, Alice had to squint in the dark to find her way to the front door even with the flashlight. The wooden front steps had apparently been taken away and tied up somewhere, because the front door was a good two feet off the ground.

She saw that the lower right-hand corner of the metal storm door was bent back, as if someone had pried it open to gain access to the front door. She pulled gently on the sharp metal corner of the storm door and it opened freely.

The inner front door was closed but unlocked, and Alice pushed it open so she could get inside. She hoped it was Chris who broken in and not a couple of teenagers looking for a place to make out or smoke pot.

The inside of the camp smelled ancient, like an old trunk in a basement. But even in the dark she remembered every nook and cranny of the place. She thought a moment about the good days her family had spent here, just far enough away to make believe they were really on vacation, but close enough that a poor family like hers could afford it. She guided the flashlight beam around the place, wondering at the fact that it looked just the same, but aged. Like herself.

But the reality of what she was doing was never far. She had no weapon and no real proof that Chris was here. If someone surprised her here, they'd certainly have the upper hand.

What will be will be, Alice thought and started forward.

She took a few tentative steps in the tiny living room, headed towards the hallway which led to the two back bedrooms.

"Chris?" she hissed. "It's Alice. Are you here?"

Her voice sounded alien and frightening in this quiet place which she was starting to think didn't want her or anyone here.

"Chris? C'mon. It's me. I want to help!"

A creek. From the back.

Alice continued, tip-toeing now into the hallway. She saw the faint outline of the two bedroom doors. She headed for the one on the left, slowly creeping her way along, keeping the flashlight on target in front of her.

"Alice?"

The voice was weak, tentative, and slurry.

"Oh my God, Chris! I knew it!" Alice said and ran into the left bedroom, shining her light around until she found him. She gasped.

He looked a hundred years old. Far older than she. More like her mother. He was curled up in the corner of the room, his legs stuffed into his large winter parka for warmth. A blue knit cap was parked on his head. A patch or two of greasy hair poked out from underneath. He'd lost weight. His sunken eyes swam as he tried to focus on Alice. She saw why. Next to him was a nearly empty bottle of vodka. A big one. On the ground next to that was a half-empty pack of Marlboro Red cigarettes. Chris's face was bright red, and she saw several angry red splotches on his face. Burst capillaries from years of hard drinking.

Her flashlight shone on his shockingly red eyes and pale-blue pupils. He held up his hands to block the light and let out a weak moan. She realized his eyes must have become sensitive in the dark. Alice pointed her flashlight away from his face, and he let his hands fall to his lap. The ambient light cast an eerie silver glow over the room.

This person before her couldn't be her brother, could it? He was too old, too damaged.

He smiled at her. "Am I dead, Alice? Is that why you came for me? I hope I'm dead."

Oddly, Alice suddenly felt wrong about being here, about seeing him. He was too far gone for her to help. She'd been naive to think it. She wanted to leave. Get the detective somehow. The shock of seeing her twin brother was too much. But it was too late now.

She approached him and said, "You're not dead, Chris. I'm going to help you."

But Chris's eyes widened as she approached. His mouth worked up and down as if he was trying to scream. He was terrified.

Alice was confused. Why was he scared of her? She realized in terror that there was someone behind her. She whirled around and pointed her flashlight at the dark figure standing in the doorway.

She nearly fainted when she saw him. He looked exactly like Ray. It was the man she'd seen next to the CVS and at the bottom of her driveway. It was as if Ray had never aged a day since high school. But there was something oddly familiar about him.

The dark figure said, "Hi, Mom. Long time never see."

THIRTEEN

Don Lambert was really huffing and puffing now and felt the sweat accumulating on the back of his shirt underneath his winter jacket. Michael trudged alongside. The heavy walking didn't seem to bother him much. They were following the long road towards the cabin. The snow hadn't eased up at all.

"You okay?" Michael said.

"I'm fine," Don said. "Let's just keep walking. And keep your eyes peeled for Alice's snowmobile."

Both Don and Michael had powerful flashlights, the beams of which bobbed up and down as they continued their way slowly down the road.

"Any idea how much further?" Don said.

"Shouldn't be too much longer. There are a bunch of camps coming up on the left. Maybe a hundred yards or so. This road will take you right to Lake Magaskawee. Ends with a small boat launch."

Uh-yuh was Don's response. He wondered what his wife Gaye would say if she could see him now. Probably, *you're a damn fool.* Don promised himself to lose weight just as soon as this was over. He wasn't getting any younger. Maybe the doctors were right. Retiring seemed like a better idea now. It's all fine and well driving around in your Crown Victoria, but when the shit hits the fan and you're out in the thick of it, well, that's when you start showing your age.

They walked onward through the dark trees and blinding snow. Even Michael was starting to slow down now. Don wasn't sure how much longer he could go. His legs were getting heavier and heavier and an unsettling dull tightness had settled into his chest, no surprise, he guessed, breathing in all this frigid air. His stomach was roiling with nausea. Walking in snow this deep—Don figured it was well over a foot if it was an inch—without snowshoes was tiring work, even for someone in shape, and a fool's game, like trying to fight a rip-tide in the ocean. Inexperienced hunters died out here every year, getting tired and dehydrated walking in deep snow like this. He was about to call a halt so he could rest when—

"There!" Michael cried. "Thank God! Don, there! Just ahead. Up on the right."

Don scanned his flashlight in front of him and soon saw the abandoned snowmobile, covered with a thick layer of fresh snow.

Michael raced on ahead to investigate it. Don put his hands on his hips and doubled over to throw up in the snow. He was breathing too hard now and winced. He didn't feel well at all.

"Jesus, you okay?" Michael asked. When Don didn't respond, he said, "Don?"

Don waved him off and eventually caught up with Michael and felt underneath the machine, at the engine. Still a little warm. "Yep. It's hers all right."

"Alice?!" Michael screamed into the wind.

"Shh! Shut your mouth!"

Michael looked at the detective confused.

Don shook his head. He said, "We don't know what we're dealing with here. Until we do, you keep your mouth shut and let me do all the talking if it comes to that."

1984

After an hour or so, Chris sat up on the ice and rubbed his head. A light snow had started to fall, and he decided to head home and maybe talk to Alice about what had happened. His head was a little clearer now, and he had gone a long way to convincing himself that what Ray had said was a lie. Just to scare him.

Chris stood up and checked on his wounded snowmobile. It wasn't badly damaged, but one of the skids on the front was twisted. He wouldn't be able to ride it home. With some effort, he managed to turn it around and began his long walk home, pushing the snowmobile alongside himself.

His head throbbed. He was tired. And he wanted a beer badly. He promised himself he'd steal another 6-pack from the stash Papa kept in the basement, underneath the stairs. He kept so much under there he hadn't noticed Chris pinching a couple of 6-packs over the last few weeks.

Chris pushed the snowmobile past the camps on his right and up into the woods, more or less following the trail Ray had left earlier. Chris was not thinking about Ray, wouldn't allow himself to. There was no point to it now.

A quarter mile now. Then a half. Then a full mile. Chris's legs ached, and he was cold right down to his bones.

"H-e-l-p!"

Chris stopped pushing his snowmobile and listened. He heard another cry. It was weak and out-of-breath:

"Jesus! Help! I'm hurt. Oh, God!"

Leaving his snowmobile, Chris walked in a small circle, scanning the trees, thinking it might be a joke or a trick.

"Oh, God, I can't feel my legs!"

It was no trick. Chris now recognized the voice. "Ray?" he said tentatively. "Ray? Is that you?"

"Chris! Chris, thank God. You got—" This was followed by a wet cough and a loud moan.

And then he realized. This was the very ravine where he'd nearly bought it himself. Only Ray hadn't been so lucky.

Chris ran to the edge of the ravine to his right and looked over. At the bottom, perhaps 25 feet below, was Ray's overturned and badly damaged snowmobile. Ray was lying underneath it. He held a hand out to Chris.

Chris carefully worked his way down the slippery rocks and fallen trees. He knew he'd been lucky. It could have been him lying down here, broken and battered. But it had happened to Ray and not him.

When he got to the bottom, he said, "Ray, what happened?"

He thought of Alice when he looked into Ray's eyes. Couldn't get her out of his mind.

The snow around Ray's head was bloody. Ray turned to cough and a spray of blood came out. He said in nearly a whisper, "Didn't see the ravine." He tried to smile and winced. His teeth were bloody. "It hurts. I'm freezing."

"Good," Chris said.

"C'mon, man. I'm hurt. Please."

"Where's Vic?" Chris asked.

"He didn't come with me. He had something he had to do with his old man."

Chris remembered watching Vic peel off away from Ray into the woods earlier, after they'd left him lying on the ice. This was no trick, no elaborate scheme. Ray was in real trouble.

Chris thought of Gartlin and heard his wife's words again as he had hundreds of times before: *Honey? Who's that at the door? Is everything okay?*

"What did you guys do to Alice?" Chris said.

Ray closed his eyes and mouth and turned his head away.

It was as much of an answer as Chris needed. He backed up several feet. His eyes never left Ray. He sat down heavily on a large rock and put his face in his hands and cried. He stayed this way for a long time. He didn't know how long and didn't care. He thought about Alice and Gartlin's wife and the Orange Products fire and about Nora Strawser. She didn't have problems like this. As big as these.

Ray had fallen asleep, or passed out. His breath was rattling but regular. Chris stared at him and the wrecked snowmobile.

If he made it this long, Chris thought, *he'll be okay. I just need to go get help. It's that easy. I would just leave my snowmobile here and run out to Route 6. I could flag a car in a few minutes probably. He'll be fine. Then everything between us can be normal again. As normal as it could be.*

But he thought about Alice again. How she'd have to face Ray at every family party. How they'd both have to face him. How they'd have to pretend nothing was wrong, when they both knew that Ray'd gone too far. Way too far. Chris thought about Gartlin's kids and how they'd never know their father because of what Ray had decided to do one night when they were out screwing around as the Masters of Chaos. Just saying it made Chris feel ashamed. It was stupid. Really colossally idiotic what they'd done together. What they'd become.

And I got off on it in the warehouse fire, Chris thought. *I actually came in my pants looking at that fire.*

He was too ashamed to even face his own thoughts. Chris thought more and more about suicide lately, and right now, it seemed like a fine idea. But he knew he wouldn't go through with it. He was no better than a piece of shit in his own mind and always would be, but he wasn't a quitter.

Ray woke up then. He turned to look at Chris and coughed. "I think I fell asleep. You go for help?"

Chris nodded.

"Thank you, man. Seriously." He wheezed. He said, "Starting to feel a little better actually. Why don't you get this thing off me?"

Chris shook his head and stared at Ray coldly. He said, "Might make it worse."

Ray nodded.

They sat in silence for a few minutes and then Ray said, "I'm sorry about Alice. It was stupid. It was a stupid thing we did."

Now, trapped under a wreck, potentially paralyzed, the fucking guy finds God, Chris thought.

Ray wept. Quietly at first, as if he was embarrassed and then a little louder. He said, "I'm scared, Chris. I'm really scared."

Chris grunted in mock agreement, "Uh huh."

"I can't fucking feel my legs. Chris, I still can't feel my legs. When are they gonna get here? How long ago was it that you went for help?"

"A little while."

"Jesus, this sucks. I'm fucking scared, man. What if I'm, you know, paralyzed?"

"I don't know, man."

Ray cried again.

It was hard for Chris to listen to. He wasn't sure why he was lying to Ray about going for help.

Because I haven't made up my mind yet, Chris thought. *About how this is going to end.*

Gartlin. Vic. Nora. Fire. Death. The bow. Chaos. Ray and Vic fucking his sister. The images swam in Chris's mind. He put his head in his gloved hands again and tried to will this away. He cried for a minute.

Chris stood.

"W-where you going man?" Ray said pathetically. "You can't leave, man. C'mon, seriously. I'm family."

But Chris had no intention of leaving. He thought he might end this story right here and now. Thought it might be a fine idea. Karma and all that. For Alice. For Gartlin.

He bent down and picked up a heavy branch and broke it off just right with his boot on the rock he'd been sitting on. He hefted it a little in his hand and nodded. He wasn't thinking about anything except that Alice was going to be all right now. They all were.

He turned towards Ray, who let out a sob and whispered, "Chris. Please don't do this."

"Dear God," Alice said, her flashlight beam shining on what appeared to be Ray's ghost.

Chris screamed and whimpered.

The young Ray smiled. He said, "Looks like we're having a little family reunion. It's kind of cozy, don't you think? By the way, the name's Ricky."

Chris said, "I killed you! I killed you!"

Alice's mind was reeling. She felt dizzy and sick. She said, weakly, "B-but, why . . .?" She thought for a moment and then said, "What do you want?"

Ricky shook his head a little to dismiss the question. "Well, for one thing, I have to kill your brother there. He's seen my face. Come to think of it, so have you. I ain't going back to prison."

"Alice?" Chris said. "I killed him. I killed Ray. That's why he's come back. Me and Papa took care of the body. Dumped the snowmobile in the lake. Sunk it. That's why he came back. He doesn't want you."

Alice listened in horror to her delirious brother. "Chris, I . . ." But she couldn't finish. All she could think about was holding that baby in the hospital, Ray's baby, and hating it and loving it all at once. Hating herself for not knowing she might have been pregnant before it was too late, before she could have done something about it. And now that being was standing here holding a gun. No one had known.

She was in college and hadn't yet met Gerald. That came a couple of months later. They told her the records would be sealed.

Chris said, "We killed that teacher. Me and Ray and Vic. Only I didn't want to. It was Ray. Alice, I'm so sorry. I'm so fucking sorry." He began to sob again and reached for his vodka. He looked disturbingly like a child clutching a feeding bottle.

"What?" Alice said. She heard her brother's words, but they wouldn't process at first. *That teacher?* And then she remembered. The history teacher. In high school. And then it all clicked into place.

"I wrote the police a note. To tell them about Ray," Chris said. "Ray and Vic got mad. They did that to you because of me. It was all because of me."

Ricky said, "Well that's just fine, you alcoholic sack of shit. Thanks a fucking million." He rolled his eyes, silently saying, *do you fucking believe this guy?*

"Chris, no," Alice said. "Please tell me that isn't true. All these years. You and Papa hid that. Did Ma know?"

Chris nodded and began crying.

That's why he never left, Alice thought. *That's why he and Papa clung to each other. Spiraled together.*

A shot rang out from Ricky's gun. He held it high pointed towards the ceiling. Alice screamed. Chris jerked and then stared at Ricky, wide eyed.

Ricky said, "Hi. Remember me?"

He lunged at Alice, grabbed her neck, and forced her against the wall. He was incredibly, impossibly strong.

"Why did you kill my father?" Alice said, her voice harsh and forced.

"I think I'm going to take care of you first."

Alice shook her head no.

"You know what it feels like? Huh? To not have a home?"

Alice shook her head again.

"Leave her alone!" Chris said and went for Ricky.

Ricky kicked Chris in the gut and said, "Would you *please* shut the hell up?"

Chris gagged and struggled for air.

Ricky turned back to Alice. He said, "I'll tell you what it was like. It fucking sucked. How's that? Huh?"

"I'm sorry," Alice mouthed. She was. For all of it. She began to cry. She said, "I was just a kid. I didn't know what to do."

Ricky's face creased up in frustration. He stared at her intently and worked his lips across his teeth. He said, "I didn't come here to kill you or him or anyone. I didn't, you know."

Alice didn't say anything.

"I came here to see where I came from. That's all. It was your father. I had to kill him. All I wanted was a little meet and greet, was planning to find work up North."

Chris was crying, balled up on the floor. He said, "But you shot him. You shot him and left him out there. He never did anything to you."

Ricky's eyes widened.

Alice saw it then. That same look Ray had in the basement. It was a crazy look. A scary look. An out-of-control look.

Ricky said, "NOBODY calls me a bastard. And that's what he did. Right fucking there at your goddamned precious breakfast fuckin' nook. Him and that mother of yours.

My lovely grandparents. Didn't want to have thing-fucking-one to do with yours truly. You know what I'm saying? Called me a bastard and told me to get the hell off his property. All I was trying to do was set a few things straight. Trying to get my life in order. Just set a few things right."

Ricky casually aimed at Chris and shot.

Alice screamed, "Chris!" She tried to wrestle away from her son. His grip on her throat tightened.

Chris moaned softly and rocked back and forth. He said, "I'm sorry. I'm so sorry," over and over again to himself. He clutched his belly.

"Now, where were we?" Ricky said, returning his attention to Alice. "Oh, yeah, right. And you know what?"

Alice shook her head a little. She stared at Ricky in horror, realizing that her mother had tried to hide all of this from her. This whole time. It was why she was acting so strangely. She knew.

"It's your fault." Ricky pointed his gun at the base of Alice's throat. "Mother."

Alice said quietly, "No."

"You left me for dead. Like throwing a sack of puppies from bridge. You're no better than that. A whore."

"No."

Ricky pooched out his lips and glanced sideways. He said, "I gave him one more chance. Outside that stinking bar."

"You didn't give him a chance," Chris said. His words were wheezy and wet.

"I GAVE him a fucking chance!" Ricky said, turning towards Chris. "Besides you two were so drunk what the hell would you know?" He turned back towards Alice and said calmly, "Personally, I don't touch the stuff. It'll kill you."

"So you shot him and tried to get Chris. That's what all this was?" Alice said.

"Had to. Chris saw me. And well, it was a long hike up here, so there's that. Can you believe this weather?"

"And my uncle?"

Ricky nodded. He looked sheepish. He said, "Yeah, well, that one kind of got away from me, but he did tell me that Jackie Ruth knew where Chris was. And you, well . . . That was just fucking gravy. You know what I mean? Who knew you'd come all the way home? My mother."

Chris said, "Then leave her. Kill me and get outta here. That's what you came here for. Because of me. I'm a piece of crap. This is all my fault. It always was. Alice made something of herself. I'm nothing. Nobody. I got nothing." He cried. "I'm already dead."

Ricky nodded vigorously and said, "Oh, you're right on the money about that, partner. You are dead already. I'll just be speeding up the process a little."

"Let her go," Chris insisted.

Ricky cocked the trigger on the pistol he was holding at the base of Alice's neck. He smiled a little and stared into her eyes.

Then, they heard someone call out from outside. "*Alice*?"

FOURTEEN

"Okay, okay," Michael said, a little stung by the detective's rebuke. The guy was right, of course. He shouldn't have yelled out like that. It was stupid. They were tense and Michael was a little scared.

"And another thing," Don said. "You're going to stay put while I go check this out. You hear shots, you get down until you know what's going on."

Michael said, "No way. I'm coming with you."

"Oh no you're not. I'm going to be in enough hot water explaining why you got this far."

"But—"

Don cut Michael off with a raised, gloved hand. Almost out of the side of his mouth, he said, "There's a shotgun in the car. Rounds are in the glove compartment." He reached for a set of keys attached to his belt beneath his coat and pulled one out, removing it. He placed it in Michael's hand. "If things go bad, and I have no reason whatsoever to believe the only thing we're going to find in that little camp is a dead alkie and Alice sobbing right down next to him, I want you to have protection. But, do not go for that gun unless something real bad goes down. We understand each other?"

Michael nodded.

Don continued. "The only reason I'm making you an honorary detective here is because I have no other choice. I have reason to believe Alice Wynter and her brother Chris, a wanted fugitive, might be in trouble in there. I am tasked with protecting the citizens of Somerset County by doing everything in my power within the boundaries of the law."

Michael understood that Don was trying more to convince himself and give Michael something to say if he were questioned about what happened out here.

Don winked and smiled a little. "We still understand each other?"

Michael nodded again. "You got it, boss."

Don took a deep breath and said, "Okay, partner. I'm going to investigate here. You watch. Keep me lit up the whole way. I don't want anyone sneaking up on me. You see that and you scream."

Don was scared. Michael could see it in his eyes. They just didn't know what they were dealing with.

The fat man walked slowly towards the camp with his gun drawn. He cast a long shadow that reached nearly to the camp's front door. His heavy boots dragged through the snow as he crept closer. Michael heard the man's rapid breathing.

The snow fell relentlessly. Alice's snowmobile was nearly covered again. In another few minutes all it would be is a long lump underneath several inches of drifting snow.

Suddenly, a shot. A scream from the camp.

Don turned suddenly and put his finger to his lips, urging Michael not to yell back. He crept closer still. He was within fifty feet now.

Something was going on in that camp. Michael could feel it and knew Don could as well. Alice was in danger. They all were. Michael's stomach clenched, and he fought his growing urge to break loose and run towards the camp while he watched Don helplessly.

Alice opened her mouth to scream in response to the cry from outside. It was Michael! He must have followed her somehow!

"Oh my fucking Jesus," Ricky said, shaking his head. "You gotta be kidding me." He clamped the gun hand on Alice's mouth before she could respond. "What a fucking thing this is. Who the fuck is that? Huh? Who the fuck followed you?"

Alice shook her head as if to say she didn't know. She swallowed hard. It hurt her Adam's apple and she winced in pain.

"You," Ricky said, pointing the gun at Alice. "You better keep your mouth shut. No more of that shit. I'm in charge of this thing here. All I wanted to do was set things right and look what you fucking went and did. Real noble. You really fucked things up for me, you know that?"

Alice saw a flash of movement beneath her. It was Chris. He'd pulled himself over close to Ricky's legs in the confusion.

"Ow, fuck!" Ricky said and let go of Alice, grabbing his shin.

Chris had kicked it hard with his work boot and was now climbing up Ricky's leg and punching up at Ricky's crotch. But Ricky was too fast for him and swiped down with the gun, narrowly missing Chris's head. Chris kept coming. He was up to Ricky's stomach now and pushed both fists into Ricky's middle and grabbed hard, squeezing. Ricky hissed in pain.

And then Alice went down hard. Ricky threw her, trying to buy some time to get Chris off him.

The men struggled. Alice recovered quickly enough to stagger forward and grope for the gun in Ricky's right hand before he could think to shoot Chris.

And then with a low cry of effort, Chris tackled Ricky and they both crashed to the floor. Chris wouldn't let go and was now screaming with effort and pain. Alice lost sight of the gun. She remembered the flashlight.

I can hit him with the flashlight! She thought.

But it was no use. The two men struggled mightily. Alice heard them grunting with effort. They were a tangle of arms and legs. Alice knew that even pumping with adrenaline, Chris had no chance. He was old now. And tired. And he was nursing a bullet wound somewhere in his gut. But she had to try.

She tried to get a better sense of their movement. She managed a few weak blows on what she thought was Ricky's back before realizing that she'd be better off running outside, towards help. She was caught in a terrible moment of indecision, torn between leaving Chris here to fend for himself in a battle he couldn't win and running outside towards safety. But it was no use. Before she could decide, she heard a muffled shot and the scuffle stopped.

She felt an arm reach around her neck and felt cold sweat on the side of her face as Ricky grabbed her arms and pushed them up behind her back. His face rested against hers. His grip was vice-like. She smelled the acrid scent of pure fight, pure male aggression. There was no reasoning with the man now. He'd kicked into full-on survival mode.

He said, "One down. C'mon, Mommy dearest, we're going for a little walk, you and me, before I blow this god-damned popsicle stand and head north."

Don Lambert was sweating like a pro wrestler under his winter jacket as he made his way slowly through the deep snow towards the little house, gun drawn, flashlight pointed at the house. The image of Bruce Wynter's corpse slumped over the kitchen table haunted his thoughts, and he tried to focus. He risked a look backward and saw Michael standing next to Alice's snowmobile watching intently.

He thought about his wife Gaye. She would be furious with him when she found out what he'd been doing this night. She'd tell him that he was too old and too out of shape for this sort of thing. She'd tell him that he should have waited for proper backup. He'd argue with her, but it wouldn't do any good because she was right. But tonight he still had a damn job to do.

Closer he crept, straining his ears, hoping to hear something that might reveal what was going on within, but the snow muffled all but the loudest sounds. The snow silence was unnerving, but Don didn't feel like anyone was watching him, other than Michael.

He reached the front door. The front steps had been removed and tied up by the side of the camp. He saw that the corner of the storm door was bent, as if someone had pulled it loose to break in. The inner front door was wide open. He saw the dark interior of the cabin through the glass on the storm door. Someone was either inside or had been earlier.

He opened the broken storm door and unhinged the spring so that it would stay open. He poked his head around the door frame and saw nothing inside but the pale silver light his halogen flashlight produced. The place felt empty.

Don put his gun and flashlight on the floor and hoisted himself up and onto his stomach. The floor of the camp was a good few feet off the ground. He wiggled around a bit like an overturned turtle, trying to coax his heavy body to roll over far enough that he could shift his weight and right himself.

Then he was on his feet. He'd have no chance of surprising whoever was in here. He'd rolled the dice and gotten lucky. The air was dead. He was sure there was no one in here with him. He took a look outside and saw Michael still there, holding his flashlight.

Don crept through the dark camp, listening at every few steps. He checked the rooms methodically, one after the other.

Finally, at a room on the left, down a short hallway that led to the back, he found the body. It was curled up and facing the wall. He held out his gun and approached it. The man was wearing a blue winter jacket, the kind you get in a uniform supply store. He had on heavy boots. Don reached out with his boot and turned the body over. It was Chris Wynter. He was clearly dead as a stone. A quick glance around the room revealed disturbances in the dust. A scuffle. There'd definitely been a struggle of some kind. Blood stained the floor near the far left corner. He took off his glove and felt Chris. The body was still warm. This had just happened. He wondered if this was the shot they'd heard, or if there was another, muffled at close range. The hair on the back of Don's neck went up and a rash of goose pimples rushed over his body.

Don backed out of the room and down the hall, trying to find where the killer had escaped.

Just then a woman's scream came from outside. "*No! Let go of me! Please!*"

Michael heard Alice scream. She was outside. He started to run towards the scream and stopped himself. He wasn't armed. He groped for the key to the glove compartment in his pocket. He glanced back towards the disabled car and then towards the camp.

Don had told him to stay put. But he couldn't. Something bad was going down. He heard Alice. Where was Don? For all Michael knew, there was a killer in there with one of those silencer attachments on his gun. Don had told him to stay put unless something happened. Michael definitely considered this a big *something*.

He didn't think a moment longer. He turned and stumbled his way back through the snow towards Don's car. He was good quarter mile away. His legs burned with the effort. He wouldn't make it like this. He then concentrated on every step, making each one count. Up over the snow, down through it, up over the snow, down through it. He was in good shape and quickly developed a rhythm. It wasn't snow shoes, but it would have to do.

Several minutes later, he reached the car and slammed open the driver's side door and launched himself inside. He thought of nothing but Alice. She was in danger, and that was all that mattered right now. He reached round behind the seat and found the shotgun Don had mentioned. Next, the shells. He threw off his glove and jammed his hand into his pocket for the key. He struggled for a moment with the lock but finally managed to get the key in the lock. The large glove box fell open. Michael reached inside, frantically searching for the shells. He found a packet likely containing the manual and threw it aside. He found a tire-pressure gauge, discarded napkins, a couple of Wet-Naps from a lobster shack, and a cigarette pack containing 2 smokes and some matches. No shells. Don had been wrong.

"Shit!" Michael said.

He looked on the floor. He checked underneath the seats, doing the same in the back. He sat for a moment, watching his white breath fog in the cold, still air.

Michael wasn't much of a poker player, but he knew what a bluff was. He could still use the shotgun, could still bluff his way out of a tight situation with it. Besides, he hadn't hunted since he was a kid. He wouldn't know what to do with a shotgun anymore. He'd probably be more of a danger to himself than anyone else with a loaded shotgun.

Don reacted immediately and without thinking when he heard the scream from outside. Presumably it was Alice, and now was the time to act, while whoever was holding her was distracted. He might get lucky. He lumbered back down the dark hallway, forgetting about Chris Wynter's body for the moment.

He passed the living room on his right and went into the little galley-style kitchen, where he saw a back door, slightly ajar. He pushed the door open and looked outside. He saw nothing but blowing snow and the black, skeletal outlines of leafless trees reaching heavenward. He jumped down gently onto the ground from the back door and winced when his heart gave him a little uncomfortable jolt. He was anxious as hell and scared. Don figured his blood pressure must be through the roof. He really should have waited for backup. He wasn't prepared for this, and if someone was watching this spectacle, they'd know that too.

He aimed his flashlight downward and saw the shallow indentations of two sets of footprints. The snow was filling them in fast.

"Alice!" Don called. "Everything's gonna be all right. We've got plenty of backup on the way. Alice! Can you hear me?"

Nothing.

Jesus H. Christ, I don't like this, Don thought miserably.

"Alice?" He tried again.

Nothing.

He walked slowly forward, keeping an eye on the footprints, which led off to the side of the little camp into a pocket of sparsely spaced trees. Beyond them lay a forest. God help them all if he had to go in there. At least here he could see.

The snow was masking sounds and making him jumpy. He heard the branches creaking as the winter wind howled through them. Occasionally, a clump of snow falling from the buildup on one of the branches landed with a loud *whump!*, once loud enough that he aimed his gun towards the sound and nearly pulled the trigger. He was beginning to panic now. He had no chance. He hoped Michael had the sense to get the shotgun.

The footprints were fading fast and soon were gone altogether.

Don Lambert stopped dead in his tracks. He no longer knew which way to turn.

Where was Michael? He wondered.

"Michael!" he yelled.

But it was too late.

A dark figure stepped out from a tree on his left and rushed him. The minute he saw it, he heard Alice scream.

"Look out! He's—"

Don felt a dull thud on the left side of his head and an unusual taste filled his mouth. He was suddenly incredibly dizzy and tired all at once. His eyes wouldn't focus.

Another thud, harder this time.

Don looked towards the ground and the whiteness seemed to call to him. It filled his vision and then rushed towards him at an impossibly fast speed. Then . . . nothing.

FIFTEEN

"Please, Ricky, please. Let me go. Let us all go. It's not too late," Alice said after Ricky had beaten the detective down. He now lay in a lump in the snow. She wondered if he was dead. She tried to run then, but Ricky caught her easily.

"No you don't. Where you going? Huh?" he said. Then he had her tight by the upper arm and seemed to be dragging her aimlessly, not sure where to go.

"He's not dead. I think I can see him breathing. It's not too late. We can just go back. Tell them it was an accident."

"Would you shut your yapper? Seriously, for just one stinking fucking minute? I gotta think. Gotta think. What the fuck am I gonna do, huh? You see what you people did? Jesus!"

He dragged her along and Alice did her best not to make it easy for him. She fell several times, but each time, he simply scooped her up and dragged her on. They were on the lake now, moving East, away from the camp. And help.

Even if Michael were there and hadn't gone back for help, he'd never hear her out here.

"Ricky, I was young. I was scared. I didn't know what to do. Your father raped me."

"Yeah, right."

"Why would I lie?" Alice asked. She wanted to keep him talking. The more they talked the better the chance she could find a way to get away from him. "I thought you'd have a better life."

"You knew what you were doing. You knew what would happen to me, a little bastard kid, an incest baby, maybe not wired up right because of it. Probably had a big laugh after."

"That's not true. That's not TRUE!" Alice cried, angry with herself for letting his words get to her. She dissolved into tears and frustration. She didn't know what her son's life had been, but it hadn't been good. And it was her fault. She could have aborted the baby, but she hadn't known. She hadn't goddamn known until it was too late. What would she have possibly known about how these things worked then? She'd been a virgin until that horrible afternoon in Ray's basement. She'd never even let Michael touch her much. In her mind, she'd gone right back to being a virgin after it happened. Just put that in a lockbox in her mind and shut that door forever. Or so she'd thought. It wasn't until Gerald came along that she'd even begun to feel safe around men again and *that* took two years.

But she had to keep him talking. Had to focus. She had to deal with her emotions later.

Softly, through her sobs, she said, "You were better off on your own."

"You think so? Do you now? Well, how do you figure? You think getting beat up and burned by your step-dad was better off? You think stealing when you was hungry was better off, do you? Or getting caught in the shower alone when you were fourteen in juvi? What the fuck do you know anyway? I'll tell you. Nothing. That's what."

"Why did you come here, then?"

"To make it right. To make things fucking right. I didn't want to hurt anyone. But your fucking brother got in the way. He fucked things up for me. I shouldn't have fucking come here!"

He pulled her hard then and shoved her forward in front of him, tired of dragging her.

"Goddamn bitch," Rick muttered. "All I was trying to do was make a clean getaway. Could have gotten away clean. Started over. Maybe settled down. Maybe logging. Whatever. Don't matter. Now I gotta deal with this shit. So help me, if that fat fuck cop dies they're gonna put me away forever . . So help me, I swear to Christ. Still time. Still time."

She said, "So why don't you just shoot me and get it over with? Huh? Why don't you just pull that trigger and be done with it?"

"Oh sure. What if that fat pig over there wasn't lying? What if about two thousand goddamned state troopers are on their fuckin' way right now? Won't have any collateral, now will I? That's where you come in. Mother." He spit the last word out like a curse.

He wasn't going to let her out of his sight. Talking wasn't working. She had to try something different.

"The snowmobile," she said.

"What?" Ricky said.

"I came up here on a snowmobile. We can use that. You know, to get out of here."

"Where is it?"

Alice pointed vaguely towards the front of the camp, now several hundred yards away.

Ricky squinted.

Alice said, "You can't see it. It's covered with snow. How do you think I got up here?"

"How the fuck should I know?!" Ricky said and slapped her across the face hard. "What do you think, you're smarter than me? You could've walked. I did."

Alice reeled and held a hand to her cheek. She didn't like the look in his eyes. Whatever this was, whoever he was, Ricky was crazy. He was out of his mind.

She said, "No, I-I just—"

"You just what?" Ricky said, grabbing her arm again. When Alice said nothing Ricky said, "That's what I thought. Nobody tells me what to do. Nobody. We clear? As far as you're concerned, I'm goddamned freakin' Einstein."

"I'm sorry."

Ricky's face softened and he laughed at her. He turned towards the camp and rubbed his chin, thinking. "Now that's better. That's what I like to hear from—"

Alice lunged out with her hand and poked two gloved fingers in Ricky's eyes.

He doubled over, clutching his eyes and howling in pain. "You fucking bitch! Jesus Christ! What the fuck?"

Alice looked around desperately for a moment for the gun, sure he'd dropped it because she didn't see him holding it any longer, and decided it wasn't worth it. There had to be sixteen inches of snow on the ground now (if not more).

She'd never find it, and hopefully Ricky wouldn't either. Now was her only chance. He was in a rage now and would surely kill her.

She turned and ran back towards the camp as best she could through the thick snow. She fell but didn't look back. She was so scared she thought her heart would beat right out of her chest.

Ricky was either too far away for her to hear his howling or he'd stopped altogether and was coming after her.

Alice didn't dare turn her head to find out.

Michael climbed out of the car, closed the door, and took several deep breaths, trying to come to grips with what he might face out here.

He once again began his odd, hurdler's run back towards the camp, his legs swinging from side to side as he bounded over the snow, holding the shotgun high in his right hand and the flashlight in his left.

Back at the camp, he dropped the pretense that his presence would be a surprise to anyone here. Whoever was here, whoever had made Alice scream, knew someone was here.

"Alice?" Michael said at something a little louder than his regular voice but softer than a yell. "Don?"

Nothing.

Michael deftly hoisted himself up and into the camp, holding the shotgun in front of himself. He said, "I've got a pretty big gun here, so don't mess with me, okay?" He felt like an idiot. *Yeah, that'll scare 'em out*, he thought.

Snow was blowing in and around the place. The air was somehow colder in the camp as it blew across Michael's face.

In one of the back bedrooms, he found Chris Wynter and thought of what Alice had told him of the man. Whatever he was, he didn't deserve this. He'd been bleeding in the gut. His blue winter coat was stained a dark red in the front. Whether he was stabbed or shot, Michael didn't know.

He walked back towards the front of the camp, intending to go back outside, when he realized suddenly that if he could feel air moving *through* the house, there must be a door or window open. Maybe that's where the attacker went. And Don would surely have realized the same thing.

He found the open kitchen door and peered outside, his eyes catching on a something not far from the door. He turned off his flashlight, fearing that he might give his position away.

He jumped down to the snow-covered ground and ran cautiously towards what he was sure was Don. Sure enough, it was the detective. He had a thin layer of snow covering him. Michael rolled him over, brushed him off, and listened to his chest. He was alive. Thank God.

He glanced around him. Without the flashlight, he could just barely make out the haunted black shapes of the barren winter trees and see the slope that led down towards the lake. Snow reflects more light than earth, and some nights, even without a moon, a snowy night can be brighter than normal.

He picked up Don's legs and dragged him towards the camp. It wasn't much more shelter than he had out here, but at least . . .

Michael suddenly realized that it had stopped snowing. The wind had picked up and was blowing snow around. The temperature had also dropped at least 10 or 20 degrees. But it wasn't snowing.

After he'd dragged Don back under the camp's eves (there was no way he would have been able to get the heavy man into the camp itself), Michael unholstered Don's gun carefully and released the safety. He buttoned up Don's jacket to the top and made sure he was as covered as he could be. There was nothing more he could do.

The wind screamed out on the lake. Alice ran as best she could towards shore, but the snow was deep and it was slow going. The visibility had gotten a little better, and she could make out the shoreline clearly.

When she reached it, she risked a quick glance and was dismayed to see Ricky rapidly approaching. She let out a little groan of despair and tried to pick up her pace. It was impossible. The snow was simply too deep. Ricky was much taller than she and had longer legs. He seemed to bound over the snow.

She ducked left into a gathering of pine trees. The wind whistled through them.

Behind her, he heard Ricky yell, "You're not going to win! Give up! I'm gonna catch you!"

Branches loaded with otherwise soft pine needles now stung her face as she whipped past them, trying to get to the snowmobile, but knowing that she'd never reach it before Ricky got to her. But it was all she had to hope for.

"You did this to yourself!" Ricky said. "You hear me? All this crap! All this shit! It's your own damn fault! Ooh, it's gonna be fun when I get to you. You won't last forever. I'll just keep coming at you!"

He was only perhaps 10 feet behind Alice now. The snow wasn't as thick in the midst of the pine trees. Alice darted in and out among the tree trunks, smelling the pine tar, her mind screaming in near panic. She was struck by the contrast between the almost angelic appearance of the beautiful snow covered branches and the horror that was chasing her, literally born out of hatred and anger.

And then a wall of snow caught in the branches let loose because of the vibration. Everything was white. She was disoriented and fell, covered in the wall of snow that had fallen on top of her from the branches above. When she got up again, Ricky was nowhere to be seen. Or heard. She felt alone and trapped, like a little rodent caught in a cat's murderous gaze.

Alice crawled along, inch by inch, being as quiet as she could possibly be out here, out of breath, scared out of her mind. She had one thing on her mind. The snowmobile. Must get to the snowmobile. She glanced around nervously, listening intently for any noise, trying to catch any movement at all.

Despite her panic, she was bone tired. She felt it all the way down. She was dizzy and felt oddly like curling up beneath one of the large pines and sleeping. Anything for sleep. Anything to be somewhere else.

She resisted the feelings and willed herself forward, crawling slowly from trunk to trunk, trying desperately to remain hidden. She could see the snow-covered lump that was the snowmobile in the distance. She wondered how she would ever get to it. If it was even possible.

Then, in front of her, a huge branch let loose and raced toward her like a monstrous baseball bat swung by a giant. The branch struck her in the face and stunned her. She fell forward on her chest. Her breath escaped her in a loud *whoosh*, and she struggled for air, gasped for it. Her mouth was filled with snow and bark and dirt and needles, which she tried to spit it out, managing only to breathe a fair chuck of the stuff in. She coughed and heaved violently, trying to catch her breath.

"Hee hee!" Ricky said, walking out from behind the large pine wiping his hands. "Lookey what I caught, Pa! Whaddaya suppose it is?"

His left eye was bleeding and the right was dark. She struggled to run, to get up, to do anything, but she couldn't breathe. He'd hit her with a branch. He must've pulled it back and sprung it like a mousetrap.

Then he was on her. He pinned her to the ground. He said, "That was a mighty stupid thing you did back there. Of course, it didn't make any difference. I don't like you. I thought about what kind of a selfish bitch you must really be. Like the rest of them. But still, it's a shame to kill you because I never meant to. I just gotta end this thing up right. Get a fresh start. You understand, right?"

He put his cold hands on Alice's neck and tightened his grip. Alice stared up at the dark figure. Her mouth worked to try to say something, anything, but nothing would come. There was nothing left to say.

Ricky pushed his thumbs into Alice's neck and said, "Bye, Mom."

A shot.

Alice flinched, expecting pain, numbness, an out-of-body experience, anything. But she felt nothing. Ricky groaned on top of her and slumped, clutching his left side. Alice saw veins on his face and forehead bulging angrily. His face was taut with pain and rage.

She heard a grunt and watched as a boot connected with the side of Ricky's head and sent him the rest of the way to the frozen ground.

The next moments were a blur for Alice. One moment she'd been expecting death. Then suddenly Ricky had slumped thanks to a bullet from—

Alice looked up to see Michael, his eyes wide and scared, shakily holding a gun on Ricky, who'd rolled off to Alice's right. Michael's savage kick had unfortunately given Ricky the momentum he needed to continue his roll away from danger.

Michael shot carelessly towards Ricky as Ricky dove underneath a branch and out of site. Alice watched a little puff of snow erupt where the bullet hit it.

"You okay?" Michael asked hurriedly. Then, "Who is that?"

Alice touched her face where she felt the scratches and scrapes the fast moving branch had given her and nodded, still amazed that she was alive. "It's too complicated. Not here. He killed Chris. We need get out of here. Now! The snowmobile!"

Michael reached out for Alice's hand to help her up. He stood in front of her protectively, waving the gun madly towards the darkness of the trees.

"Come out here, you bastard!" Michael yelled and squeezed off another two shots randomly.

"Michael, wait!" Alice said. Michael was scared, panicky.

He nodded and took her hand.

They walked backward, away from the direction Ricky had rolled. They didn't get far.

Ricky crashed through the trees, screaming. In the moment before his body crashed into Michael's, Alice saw the blood streaking down the left front of his shirt. A bullet, probably the first one, had hit him on the left side halfway between his hips and rib cage.

The two men smashed together and went down in an angry fury of fists and profanity, Michael madly beating on Ricky's back.

Alice screamed, "His ribs! His ribs!"

She lashed out and kicked Ricky on his side, causing him to scream in agony. But it only seemed to intensify his attack. He held Michael's gun hand and brought it down savagely on the frozen ground. Alice heard a disturbing pop. Michael shrieked in pain and surprise. The gun fired as Michael involuntarily squeezed the trigger. It bounced away, barrel smoking.

Alice lunged for it immediately and grabbed it before Ricky dove for it. She held it up in shaky hands, desperately trying to find a clean shot.

Ricky, realizing that Alice had the gun, twisted Michael's body in front of his own. He said, "Go ahead! Shoot it! Fucking shoot me! Do me a fucking favor!"

Michael brought back an elbow hard on his left side, landing it squarely on Ricky's wound. Ricky shouted in pain and for a moment forgot all about Alice and pushed Michael away instinctively.

Alice squeezed the trigger immediately. She felt the recoil of the gun and watched as a cone of sparks exploded from the barrel.

She missed. She heard the bullet crash through the pine branches.

Ricky looked up and smiled, reaching for her with one hand, while trying to keep Michael down with the other.

Alice fired again.

Click.

The gun was empty. She fired again and again to no use.

Michael, holding his broken wrist protectively to one side, squirmed out from underneath Ricky and twisted himself onto Ricky's back, reaching under with his good arm, holding on for dear life.

Ricky stopped his advance and screamed with rage at Michael.

Michael shouted, "Alice! Go! Get to the car! He can't get to both of us! The car has a CB. Call for help! I can hold him! Quarter mile up the road on the left! It went off the road!" He was desperately out of breath and barely managing to get the words out.

Alice hesitated, unsure of what to do. She couldn't leave Michael to this monster. Ricky had grown up fighting in jails. Michael was no fighter, surely he would lose.

"Go!" Michael insisted, wrestling with Ricky.

She dropped the gun and ran towards the snowmobile. Behind her, she heard the men struggling and grunting with rage and pain. One of them would drop soon.

Bounding through the snow, blind with fear, expecting Ricky to take her down any second, Alice approached the snow mobile. She dusted off the seat and handlebars quickly and jumped on, simultaneously reaching beneath her for the key. Her fingers closed on it and she twisted while gunning the accelerator, hoping to flush out the fuel line.

But it wouldn't start.

She tried again and swore. It was no use. The engine was too cold or the battery was dead or both. She would have to go on foot.

With one last look towards Michael, she started as quickly as she could up the road, towards the detective's car. Towards help.

SIXTEEN

Don Lambert awoke with a start. His head was throbbing with a pain so disorienting it took several moments for him to realize just where in the hell he was. The pain was centered at the base of his neck but he felt as though his forehead was going to burst open from the pressure any minute. Even the pale light reflecting off the snow hurt his eyes. He tried to blink his vision clear. No doubt about it, he had a concussion. Probably a bad one.

He sat up and realized he was desperately cold and unable to feel his fingers or toes.

His head began to clear. He was at the camp a ways north of Redding. Someone had hit him. Chris Wynter. Michael. Alice. Someone had Alice. They'd taken the car to get here, but it had skidded off the road in the snow.

Don rubbed his chest and winced, letting out a long, slow breath. In addition to his titanic migraine, he felt a dull ache in his chest punctuated by occasional deeper, sharper pains. Not good. The same feeling as before. When was it?

Yes. When he and Michael had walked from the car and found Alice's snowmobile. The implications of these feelings were not lost on Don as he willed the pain in his head and chest to subside long enough to let him complete whatever job he needed to complete this night. It had to end. Maybe it was over already, but he doubted it very much.

He wondered how long he'd been out. Not too long, or he'd be frozen. He never would have regained consciousness. Hypothermia had only begun to settle into his body. He could only have been out a few minutes. He was lucky to be alive.

He stood up and immediately vomited, overcome with unbearable nausea. His head swam and he fell backward, slamming into the side of the camp. A sharp pain radiated down his arm when he hit, and he swore, shaking his head, rubbing his arm with his right hand, thinking about Gaye, about getting home, seeing his daughters, about ending this interminable snowy night.

That's when he realized: it wasn't snowing. The blizzard had stopped. He gazed upward, holding the back of his head for support. He saw a few stars behind the curtain of thin clouds that was streaming overhead. The wind had picked up considerably and blew mercilessly. It was colder as well. Much colder.

He felt for his gun, but it was gone. No surprise. Still, he felt a moment of panic. A cop is trained to know where his gun is at all times. He stood there for a moment, gathering the rest of his senses, his courage, while balling up his hands into fists and unclenching them again. At the same time, he worked his toes back and forth, trying to get his blood flowing again. After a minute or two, he felt a dull warming sensation in his boots and gloves. His head cleared slightly. He looked around, his eyes focused on the shotgun immediately.

Seeing it there, just inside the camp's open back door, was oddly unsettling. It was the contrast between what should be and what really is. He grabbed it immediately, and then realized with growing hope what it meant.

He checked the chambers and found them empty. He smelled the barrel. Just gun oil. It hadn't been fired. Michael must have gone back to the car for it, not found the shells, and brought it back anyway. And that meant that Michael might still be alive. He was also probably responsible for the missing pistol. If the other guy, whoever that was, had taken it, Don would surely be dead.

But here he was, for better or worse. Here he was.

Michael felt his energy draining. His muscles were burning with the effort of keeping Ricky immobile while Alice ran for help. Ricky was simply too strong for him, bullet wound or no bullet wound. The two men were now locked together, struggling for the slightest advantage, like two men in a cage-fighting grudge match.

Michael's wrist hurt badly. His fingers on that hand were useless. He tried to protect it by holding close to his belly. Of course, Ricky went after it every chance he got, scraping and clawing with his free hands when he wasn't trying to gouge at Michael's eyes. Ricky was far younger than Michael and had far more experience fighting. It wasn't an even match. So Michael held onto Ricky with his free hand and his legs, which were scissored around Ricky's middle, and prayed for the strength to keep it up. His unbroken left hand held Ricky underneath his chin, pulling his back backward in a (hopefully) painful arch.

"You ain't gonna win, fucker. You ain't gonna win," Ricky wheezed, as if reading Michael's thoughts. "God's on my side on this one. Believe me."

Michael ignored him. Best to save his breath. He hoped Alice had reached the car. He hadn't heard the snowmobile start, so he presumed the battery had died in the cold. He'd just have to hold Ricky that much longer. Ricky was bleeding and that would weaken him eventually, depending on how bad the wound was. By the look of it, it wasn't good. And that was all he could do now. He had no weapon, no way to disable Ricky. If he let go, Ricky would kill him with his bare hands. The kid was strong and in a rage and single-minded.

If Alice got to the car and managed to get help here more quickly, Ricky might panic and take off. Then the police dogs could get him for all Michael cared. Or a sniper.

But Ricky had learned a few tricks over his few years, and one of them was how to get out of such a choke hold. Unbeknownst to Michael, Ricky really *was* going to get out of this. He was just waiting for the perfect moment.

That moment came when a weakened Michael relaxed his hold just enough to reposition his aching legs. The slight movement gave Ricky the barest moment of advantage. And he took it.

"Agh!" Ricky screamed and moved like an Olympic wrestler.

Before Michael could react, Ricky rolled over on his side with incredible strength, taking Michael with him. In the process, Ricky pushed all his weight on Michael's compromised wrist and then managed to bend Michael's locked legs at a bad angle at the knee.

Michael screamed in pain and lashed out, but it was too late. Ricky was up and off after Alice, who, at that moment, represented his greatest threat. Ricky apparently knew from experience that it would be many weeks before Michael would walk normally again.

Alice felt the icy air blow across her face as she ran for the car. It was wicked cold out now, certainly well below zero with the wind chill. The stars and moon were out in their full glory. She saw bright clouds streaming overhead, the last remnants of the quick moving Nor'easter that had dumped nearly two feet of snow in just a few hours. The moonlight lit up the trees and the whole campsite took on an eerie silver glow.

Despite the cold, Alice's cheeks flushed when, faintly, behind her, she heard a grunt and cry of pain. She would hate herself if something happened to Michael. Such a sweet man. But she took solace in the fact that she was sure that given the chance, Ricky would come for her, after what she'd done.

What Ray had done, she thought in counterpoint.

Ricky's rage had focused naturally on her. This meant that he might leave Michael alone, unhurt.

But that didn't matter now. There was no time for such thinking now. Alice concentrated on the task at hand. Get to the car. Find the car. Michael said they'd slid down, off the road. On the left he'd said. But was that coming in or leaving?

Alice slowed and kept her eyes open for any signs, hoping she'd see a clue that hadn't been covered by snow, a broken branch or tree, maybe. Anything. She scanned back and forth but saw nothing. She was sure she'd gone at least a quarter mile, as Michael had said.

He had *said a quarter-mile, right?*

Now she wasn't sure. Maybe it was half. She walked further up the snow covered road, if you could even call it a road. She wished she had the snowmobile. She was exhausted and out of breath. With the snowmobile she could have cruised up and down both sides of the road, searching for the car.

Nothing. Damn it.

She walked a little further up the road. She was nearly to Route 6, or so she thought. It was hard to tell. She hadn't come in this way—the shortcuts with the snowmobile were much closer to her house. She thought of her mother then. She hoped she was all right. There was nothing for it. Things were what they were.

She turned around and cried out a little in frustration. Where was the damned car?

Determined, Alice set her eyes on the right-hand side of the road, retracing her steps, hoping she'd interpreted Michael's words correctly: *on the left*. He was telling her how to find it on the way out.

On the left. On the left.

The moonlight helped. The wind didn't. It repeatedly whipped through the pines and sent little whirls of swirling snow at her, forcing Alice to cover her face for fear of getting ice or dirt or grit in her eyes.

Then, perhaps fifty feet ahead on the right, down a small ditch, she saw the unmistakable rectangular shape of a snow covered car. She ran towards it, now understanding that it would have been practically impossible to see it coming from the other direction, given the way it was situated there, well hidden. But from this angle, she could now see the blue flashers in the back window.

Hold on, Michael, hold on! She thought as she raced towards the car.

She slid and bumped down the small hill and banged unceremoniously into the driver's side door. She saw that the passenger side of the car was dented in a few inches where they'd apparently slid into a tree.

Silently thanking the universe that it wasn't locked, she opened up the driver's side door and climbed in, glad to be free of the terrible wind. She shut the door and fumbled for the CB microphone, which hung below the dashboard. Praying that the battery hadn't gone dead, that the detective and Michael had had the common sense to turn off the headlights, she picked up the CB and pressed the button on the side.

"Mayday! Mayday! Mayday!" she screamed into the microphone while holding the talk button on the side. It must be on the right channel. Had to be, right?

"Mayday! Mayday! Mayday!" she said again. "A detective is down. Don something. We need help. We need some goddamn help! Someone. Please! I'm in the detective's car now. We're at the camps at the southern end of Lake Magaskawee. Please! Someone! We're at the camps at the southern end of Lake Magaskawee! There's a man here. He's already killed my brother. He might have killed the detective. He's dangerous."

She waited.

To her great relief, she heard: "Roger that. Who is this?"

"Alice Wynter."

The voice said, "Got held up by the storm. Help is en route. I repeat, help is en route. Are you in the detective's car?"

"Yes."

"Do not leave the car. Do you understand?"

"I have to—Michael, he's—"

"I repeat. Do not leave the car. Wait for help. We'll know who you are if you're in the car."

"But the car crashed. It's—you'll never find it. Off the side of the road."

"I repeat. Do not leave the car."

Alice said, "Roger," and threw the microphone on the seat beside her.

Who knows how long it would take them? She had to go, to try to help Michael. She began a frantic search for weapons but found nothing but an empty gun rack. She found a police baton next to the driver's seat and took it, figuring it was better than nothing. The detective must have left it there.

She opened the driver's side door and found that she had to push hard to open it against the unrelenting wind. The door slammed shut behind her and she started up the hill.

It was slow going. There was ice on everything and she slipped several times. If the police car had skidded down a larger hill, the detective and Michael could have been killed. And that would have meant that she'd be dead like her brother.

Chris.

She hadn't had time to think about him until now. She still didn't have time. She pushed the thoughts of her lost, dead brother aside and focused on getting up the hill, which she did a few moments later. She had to help Michael now.

In the distance, towards the camp, a snowmobile engine whined to life. Her snowmobile.

She froze.

Don heard the grunting, fighting men as soon as he rounded the corner of the camp. They were in a cluster of pine trees perhaps twenty-five feet from the front of the camp. Occasionally, Don saw a branch shake. He heard no shots. The fight had moved beyond that presumably.

But where was Alice? Don blinked as he surveyed the area looking for any sign of her, still trying to clear the last of the blurriness from his eyes. His arm and chest still hurt. He was worried about that. Very worried.

He was moving slowly and deliberately. He was nauseous and dizzy. His body ached in every joint. He felt like a 10-year-old kid with a bad case of the flu. Every breath was a battle. He felt as if he couldn't get enough air into his lungs. He wouldn't last long if things came down to it.

He ducked back around to the back of the camp. Perhaps Alice took refuge in there after fleeing from her attacker. He called inside as quietly as he thought he could. She didn't answer. She was either dead, incapacitated, or had taken off for the car. He hoped it was the car. He needed medical attention badly, not only for his woozy head but for the much more sinister persistent ache in his chest.

He crept around the corner again, keeping himself steady, stopping when he had to dry heave or catch his breath, which was too often.

Don concentrated on the ground in front of the camp now, trying to forget just how much trouble he was in. He saw no footprints and no other markings on the snow, but that didn't surprise him. The way this wind was whistling out here, any tracks would be covered up in seconds. A 10- or 15-foot snow drift climbed up the side of the camp. Others drifts climbed up trees. Don looked for the snowmobile and noted another, smaller drift threatening to cover it up, but the top had been cleared.

Alice's work? Maybe. Maybe not. Could have blown off just as well.

He moved out a little further, tilting and turning his head a little to face his left ear into the wind, so he could hear. The fighters were silent now. Don crept out a little further and waited.

He didn't have to wait long.

He heard a pained scream, followed by a long moan. Then, a man ran out of the trees, hell bent on getting to the snowmobile. He wasn't paying any attention to Don. This was the man who had clocked him, who had killed Chris and Bruce Wynter, who had attacked Jackie Ruth, and who may have just killed Michael and Alice. This was a dangerous man. And Don was unarmed and quite sick.

At first, Don thought he had fainted or was dreaming because the man that ran out of the pine woods looked exactly like a young Ray Wynter. He was a dead ringer, right down to the long black hair that poked out of a knit cap. He seemed like a strange anachronism, this man, like something that just didn't belong in our time.

Don instinctively held his breath, all the while knowing the man couldn't possibly hear his wheezy breathing yards away in this wind. Besides, the guy was too focused on the snowmobile.

Don watched him for a moment longer and then broke into a light jog, trying his best to keep his breathing as normal as it could be and his queasy stomach from turning over. He gained some ground. This was real. He wasn't dreaming.

The young Ray in front of him was on the snowmobile now, trying to start it. He wasn't having any luck. The guy swore and looked upwards towards the road. He got off for an instant and then back on. He wasn't sure what to do.

Don was within ten feet.

The man hopped off and got down on his knees in front of the snowmobile's engine and reached his hands in. He knew his way around a machine like that.

Don kept coming. Five feet now. The wind was protecting him by disguising the sound of his approach. He squeezed the heavy shotgun, making sure it was real, that it was heavy enough to do the job.

Then the snowmobile started, and the young Ray howled in triumph.

Don gave everything he had left and broke into a flat out run, swinging the shotgun up behind his head as he went. When he was close enough, he closed his eyes and prayed he'd connect.

SEVENTEEN

"Coming to get you, mother," Ricky said as he dashed off through the trees.

Mother? Michael thought. *Was Ricky Alice's son? Was that why all of this was happening?*

He couldn't possibly comprehend this information here, now. He had to get out of the trees. Somehow manage to find help.

His knee was exploding in pain with every beat of his heart. At first, hoping against hope that Ricky had only managed to twist it a little, that it was going to be okay, Michael tried to bend it. No luck. He felt the insides popping and clicking and realized he was really hurt. If Ricky managed to get to Alice and run off, he'd die out here, hidden from view in the middle of the pines.

Frustrated and angry, Michael braced himself with this good arm and managed to stand up, keeping off his bad leg, hissing through his teeth, trying to ignore the shooting pain. He hopped and fell down again immediately. The pain was too much. Ricky had known what he was doing. This was no accident.

He rolled over on his stomach and tried pulling himself through the thick snow. He could manage a few feet at a time. It was too slow. He forced himself up on all fours and tried that way. He was at least level with the depth of the snow that way. He relaxed his bad leg and tried moving forward. That was better. The pain was excruciating, but he was moving.

He didn't look forward. He didn't want to see how far he had to go or how far he had come. Nothing mattered now except moving forward. Just keep moving forward.

Finally, after several minutes, he risked a look and saw the cold moonlight through the branches. He'd at least made it out of the pines. Small miracles.

He allowed himself no rest for the accomplishment. It all meant nothing if he couldn't get out there.

When he was clear of the trees, he saw two figures. One was Ricky, he was hunched over the snowmobile. Trying it get it running, Michael figured. The other figure was Don.

By God, Michael thought. *The detective is close enough to—*

Then Michael spotted the shotgun and his stomach dropped. Don doesn't know there are no shells in there! He must be delirious or intent on bluffing Ricky to give up. But that wouldn't work. It just wouldn't—

Then Michael watched Don charge and raise the shotgun high over his head. He brought it down with a force Michael wouldn't have thought possible from the fat old man. The gunstock swung through the air in a wide arc and hit Ricky square on the back of the head. He never saw it coming and had no chance at all of deflecting the blow.

Michael heard the sickening pop a second later, dampened by the wind, and watched in horror as a spatter of blood shot from the back of Ricky's head. Ricky slumped and then fell over. He must be dead. Had to be dead. Michael called out to Don, but Don never heard him.

Don Lambert felt the gunstock connect with the young man's head and knew that he'd likely dealt the kid a deadly blow. He staggered backward and watched the man keel over onto the snow. A bright red stain spread beneath his head, and Don nearly screamed at what he'd done. He'd never killed a man before. Hell, he'd only drawn his service revolver a handful of times in all his law-enforcement years. And now he was standing over a man he'd likely killed. He felt suddenly like vomiting again.

That's when an invisible hand seemed to tighten on Don's chest like a vice. His breath left in a whoosh and pain shot down his left arm. He dropped the shotgun.

He wondered if he'd ever see Gaye and his girls again.

Alice, at the car moments earlier, heard her snowmobile start and jumped with fright. Ricky was coming for her. He'd probably killed Michael. The detective was down. She could be the only one left.

Frantically, she edged her way back down the hill and into the detective's car. The keys were still in the ignition. She tried the engine. It was dead and only clicked from somewhere deep under the hood. She got out again, thinking that it didn't matter anyway because she would never be able to get the car out again.

She scrambled back up the hill. The snowmobile was still running. Idling. Why wasn't Ricky coming after her? Maybe he hadn't gotten to it? Maybe Michael or the detective—?

Alice started down the road cautiously. What was happening? The moonlight was lighting the way well now, so she could see a good distance ahead of her.

"Alice!" a voice cried. "Alice! Are you there?!"

It was Michael!

She broke into an awkward run, pushing her way through the heavy snow.

A few minutes later she rounded the curve that led to the camp. She saw Michael immediately, hovered over the large shape of the detective. Another body, Ricky, lay on the ground next to the snowmobile. Michael's face was twisted up in pain as he pushed down on the detective's chest.

When she was close enough, she said, "Michael, are you okay? I called for help."

"I'm hurt, but I'll live," Michael said.

Alice side-stepped around Ricky and tried not to look at the pool of blood surrounding his head. She knelt down beside Michael and gasped when she saw Michael's wrist. It was swollen and bent abnormally.

"It looks worse than it feels. Mostly numb now," he said when he saw her stare. "You have to take over. It hurts me too much. 5 pumps, 3 breaths. Nice and easy."

Alice nodded and tried to remember the various CPR classes she'd taken over the years. She looked down at the detective's ashen face as she started.

"When did you call for help?" Michael said.

"Just a few minutes ago."

He looked up at her and said, "Jesus, he saved our lives. I'm not sure he's gonna make it."

EIGHTEEN

Ten Days Later

"Ma, you can't stay here by yourself," Alice said. "You have no one to help you."

"Ah, your old mother can manage just fine by herself, thank you very much."

Her mother's wounds were healing. The physical ones. But Alice saw something in her eyes that wasn't light. A dimming. Grayness. Everything her mother had on this earth was gone. Everything but the ashes of her husband, which she clutched in her bony hands, and Alice.

Edward Papa Wynter hadn't wanted a funeral or memorial of any kind. He hadn't left a will. Alice and Jackie Ruth had agreed that they'd spread his ashes out back before going to the funeral. Perhaps that would have made him happy. As if anything could, even in death.

This little house was more Papa's than anyone else's. Alice certainly felt little attachment to it. Her mother was a different story. She couldn't quite let go. Not yet.

Alice said, "We'll sell the place and—"

"Sell the house? Forget it. Never. You grew up here. How could you sell it?"

"—get you a nice condo Down East. Portland maybe. Ma, please."

"You just get back to your life, Alice. That's what you want, isn't it? To get back to your nice house and highfalutin' job in the city?"

Alice shook her head in frustration and looked out at the driveway, at her black Mercedes. In many ways, her mother was as stubborn as her father had been. They all were. This stuff that her mother was saying was just . . . a tenuous connection to a past that never was, a world that existed only in her mother's mind, a place where Alice and Chris were raised as if plucked from a painting by Norman Rockwell himself. And a lot of the fight had left her mother. Her words sounded hollow to Alice.

"Ma, did you know about what Ray did to me?"

Jackie Ruth sighed and looked at Alice with a barely disguised look of defiance. She said, "No."

Alice furrowed her brow.

Jackie Ruth's face softened. She said, "Not entirely. Over the years, with Chris here, he'd let some things out. Sometimes when he was drinking. By accident. But I didn't know. Not everything."

"What about Ray? Did you know about what happened to him?"

Jackie Ruth nodded her head a little and looked at the floor. "I knew. Papa told me years ago. Said he needed to protect Chris. That Bruce would kill him if he found out. But I didn't know about the teacher. Not all of it anyway. What a mess those boys made."

Alice shook her head in sadness.

"Never let Chris forget it, your father. Held it over him. I suppose in his own way it was how he dealt with his own guilt. That and booze. The two of them were a pair for it."

"I'm sorry, Ma."

"Sorry?" Jackie Ruth said, laughing. "Oh, that's rich. *You're* sorry? Dolly, dear, you have nothing to be sorry for. I didn't tell you enough growing up. It wasn't your fault. You were born into this family and did your best to get along. And you . . ." She brought a quick hand to her mouth. Her eyes watered and she smiled, looking at her daughter lovingly. "I love you, Alice Wynter. I do. You were always special to me. You know that? Somehow, you managed your way out of all this. Just hurts sometimes because I want you here with me. As much as I wanted for you to see and experience, I wanted you here with me. It hurts a mother sometimes." She tightened her grip on Papa's ashes as she said this.

Alice leaned over and hugged her mother. She said, "I love you too, Ma. I'm just sorry about everything that's happened."

"Well, it's over now."

"I guess."

Alice let go of her mother and sat back in her seat, picking up a cup of hot tea in front of her. She wouldn't be the same, and she knew it. A stranger named Ricky had blown in like a tornado and laid waste to her old life. To all their old lives. Alice Dunn and Alice Wynter had collided that snowy night out at the camp. They'd met like a match to gasoline and exploded, leaving something new, and here she was sitting at the kitchen table in the house where she'd grown up, loving and hating her mother all at once, just the way it should be between a mother and daughter. Alice would go back to her life in New Jersey a different person. And that was scary. She wasn't sure what she'd find there.

Perhaps her life there *was* a house of cards. A facade. She wondered if she'd be terrified of the things she found there, of the people who expected her to be something she no longer was. She wondered if she'd see signs of the way her past had infected her carefully constructed after-life. She wondered if everyone there somehow knew about the dark stain in her old life but couldn't quite put their finger on it. Sensed all this time that she was different in some way. Fundamentally different. Sometimes what's obvious to others isn't obvious to ourselves.

Alice watched her mother delicately sip her tea. She looked older now. Yes. That was it. Her grayness. But that was okay. *That* much at least *was* normal.

"Ma?"

"Yes, Dolly?"

"What did you think when you saw him? Ricky, I mean."

"I knew what it was right away. I could see so much of you in his eyes. Ray as well obviously. Papa did too. It was a strange thing, seeing someone that looks so much like family sitting here at the table but not knowing who he was. He sat right there." She pointed at the empty seat across from Alice. "But at the same time, I just couldn't bring myself to face what he was."

Alice tried to imagine it, her parents sitting at the table, forced to confront something about their family that they wouldn't admit to anyone, even themselves. Papa especially, knowing what he knew about Chris. About Ray. And he might have known more than her mother knew. He might have known exactly who Ricky was.

"But Ricky didn't know he was a secret," Alice said.

Jackie Ruth shook her head a little. "No. No, I don't believe he did. He asked about you, what kind of person you were. We didn't say much. We didn't know what to say."

"I feel bad about it."

"Don't, Dolly. Oh God, I'm so sorry I didn't say anything right away. But, I just couldn't. I knew it would hurt you. You were in an impossible situation. You did the best you could under the circumstances. Besides, he wasn't right. Both your father and I saw it right away. He had a funny way about him when he was here. We just wanted him to go away. I really thought he would. And then, he did what he did."

"Dad chased him out. Called him a bastard."

"I think that boy scared your father worse than anything ever had in his life. He was scared of what it meant. Here was this man, this strange man, who walks into our house, our lives, uninvited, and just manages to get right under the skin of the oldest most terrible thing in our family. Things we thought were long buried. And the worst part of it is that if we hadn't been home that day, things might have turned out differently."

"Don't say that, Ma. You don't know that. He was sick, Ricky was. He might've thought your not being home was a snub. He was probably looking for an excuse."

"You're probably right about that, Dolly. I just don't know. But I'll never forget that look in his eyes."

Alice had seen that look too, that crazy look in Ricky's eyes that reminded her so much of Ray. Alice suddenly remembered those days after Ray's basement when her life had become a blur of pain and self-hatred. She remembered the hurt look on Chris's face when she'd slammed doors in his face, ashamed to face even her twin brother, not realizing his role in it, not realizing what kind of hell he himself was in.

Since that night out in the blizzard, since coming home wrapped in a blanket in the back of an ambulance, watching Michael trying to put on a brave face while the paramedics examined his broken wrist and knee, she'd thought a lot about her brother Chris.

She was going to bury him today. This afternoon. He'd bled to death running from his demons that night and perhaps it was better that way. She believed him at his word that Ray had killed that teacher way back when. He was a follower, Chris was, he'd always been. First he'd followed Ray. And then Papa.

She'd believed in Chris. He was a good person with a good heart. He'd been in the wrong place at the wrong time. Maybe that was it. She wasn't sure it was true. Maybe there was something he could have done to stop this craziness and maybe there wasn't. She'd never know, and that didn't matter now. Chris, for all his faults, or all his demons, was her brother after all. And she was going to bury him this afternoon. She forgave him, for whatever he'd done or had not done.

"I think I want to go, Dolly." Jackie Ruth's fingers massaged the container of ashes. "I think I'm ready now."

Alice looked at her watch and said, "Ma, we've got hours yet until the funeral. You want another cup of tea?"

"No, that's not what I meant."

"Tell me, Ma."

"I want to sell the place. You're right, Alice. I'm . . . I'm just remembering the good things. Truth is, I've spent a lot of unhappy years here. I think maybe it's time for a change. You're all I have left now in the world."

"You sure?"

Jackie Ruth nodded and set her cup of tea down. She said, "Maybe a little place. A . . . oh, what do you kids call them again?"

"Condo?"

"Yes. A condo Down East."

"Okay, Ma. We can make that happen."

"I don't have much and God knows this place isn't worth much to anyone but me."

"That's okay, Ma. I'll help you. We'll take care of it."

"Thank you, Dolly."

They sat in the kitchen together in the old house, talking a little about old times, the good bits, anyway. A little later, when they agreed it was time, Alice and Jackie Ruth walked out the back door, dug a spot in the snow, and sprinkled Papa's ashes on the ground. Alice didn't feel much of anything.

When they were done, Jackie Ruth said, "Well, that's that."

They returned to the kitchen and talked some more about the old days. After an hour or so, when the tea had dried in the bottoms of their cups, Jackie Ruth stood and left to go get ready for the funeral.

Alice Wynter put her head in her hands and cried.

In the end, few turned up for Chris and Bruce's funeral, late because of the mandatory autopsies. A couple friends from years ago came by, but not many. Bruce's 93-year-old neighbor Nick Orick was there. And so was Chris and Alice's third-grade teacher, Jane Whitson. She said she'd read about what happened in the paper a few days before and that Alice had grown up into a fine young lady and what a shame it was about what happened to Chris.

The day was cool, but the sun was brilliant and warm. It was one of those winter days Alice loved as a child, when she could smell a little hint of spring in the air long before she knew winter would end. It was a nice way to send off her twin brother.

The rumor mill had been churning double-duty since the night of the blizzard. Alice heard snippets of whispered conversations and tried her best to ignore the troubled, furtive glances. It seemed as though the entire town of Redding was speculating about what had happened. One theory was that Papa had made a business deal that went sour. Some said Papa and Chris had finally pissed off the wrong people in Flynn's Tavern.

And that was just fine with Alice. Not many knew the truth about Ricky, about who he really was. Only two people besides Alice and Jackie Ruth knew, one because it was his job, and the other because he had a kind heart.

Don Lambert stood beside Alice, next to his wife Gaye, with his head bowed reverently. He nodded in all the right places and delicately threw a flower on the casket when the Reverend was done with his short homily.

Ashes to ashes and all that jazz.

Alice kissed her hand and touched the caskets, trying not to cry. What can you do? This is the way it turns out sometimes.

In a few moments, the small gathering dispersed, leaving Alice and Jackie Ruth left to shake the hands of the attendees as they left. Alice was glad it was over. Glad to move on, but there was a little business that needed taking care of and the detective seemed to know that.

He was last on line. "I'm sorry about everything that's happened," he said to Alice and her mother. "It's been a tough couple of weeks for you. Neither of you deserved this." His voice was thick and tired. Raspy. His face was pale and drawn.

Jackie Ruth said, "Thank you, Detective."

"Alice, do you have a minute? I've got some information for you."

He led Alice off, away from Jackie Ruth and away from the remainder of visitors now slowly heading back to their cars.

Alice said, "Don, you didn't have to come. You're not well. You—"

He held up a hand. "After all we've been through, I felt I had to come. I wasn't supposed to. Gaye'll probably never let me live it down."

Alice smiled and nodded. "Fair enough. Don, you look much better."

"Than the last time we saw each other? I hope so." He let out a long, friendly chuckle and then gripped his side and winced.

"Well, you do."

"Lost a couple pounds in the hospital," Don said, patting his sizable gut.

"I can tell." Alice smiled.

Don laughed. "It's gonna be a few weeks before I'm

back to my old self, obviously. The doctors tell me that if hadn't been for you and your friend, I would have died."

"Michael."

"Yes. Michael."

Alice said, "No sweat. He's feeling better, but he said he just wasn't up for it today. His knee is—"

Don nodded and held up a hand. "Had a back thing once years ago. I understand. So, while I was in the hospital, I had my associate do a little poking around."

"Oh?"

"You know, about Ricky."

"I see. Do I want to know?"

"Up to you," Don said. He reached into his inside jacket pocket and took out several folded sheets of paper. "I'm just as happy to toss this out and forget it. What's done is done."

"No, I want to know. I think it's important."

Don opened the papers and scanned them, refreshing his memory. He said, "Where to begin?"

"How about at the beginning?"

"Well, I'll tell you what. I'll start even before the beginning. You see, at first, we didn't think the cause of all this was anything like Ricky. Personally, I figured Ray's friend Victor Acree had come back. Before the blizzard, I was doing some thinking on it and figured I'd found my man while looking through the records in the basement. Had a real Perry Mason moment there. Or thought I did. Just found out that Vic had died of a drug overdose just a few years after high school."

Alice said, "So Chris was the only one left of their little gang."

"Only one. That's right. Although, I swear. I'm not ashamed to admit that the thought had crossed my mind that Ray wasn't really dead."

"In a way he wasn't."

"Uh yuh. You got that right."

"So. About Ricky." Alice took a long breath.

"Right. Birthdate, July 2, 1985. He was a 7 ½ pound boy, given up for adoption."

Alice looked away.

"He was adopted by Mr. and Mrs. Frank Dawkins just a short time later. Based on the lack of records from this point, we have to assume that things were okay for a while. No sign of trouble until two years later, in 1987, when Frank is arrested for driving under the influence with Ricky in the car. Court ordered alcohol treatment apparently didn't take, as Frank was picked up again the following summer in a domestic dispute during which Ricky was repeatedly slapped by his drunken father. Ricky was removed from the home at this time and placed into a group home for foster kids."

"Where was that?"

"Just outside of Boston. Braintree."

Alice felt an odd mixture of emotions. Detachment, guilt, and sadness. In 1987, she was a junior at Boston University and deeply in love with Gerald. She'd only been home a handful of times. Her scholarships kept her busy and away, just as she wanted it.

"Alice?"

"Hmm?"

"You okay with this? You don't have to hear this."

"No, I want to. Go on."

"I'm telling you this right now. It gets worse."

"I need to hear it."

Don nodded and looked down at his notes. "Social workers were unable to place Ricky in anything permanent due to what they were then starting to call his 'special needs.' These being hyper activity, social dysfunction, impaired learning skills, you name it. These problems were probably related to the fact the father was your cousin, but I'm just guessing. The social workers had no way of knowing that, of course. Ricky's natural father had been marked as unknown."

Alice nodded.

"He bounced around for years, until he was ten. He was placed in any number of temporary foster homes, either being removed at the request of the volunteers or simply spending his allotted time and moving on. He was by all accounts unruly, violent, and belligerent. It's a damn shame, you know? A lot of people think all adopted kids are like Ricky. A kid like him comes along and spoils it for all the other kids who are mostly just fine."

Alice said. "You said it gets worse?"

"I'm getting to that. When he was ten years old, Ricky killed the youngest son of the latest set of folks taking care of him. Pushed the boy out of a tree during an argument."

"Dear God."

"And so, there goes little Ricky to juvenile hall in Boston. Things wouldn't have gotten that far, in my opinion, but Ricky showed no remorse whatsoever according to the judge."

"Let me guess. He fought there. Got into trouble."

"Bingo. A lot of it. The list is endless. He racked up more time because of it. But on his sixteenth birthday Ricky rigged a boom box with an explosive he made from plant food from the garden to kill a kid he'd had an argument with the afternoon before. Blew the kids head off. Literally."

"And he went to adult jail?"

"Yep. In Massachusetts, 16-year-olds can be considered adults. He was sentenced to eleven years for manslaughter and moved in a few days later. Damn lucky to get manslaughter you ask me. He got into trouble there as well, so they kept him for the whole sentence. The parole board shot him down every few years or so for one reason or another. Didn't get out until last year, just a few months ago. He was twenty-seven years old. My guess is that gave him plenty of time to think about his life."

"So how did he find us? My parents?"

Don shook his head. "Not that hard nowadays. If you've got plenty of time. And that's all he had. He must've spent his time writing letters, trying to figure out where he came from."

"He said to me that night that he was just trying to set things right. To move on. That kind of thing. Do you think that's true?"

"No. Not really. I think he wanted revenge for the cards he'd been dealt. I think he was planning on using your parents to get to you. You'd gotten married, changed your name, didn't have much contact with your Maine roots. The Wynters were easier to track down."

Alice finished the story: "And when he did, he got another earful of rejection, courtesy of Papa Wynter."

Don shook his head. "Uh yuh. That's about it, I'd guess. Set him off."

"And my father? How did that happen?"

"We had a tip from Flynn's Tavern that Papa and Chris

had been arguing about Ray. Another man told us that he's seen Chris and Papa arguing outside with another man. After that it's speculation, but we think Ricky forced them into the car. At some point, there might have been a scuffle, maybe Ricky shot your father on purpose, or maybe the gun just went off. Either way, your father was dead. Chris, drunk as he no doubt was, managed to escape to the camp. We think he threw the gun, maybe thinking *he'd* shot Papa. Hell, maybe he did. I guess we'll never know. Miracle he didn't die out there in that cold."

Alice hugged Don and kissed his cheek. She said, "Thank you, Don. Again. For everything you did. I'm glad I know. About Ricky. About my father. Everything. It somehow makes me feel better."

Don rubbed his cheek were Alice had kissed it. "Truth is, that kid shouldn't have been born. He didn't belong here. Seems to me a little like he knew that too."

That made Alice sad.

"And Alice?"

"Yes?"

"I want you to know that I'm burning these papers today." He held up the folded papers he'd been reading from. "No one needs to know anything except Ricky was a drifter who happened to cross paths with your family. You've been through enough."

Don Lambert walked slowly towards his car. Gaye was waiting for him with the passenger door open. He'd managed to convince her that despite the doctor's warnings, he needed to be here for Alice, but she hadn't even entertained the idea of letting him behind the wheel. Besides, he was still a little sore from the emergency angioplasty. His other surgeries were coming.

She was smiling.

Don wasn't much in a smiling mood, having gone through Ricky Dawkin's history with Alice, but the sight of Gaye standing there warmed his heart and made him think of better things: his daughters. Erica had called just the day before and announced that she and her husband, a lawyer Down East, were expecting. Gaye was calling it a sign from God, saying that's why he decided Don needed more time on earth. Don figured she was probably right. And with any luck, maybe Erica's sister Kim would find the right guy and finally settle down. But there would be plenty of time for that. He hoped.

Don said, "What are you smiling at?"

"You. You're cute when you're not feeling well. You know that?"

"Yeah, well, don't get used to it."

"C'mon, detective. Let's get you home and back into bed. You're here against doctor's orders, and I don't like it."

"Ah," Don said, waving a hand dismissively. "They don't know everything."

"And neither do you, mister. Now scoot. Get settled in."

Don did as he was told, carefully lowering himself into his seat. He closed the door and saw Alice walking with Jackie Ruth towards Alice's black Mercedes.

Gaye opened the driver's side door and got in. When the door shut, she immediately began crying.

"Hey, hey," Don said, stroking her leg. "What's wrong?"

She shook her head and looked up at him. Tears ringed

her eyes. She said, "I just can't imagine what I would have done if I'd lost you. Being here, seeing this—"

"It's okay. I'm okay. I won't live forever, but I'm doing all right."

"I know," Gaye said. "It's just been getting to me these past couple of days with you so sick and all."

"I've been doing a lot of thinking myself."

"Oh?"

"Yeah, well, Matt's been handling things real well down at the Sheriff's office, and well, I'm obviously not getting any younger. And then there's Erica and—"

"Don, what are you trying to say?"

"That I'm retiring."

Gaye's face lit up and a smile spread across her face. She let out a peal of laughter so loud it nearly hurt Don's ears.

"What?" he said, smiling.

Gaye smirked and started the car, looking out ahead as she accelerated. "Honey, I love you. You know I do. But, I already made up my mind about that. You and I have a lot of grand-parenting to do now."

Don gazed on at his wife in amazement for a moment and then turned to watch the Maine landscape roll by.

The next day, Alice kissed her mother goodbye in the kitchen and promised her that she'd be back soon to talk to a realtor and maybe start looking at condos in Portland. Next month, no later than that, she promised. This time she meant every word.

Gerald was expecting Alice home in New Jersey sometime that afternoon. She hadn't yet quite told him everything, but she would. He'd sounded different this morning on the phone. Maybe they would find a little of that spark again with everything in the open, but she wasn't sure. A lot of time had gone by and Gerald hadn't ever really known her, not completely. She'd hidden a lot of things from herself and those she loved. He might react badly. All was possible. And Alice was okay with that. This was all part of her new self, the smashed together Alice Wynter and Alice Dunn. Things might be a little hinky at first, but she'd grow into her new skin before too long. She was sure of that. Absolutely sure.

She blew a kiss to her mother out the driver's side window before heading down the driveway. She watched her mother in the rearview mirror waving. The dimness seemed less now and her mother looked healthier than Alice had ever seen her, perhaps even radiant. Alice thought maybe her mother saw hope for the future too. She liked to think so anyway.

She had just one last stop before winding her way east to 95 South.

The last time she'd been parked in his driveway, she and Michael had just broken from what was sure to turn into a heated affair. She'd loved Michael once a long time ago and supposed that if things had gone a different way, she might have even married him.

She turned off the Mercedes and got out. She saw Michael waving from the living room window. She walked up the front steps and let herself inside.

He was sitting in a wheelchair in his pajamas and robe. A thin paperback book opened midway was perched on his bad leg, which was elevated in a fiberglass cast.

"Hi, Michael," Alice said.

"Alice. I'm glad you came."

"How are you feeling?"

He wiggled his good hand. "So so, I guess. Just doing a little reading. Philip Craig mystery. The meds they gave me for the pain make me a little sick. On the flip-side I've been sleeping like a log. How about you? How was the funeral yesterday?"

"It was good, yeah. I mean, as good as, you know, it could be, I suppose."

Alice took off her coat and lay it across an overstuffed chair. She was suddenly uncomfortable. The memory of their coupling on the couch was vivid and somehow shameful to her now. She was sure she was blushing.

She sat down on the couch. Michael rolled himself over to her.

"You want me to help? Doesn't that hurt your bad wrist?" she said.

He shrugged. "Unless you're planning on staying, I suppose I gotta get used to it."

Alice nodded.

"*Are* you planning on staying, Alice?"

"No, Michael. I'm not. I'm leaving for New Jersey from here."

A unmistakable look of disappointment fell on Michael's face. "I see. Things worked out between you and Gerald?"

"I don't know. Maybe, maybe not."

"Hmm."

"I'm sorry, Michael, but this is just the way it has to be. I've changed. Things have changed for me. Really changed. Can you understand that?"

"I just thought, you know, after what happened that—"

"I know. But it's not going to happen. I was vulnerable. You were here. I didn't mean for it to go that far."

He smiled. "As I recall, we didn't get very far anyway."

She laughed. "True."

"Will I see you again?"

Alice nodded but knew she was lying. She intended to leave Redding behind for good once she got her mother settled somewhere else. But there was no use telling Michael that. She hoped he sensed that in her. "You saved my life, Michael. And I can't thank you enough."

He smiled. "I'd do it again in a heartbeat."

They stared at the floor for a moment, uncomfortable. Alice knew he was going to ask, so she said, "I'm sorry I didn't tell you about what happened with Ray." She'd confessed to Michael the entire story while kneeling over Don's body next to the snowmobile that horrible night.

He looked up at her. "I understand."

"I really am sorry, Michael. You were a good guy. Still are. One in a million, really. I just didn't know how to tell you. I thought I could just go on, the way things were, but I was wrong. I was young and naive, and I just didn't know how to handle things. My life just seemed to unravel. And then, when I got word about B.U. and the scholarships, I just jumped. Ran away. Or thought I was, anyway. I left you behind. You deserved better than that."

"It's okay, Alice. I'm just glad you're all right. That *we're* all right. Besides, I never would have met Kerri if you hadn't left me."

Alice smiled at that and stood to pick up her coat. She said, "You're not mad, are you? At me, I mean? For leaving things the way they are?"

"Nah."

"Sure?"

"Sure."

Alice smiled and put her coat on. "If I don't, you know, see you again—"

"We will."

"Well, if we don't, I want you to take care of yourself, okay? No more heroics. Just get better."

"I will."

Alice bent down and kissed him gently on the lips and then was out the door before they had a chance to say anything else. She didn't even look up to see if he was waving goodbye. She was afraid she'd burst into tears if she saw that. Alice had no doubt that Michael would find someone eventually. He deserved that. The universe would make it so.

She drove her beloved black Mercedes through the Maine countryside and at long last turned onto 95, headed home.

Alice turned her thoughts southward as she raced along. She found herself making plans for the house, for her career, for her life. Things seemed possible now in a way that they hadn't before. She felt lighter. Not everything was going to be all right. She knew that. But she had a feeling that no matter what was coming, it would all be what it was supposed to be. And that was good.

When she passed over the Piscataqua Bridge into New Hampshire, she thought about the little girl that had come the very same way to Boston University, to her new life away from Redding. That Alice seemed to belong to a different lifetime now.

ABOUT THE AUTHOR

Photo by Chad Hunt

Spencer Seidel lives and works in suburban New Jersey, but has also called Washington, D.C., Pennsylvania, Massachusetts, and Portland, Maine, home. He is an honors graduate of Fairleigh Dickinson University and attended the Berklee College of Music to study guitar, which he has been playing for over 25 years. His love of reading and books began as a child after discovering Roald Dahl's *Charlie and the Chocolate Factory*. Later, he was drawn to authors such as Stephen King, Peter Straub, and Jack Ketchum, who continue to influence his dark mysteries and short stories.

Read more about Spencer Seidel and his books at **www.SpencerSeidel.com**. An author interview is available as well.

From *Lovesick*, by Spencer Seidel

(April 2012)

PROLOGUE

Patrolman Jimmy Preece would tell the story for the rest of his life, how on his first night out as a rookie cop on the streets of Portland, Maine, he and his partner discovered a grisly killing on the Eastern Promenade, next to the 295 overpass. It was a murder that would make headlines throughout the Northeast, especially after what happened to that shrink in the days afterward.

Murder in Portland is not unheard of, but it is unusual. At the Maine Criminal Justice Academy in Vassalboro, Jimmy had learned that Cumberland County has only one or two murders a year. This seemingly good news does little to comfort the families of the victims, however, and that's something the cadets don't always learn at the academy. Murder isn't a statistic. In real life, it's a dead family member. It's a tragedy.

The night they discovered the murder, Jimmy and his partner, Bruce Hecker, a 20-year Portland PD veteran, were making their way up Sewage Plant Road, so named because of it's proximity to a sewage plant overlooking the otherwise majestic Casco Bay. The cops had their windows cracked because the night air was crisp and felt good to breathe. It was early fall.

“Sometimes the kids come out this way to smoke pot and drink beer,” Bruce said. “The smart ones head down a ways far enough that we can’t put our spotlight on ‘em from the road to scare ‘em off. But even the dumb ones know how to run, and it’s not hard to run from us here. So unless there’s something obviously going on that we need to know about, we usually just let ‘em scatter.”

The cruiser rolled slowly up the dark road.

“Also,” Bruce continued, “sometimes we get people passed out up here. Damn drunks from Preble Street usually. They wander up here and keel over.”

A moment of silence passed in the police cruiser. Bruce said, under his breath, and more to himself than to Jimmy, who wasn’t really listening much to what his new partner was saying in any case, “Damn drunks. Come up here and keel right over.”

“There’s a car over there,” Jimmy said, pointing towards a battered old Ford Escort parked near the chain-link fence that ran along the border of the sewage plant.

“Uh, yuh,” Bruce grunted. He put the cruiser in park and opened the door.

Both cops, rookie and veteran, slide their nightsticks through the leather loops on their waists as they stepped out of the car. They both did this naturally and casually. *Just a routine stop, Ma’am.*

Bruce turned on his powerful Maglite and shined it on the car. He said, “Could be stolen. Call dispatch, see if it’s reported. Otherwise we—”

“Shh!” Jimmy said.

Bruce cocked an eyebrow, his face creased a little with concern. He looked over at Jimmy. After a moment, Bruce held up his hands. *Well?*

Jimmy said, "You hear that?"

Bruce shook his head.

"Up there." Jimmy pointed up the dark bike trail, towards the 295 overpass. "I heard something."

Bruce said, "Probably a couple kids, like I was saying." He began walking back to the cruiser.

"No, it wasn't like that. It something else."

"Let it go. Let's just—"

"There it is again," Jimmy said, his voice a loud whisper.

After arguing a bit, they walked a little farther up the dark path. Bruce looked annoyed, but Jimmy didn't care.

Bruce said, "What is it? I can't hear any—"

Jimmy stopped dead in his tracks.

He was the first to see the two figures in the silver moonlight. He stopped Bruce and pointed at them. One was kneeling, his face and clothes dark with stains. On his lap lay another, face up, unconscious, his neck and clothes also stained.

The noise Jimmy had heard was a little louder now and unmistakable: crying.

Jimmy and Bruce crept closer, guns drawn.

Bruce snapped his fingers and pointed at the two figures. Jimmy shined his Maglite on them. Bruce pointed his gun and said, "This is Sergeant Bruce Hecker. Portland PD! Keep your hands where I can see them and lay down flat on the ground!"

They walked a little closer.

Jimmy saw that the kneeling figure was just a kid. They both were. Seventeen, maybe eighteen years old. In the harsh light of the flashlight, Jimmy saw the kid's red, tear-streaked face. His lips were pulled back in a grimace. The kid gulped and let out a sob when he saw the cops. He was rocking back and forth like an autistic child.

"Can you hear me?" Bruce said a little louder. "This is Sergeant Bruce Hecker. Portland PD. Lay down flat on the ground, arms out, palms down. Do you hear me? Arms out, palms down."

Twenty feet away now.

Jimmy said, "He's not moving."

"No shit. Get on that shoulder mic and update dispatch. Get some backup out here. And an ambulance. Jesus H. Christ, the kid's got blood all over him."

Jimmy did as he was told.

Ten feet away now.

Bruce said, "Stop here."

"Can you help me? Can you help?" the kid said quietly. "I think there's something wrong with Lee."

Oh, fucking-a-right there's something wrong with Lee, Jimmy thought. *Lee is screwed up nine ways to Sunday.*

Bruce tried his good-guy cop routine. "We're going to get your friend Lee all the help he needs. Why don't you lay him on the ground and—"

"He's got a knife!" Jimmy said after seeing the glint of a blade in the kid's hand. Jimmy brought his gun up and squared it at the kid. *Christ!* Jimmy thought, his heart trip-hammering in his chest, *I might have to shoot this sonofabitching kid. And on my first night.* "He's got a knife!" he said again.

The kid looked confused and held up his left hand. In it was a serrated knife, the kind a hunter might use to skin a deer. The kid looked almost surprised to see it. He started shaking. He dropped the knife and then threw up on the ground next to the body on his lap.

Jimmy gagged at the sight and sound of it. He could smell the blood from where he stood, a coppery, biological stink. The kid sat in a small lake of it. Jimmy's stomach roiled in protest, and he thought he might throw up himself.

"Don't you fucking move!" Bruce said to the kid. "Don't you fucking move!"

Sirens in the night. Getting closer.

"Can you help me? There's something wrong with Lee. He's not breathing." The kid bent over the victim.

Jimmy said in a low whisper: "That kid isn't right. Something's wrong with him. In the head I mean. And look at his eyes, Bruce."

"Tell me something I don't fucking know, for Christ's sake."

Jimmy ignored this and said, louder, "What's your name, kid?"

Bruce looked harshly over at his rookie partner. Rooks weren't supposed to say anything unless told to, but Jimmy didn't notice the silent reprimand and wouldn't have cared anyway because he knew it was the right thing to do.

The kid looked up and stopped rocking his body. The simple question seemed to calm him somehow, bring him back into reality. He looked down at the body he was holding as if he'd never seen it before. He let it slide from his knees and crumple to the ground in a bloody pile.

The kid looked up at the cops just as several police cars and an ambulance arrived. The murder scene was lit up in seconds by the floods on the police cruisers and the harsh glow of powerful flashlights. Several police officers and a couple EMTs had jogged up the path. Jimmy heard someone gasp and retch. Flashing blue and red lights danced on the ground and off the side of the overpass.

The kid was soaked through in blood and looked scared, confused. The knife was laying in the little pile of puke next to him. Jimmy saw then that the victim had been cut ear to ear. Blood from his sliced neck had poured down his chest in a bloody waterfall.

"My name is Paul. Paul Ducharme," the kid said, his intense unblinking eyes wide with fear. "And I think there's something wrong with Lee."